FRANK O'HARA
THE LAST PI

D. MICHAEL PAIN

LifeRich Publishing is a registered trademark of The Reader's Digest Association, Inc.

LifeRich Publishing books may be ordered through booksellers or by contacting:

LifeRich Publishing
1663 Liberty Drive
Bloomington, IN 47403
www.liferichpublishing.com
1 (888) 238-8637

ISBN: 978-1-4897-0789-5 (sc)
ISBN: 978-1-4897-0788-8 (e)

Print information available on the last page.

LifeRich Publishing rev. date: 06/13/2016

ACKNOWLEDGMENTS

Foremost, I thank my family; Judy, Katy, and David Michael Pain, my deceased son 1971-2010.

Holly Nethery, Cheryl Crame, Mike Gartland, Michelle Pain, Sheila Pain, Gene Burdock, Morris Dean, Mrs. Bill Currie and all the parties at Liferidge Publications.

CONTENTS

This riveting, multilayered mystery grabs you by the throat and won't relax its jaws. It is set like a dark diamond in a bejeweled portrait of the life, character and professional experiences of the flawed sensitively souled Frank O'Hara, Private Investigator.

Morris Dean, Editor
Moristotle & Co-Reports, stories and provocations from around the world.

It has been a long time since I have read a book I cannot put down. Frank O'Hara captured my heart! What a compelling story woven with the perfect balance of mystery, intrigue, touching emotions and tears rolling down my face humor. What a ride! I eagerly await more from D. Michael Pain and his ability to paint pictures in the canvas of my mind with his masterful story telling.

Jody Chatelain

I found The last PI to be highly entertaining with elements of suspense, romance and comedy! Pick up a copy and take some time and read it; you won't be disappointed!

Cheryl Crame

CHAPTER 1

The Hit

The sound of the hammer striking the back of her head was not as loud as he thought it would be. More like a muffled thump. There was no scream. No word from her mouth. For reasons known only to him, he didn't swing as hard the second time as he could have, but still, it was hard enough. He believed she felt no pain. Her nerve ending dissolved when the hammer came back through the hole the second time.

Her long auburn hair, still damp from the shower she had taken moments before, was mingling with the stream of blood flowing down the back of her head. It gave a glistening effect, as if she had added a deep red rinse.

The last image her brain recorded was a movement to her left, which automatically caused her to flinch and turn the exact second the carpenter's hammer made its initial hard contact, but she still didn't know what hit her. She was unconscious when the second blow came.

He couldn't believe the mess death made, with blood splatters covering the wall and textured ceiling. Her terry cloth robe was quickly covered in little red spots, a polka dot pattern. The interior of the town home was decorated expensively but sparsely. The overstuffed chair she was sitting in was dark leather which matched the couch facing the TV. There were Monet prints tastefully framed in dark frames on two walls. It was a well taken care of home with no clutter. A stem glass of white wine sat on the table next to her. It had not been touched.

Wasting no time, he sifted through her purse that was lying on the table next to her eyeglass case. He took only business cards and papers that had a name or phone number. The two twenties in her purse were not touched. He went through the table drawers in the living room. Then he moved to her bedroom.

He didn't know exactly what he was looking for. All he was told was to get anything that looked "legal," whatever that meant? He hurriedly searched through her closet and dresser drawer, throwing her undergarments and other clothing out of the drawers onto the bed and floor, and then throwing the mattress onto the floor. Then he looked beneath her bed and finally through her Coach briefcase lying on a table beside the bed. He took anything that had any writing, business cards included, putting them into a plastic garbage bag he had brought with him for just this purpose. He went into the only bathroom just off the kitchen area and removed the gray poncho he had worn to catch any blood splatter. Looking in the mirror above the sink he also noticed small spots of blood on his forehead which he carefully washed off. He removed the poncho with the blood stains and threw it into the plastic bag, but left on the plastic surgical gloves and plastic shoe coverings.

He noticed the white rug was still wet from the last shower, and avoided stepping on it. On the counter behind the sink was makeup and other feminine items women use to enhance their beauty whether they need to or not.

He returned to the living area, giving it a final glance. Stepping over her twitching foot, he took the Rolodex on the table next to the phone. Looking at her body he was struck by her beauty, even in death with blood now covering her face.

She had been listening to music, Rachmaninoff's *2nd Piano Concerto*, when the fatal blows came. He bent close to her body, checking to make sure that death had arrived. Taking one last look around, he put the plastic sack under his arm and exited the front door.

He had entered her one-bedroom condo minutes earlier when he had heard the distinct sound of the shower running. She hadn't the slightest idea an uninvited guest was waiting in the hall closet for her to finish. He locked the door with the key that had been obtained just for him and just for this one time use.

He was certain no one had seen him enter or leave. He was a professional—if you wanted to call it a profession. It wasn't something that would have made his mother proud. She wouldn't be able to say at the family reunions, "Vince is doing well, he had three contracts last year and they were all clean jobs." But he knew he was good at it.

He was a 50-year old Sicilian Italian, and looked it. Dark, graying hair revealed the advancing years, along with a pot belly. He was still muscular with large arms, and had killed with his thick hands more than one time. He was not a man to make angry.

He left, marking the time on his wristwatch. It was over in less than fifteen minutes; the exact time frame he had allotted for this assignment.

He ran down the three stairs outside of the condo and, looking both ways, continued walking at a quick pace the half-block to the parked rental car. It was dark with an overcast sky. Sal had kept the engine running.

"How'd it go?" Sal asked.

Vince remained silent. He was out of breath and didn't answer immediately. They pulled away from the curb with neither noticing that it had started to rain; a rare occurrence in Phoenix.

"A mess, a shitty mess. But I know she didn't feel a thing." He felt a little pride in that information.

"Did you get anything?" Sal questioned.

"How the hell do I know? I hit her twice. She's dead, that I guarantee. I took anything that looked like it had a name on it. Here." He reached into the plastic bag pulled out the Rolodex and tossed it into Sal's lap.

"I'm going to bet there's a phone number here we can use."

Feeling the first time a bit nauseous, Vince stretched his hand over his shoulder and then to his forehead and felt the beads of sweat that had just formed.

"My God," he said softly, "the hammer went right in like her head was made of warm butter." His memory pulled up the last sound she made. The soft wheeze as the last air in her lungs escaped up through her throat and out her partially open mouth. Thankfully, he thought, her eyes were closed. That would make the memory of this job slightly easier. He had never killed with a hammer before.

They had driven only six blocks till they came to the construction site scouted earlier. Sal slowed the car and rolled down the passenger side window. Vince wiped the hammer with gloves he had been wearing. Looking to make sure no eyes were watching, he tossed it and the apartment key out the window and into the mangle of lumber and debris on the unlit construction site left by the workers a few hours earlier. They drove two more blocks and pulled next to an overflowing garbage can where Vince took off the plastic surgical shoe coverings and placed them inside. There would be no trace of him inside the crime scene.

How the hell did it get to this? Why couldn't I use a gun, he thought. The boys in Philadelphia were sending a message to someone. Put a hammer to the broad's head and take any phone directory, business cards, phone numbers, any notes from her purse and especially anything that looks like a legal folder or legal papers. His orders were explicit, especially the part about the hammer to her head. It was just as quick and painless as a bullet, he thought. BUT the simple brutality will leave a message to those who need to know. He knew it was a business decision made by someone much higher than him in what he and others like him referred as the "organization."

A 22 pistol with a silencer was his usual method. "I'm getting the hell out of this business," he said to Sal. "The old boys would never have ordered it like this. It's getting to be bullshit now." The fact that the organization had let him move to Phoenix to escape the cold snow of the east was not a big incentive right now. He didn't figure the killing would come with it. He was balding with bad eyesight.

"Why the hell are they still sending me assignments?" I've done enough, he thought.

The realization that what he did as his "job" was brutal and without empathy didn't register with him. Like many men of retirement age he couldn't wait to wrap things up, take what he had stored away in an offshore untraceable bank account and move to some small beach city in Florida.

"Damn," he said. "That's the last one like that I'm doing. It's a gun or nothing." But he knew that the big boys in Philly always got what they wanted. If it was a hammer to the head, then that's what they got. There was no room for discussion. It was the loyalty of the profession, wrong or right, that was instilled to his very core. The one thing that he considered the virtue of his life was loyalty. He didn't require or ask for a reason.

He wouldn't admit it to anyone else but he didn't like killing women. In his twisted value view it just wasn't the manly thing to do. Business is business, but his thoughts were still attempting to justify his last brutal action.

They pulled up to a pay phone and Vince got out and called the number he had memorized. The message he left was short: "The fish aren't biting anymore." Now he could go meet his friends for a beer and see how his numbers did in the weekly football pool. His assignment was complete. His small circle of friends had no idea what he did for a living or that some of those out of town business trips were to stop someone from breathing, either as punishment or to keep their vocal chords from ever singing to someone not intended to hear a song.

Like most working men, he and Sal were happy the job was finished and off work. "Drop me off at Luigi's. I'm gonna get some pasta and have a few beers before going home."

He was a lonesome man. He couldn't share his real life with others due to the simple fact that he was a killer for hire. How do you pop a cold one and tell the boys you just eliminated a beautiful young woman by smashing a hammer to her head for reasons that you didn't know?

Sal was the only one who might understand. He had met Sal earlier in the past year when he had been sent to Arizona and had been told that he had to take Sal with him on future jobs. It was another of those decisions he couldn't question. He purposely avoided Sal except when they were teamed for an elimination project. Hell, for all he knew Sal could be his next assignment. Sal pulled up in front of Luigi's and Vince got out, with no goodbye or handshake. He quietly shut the passenger door and Sal drove off in the light rain with no glance back by either one of them.

There were few like them still in the business, but all such men remaining knew the value of silence. There were no yearly conventions where secrets of the trade could be shared; no one to complain to about inadequate work conditions, and no overtime pay. And he feared that the real stress in his occupation wasn't the police, or getting caught, but rather that one of his brethren had been given his name for termination. The biggest reason for silence and the isolation of his profession was to keep his name off such a list. His one comforting thought was that it wouldn't be by a hammer to his head—it would be a bullet that he would never see coming, by someone, maybe even a friend that he would never know had the end of his life as a "business assignment." He avoided knowing too much about any of his assignments, as having too much information always carried the burden of having someone wanting your memory erased along with the body that housed it.

Lately the thought had been lingering in his mind that sure, the money was good, but the benefits of being an "organization" member were not as desirable as when he was a younger man. He unfortunately was outgrowing, simply by age, the benefits he once so enjoyed: hookers without charge and free drinks, along with fear and respect from those who knew him and his connections. That fear and respect always got him the best table at his favorite clubs.

Worst of all, he was starting to have problems sleeping. The alcohol didn't wash his memory as it once did. He was getting drunk alone more than once a week and popping Ambiens like they were jelly beans. He was up to three a night, a long way past the first one he took just a year earlier. That very first one took effect by the time he took the two swallows of wine.

He always got drunk alone, but he knew for him it was a dangerous condition. Drunks tend to talk or decide they need forgiveness for some past act. If that news ever got into circulation it would bring an intervention, only the "rehab" would take place in a freshly dug hole. Becoming a drunk or finding religion was a fast way to have a bullet heading for the back of your head. That was a fact of his profession.

CHAPTER 2

Where's Brenda?

When Brenda failed to show up for work at the law office the following morning, her co-workers were concerned, as it was not like her. In nine years she had never been late and never missed work, at least not without a phone call. After three hours her close friend Kim, working at the bank across the street, tried calling her at work, then on her cell. No answer. She left messages: "Hey best friend, where are you?" Another call. "Hey we need to talk, call me." There was more than one reason she was concerned and wanted to speak with Brenda. She continued calling the rest of the morning. Finally she learned from the law firm receptionist that Brenda had not been into work and had not called in either.

Lunch came, and finally after continued unanswered calls she called Brenda's next-door neighbor who also knew Brenda well. Kim explained her concern and asked if she would check on Brenda. "Have her call me."

Within the hour police were called by the neighbor who, after knocking several times, used the key that Brenda had given her to enter. She gasped as she dialed 911. The police were on the scene within minutes, and immediately after they arrived the mess of death was discovered. The yellow tape went up, white chalk lines were drawn, and police photos were taken. Forensics and the medical examiner soon followed. It was an investigation that found no obvious motive; just the brutal death of a young woman, with blood splattered on the open book in her lap, classical music playing, and part of her head pulverized. Blood, lots of blood.

When Lead Homicide Detective John Fordham arrived, his first thought was, what the hell is this about? He repeated that thought in his mind several times during the next hour. Forensics were dusting for prints, and the flash of the camera continued to light up the room, causing Fordham to flinch each time the click of the camera illuminated the victim and the inside of the dead girl's home. Plastic bags were placed on the hands of the body. They were dusting for fingerprints.

The medical examiner finished his initial work and left telling Detective John, "No sexual attack, just one brutal murder. I've ordered an autopsy, but the cranial damage looks like two blows by a hard object. I'm going to bet it was a hammer or something damn close to one." He was muttering to himself as he walked away.

Detective Fordham made no reply, and knew it was going to be a long night. He had already been informed by other investigating officers that it didn't look like a robbery. "Two twenties still in her purse, all her jewelry still on her dresser. Just ransacked drawers, as if somebody was looking for something, something they wanted."

Lieutenant Fordham said out loud for the third time, "What a shitty mess." Fordham much preferred suicide investigation, which wasn't nearly as complicated and were generally easy files to close, especially when a note was left.

He didn't know he and the hit man had used the same phrase. Fordham only knew he would be having a long night.

CHAPTER 3

Meet Frank O'Hara

Frank O'Hara had been hiding from his creditors for the past nine months, ever since the divorce was final. He began answering his business phone by saying, "Hello," rather than, "O'Hara here," or, "This is Frank."

His life, his money, and his work had been on a downward slide since the judge hit the gavel and said "granted." The divorce had been mentally painful and financially debilitating. He gave her anything and everything she wanted. His guilt, more than her request, demanded such payment. He wished he could have given her more.

On some occasions, when he didn't recognize the number calling, he would answer his phone with a Hispanic accent and as soon as he realized it was a bill collector he would say, "No speak English," and quickly hang up. There was no chance he would answer when the phone immediately rang again. He believed that one of the best things to come along for people who owed money was caller ID.

Sides were taken by their friends in the past year and the majority of who he had considered his friends laid their sympathies with his ex-wife who had done no wrong. It was without question he had been on the wrong side of the marriage vows. He gave her everything in the divorce he could, except the one thing she wanted above all the rest: something to take the pain of his actions away.

Lately Frank had been playing a song from the 80's over and over in his mind. He remembered the words from the part that reverberated in his head, "I want you, I need you, but there ain't no way I'm ever gonna love you. Now don't be sad, two out of three ain't bad." Damn, he thought, that guy Meatloaf was right on. He recalled not being that familiar with it when it first hit the radio waves, but now those words seemed to play in his mind and came to him at the oddest hours, like a mantra explaining the reasons for his past year's actions. But the guilt inside his mind yelled that he was selfish at the very least, and more likely a selfish prick.

It wasn't sex as most thought, that had pulled him to the new young love. Frank had spent most of his life living on, or damn near as close as he could to, the edge. Then she left.

There was no doubt as Frank looked back, that he could see her exit coming. His marriage finally ended when his wife found out and moved out. Frank filed for the divorce, which he believed was the right thing to do. The reason for the divorce, which had shocked all of their friends, was actually no big secret. In a no-fault divorce state like Arizona cause was never listed, but was common knowledge if anyone really was interested. In Frank's case it was another woman. Most of Frank's friends were well aware, and unlike the hit man, shared their knowledge with their wives. Such information was sent out faster than flowers on Mother's Day.

Not just a woman. A younger woman. Thirty years younger. The worst scenario for jilted wives, their friends and relatives, and Frank's friends and relatives. A half-assed affair that went against the laws of nature, it made for great gossip and better yet, was perfect for failure.

Frank knew they'd never understand that it was a real relationship, simple as that. He never felt the need or desire to explain it. There didn't seem to be a starting point for him to talk about it, and other than the bartender who had to listen to him on the third margarita, no one else wanted to hear or understand his side, if he even had one. He was alone, and everyone (including the lost love and the ex-wife) thought he deserved it. Frank silently and sadly agreed with them all.

Even younger men who had never met him and heard of his affair didn't like him, simply for being an "old man" who was operating in what they perceived to be their territory. The prevalent idea that it was all about sex for him and money for her didn't actually apply. Frank tried not to give a shit about what anyone thought, but still did not like hurting the woman he had married twelve years earlier, or falling off the pedestal his daughter and son had put him on before hearing about it.

She had been gone more than two years. He had thrown away all the photos, all her notes, all the items that one has from a four-year relationship. But he couldn't throw away the memories and pictures of her that still played in his mind.

Everything turned out the same, he thought. Didn't make a damn bit of difference. He should have moved in with her like she asked. But deep down he knew she wouldn't have stayed around forever. The age factor didn't bother her, or so she said. She would sometimes tease him by telling him when he got too old she would just put him in a closet "with some good books and snacks." Frank loved her not as a younger woman, but as the person she was to him at the time. The age difference didn't bother him but wisdom taught him that one day it would.

As much as he hated the thought, he had reached the sad conclusion that he didn't blame her for leaving—it was actually the right move for her to make.

He'd heard she had become seriously involved with a wealthy man from Norway or somewhere cold, and had gotten married and had a baby. He bet himself that she'd met her husband through one of those Internet dating services, but he found himself truly happy for her. He knew from many past talks with her about her tough childhood, and was glad to see a happy ending finally heading her way. It was hard, but mentally he had finally let go. Though it wasn't his choice at the time it was, he knew, the right choice. He also knew his ex-wife was, and would always be, a close friend. God had made her that way, and Frank felt lucky for that. She had always been a bright light in his often dark world.

His life had too many chains attached at the time he fell for the "other woman," and the one thing he didn't have was the guts it takes to end a marriage that outwardly and inwardly had no garbage. Frank's wife often said she had the happiest marriage she knew. All through the time

Frank was seeing another woman, he had never treated his wife badly. When he finally did make the decision to ask for a divorce it was a shock to his wife. It was the hardest thing Frank had ever done. The other woman had already left his life by this time; she had no more waiting left in her. The divorce, when it came, was now a big empty and very late gesture that Frank still wasn't sure he ever wanted. His many religious values had always seemed to mentally block a move towards divorce, along with the harsh reality that his wife always believed in him, and more importantly, was always good to him.

He picked the phone on the second ring. It was a number he didn't recognize, and he was an inch away from the Spanish accent,

"Hello."

"Hello, Frank O'Hara is this you?"

Frank did not answer.

"Is Frank O'Hara there?"

Finally Frank replied, "Who wants to know?"

"Kim Dawson. I'm a friend of your ex-wife, Julie. She gave me your number and said I should talk to you."

Doesn't ring a bell, he thought. "Who are you?"

"Kim Dawson, I work at the bank, where your ex-wife's account is."

"Shit" he said softly, then answered, "I'll get a payment in as soon as a check I'm holding clears, okay?"

"No, no," she said, before he began with his next excuse sentence. "I'm not calling about the bank, this is a personal matter. Julie said you could help me, that you could give me advice and tell me what to do. She said you know all the right people and if she was in trouble she would call you, that you're the best private investigator there is. Then she gave me your number and told me to call."

Frank sipped his coffee, making sure to wipe the corners of his mouth with his napkin.

"I'm in trouble. It can't wait," she continued.

His first thought was, his ex-wife was like that, didn't have a mean bone in her body. After all the crap he had heaped on their marriage she still referred him a client and probably gave him a hell of a recommendation. She had forgiven him, and in her own way loved him still. She remembered the good in him and as she told him when she left his life, "I was your biggest fan, and probably always will be." He replied through his guilt that he was sorry he hurt her, a phrase that seemed too trite, too insincere. But that's where it ended.

"Yeah well...what can I do for you?" He was still apprehensive, as his years in business had taught him not to trust too quickly.

"A friend of mine was murdered and I know some things, I'm afraid." Her speech grew quicker and her voice rose in conjunction with the speed.

"She told me what she did and I warned her something bad would happen, but not murder," she began to cry. "It's bad...I can't talk to anyone...why did she tell me? How did I get myself into this? I think they might get me too. I really wasn't her best friend, it's just when someone needs help...I felt...I thought..."

Before she started her next word, Frank interrupted.

"Slow down, slow down, who is going to 'get you'?"

"I...don't know, I don't know!"

A brain wave flashed in his mind: a loony-tune, my wife sent me a loony-tune.

"Well if you don't know who 'they' are, then why are 'they' coming after you?" She didn't notice the sarcasm in his voice.

"Brenda told me, she told me some things. She took some files from her work. This guy she was seeing, she did it for him. She didn't want to do it. I guess it was more than just seeing, she told me was falling in love with him. She told me not to tell anyone. He needed help, his family was going to be in trouble and lose lots of money, their life savings. Brenda was killed two days ago. The police told me she had been beaten. I heard another one say her head was bashed in...brutally bashed in."

As if there was another way, Frank thought.

She inhaled then exhaled a large sigh. "Can I talk to you in person? I'm uncomfortable telling this to you over the phone. I'm still at the bank but I can leave. I'm too upset to work now."

Before Frank agreed to a meeting with someone he didn't know, that concerned somebody being killed, he wanted and needed more information.

"Tell me again, how did you get my number?" he asked

"I spoke to your wife when she came into the bank this morning and she saw that I had been crying and was scared. She's always been so nice to me. I told her that my friend had been murdered and I needed to get some advice real fast and I had no one I could trust or talk to. I didn't think I could trust the police, and Brenda specifically said not to tell them. I wanted to see if you think I should...it sounds crazy, I know."

She paused briefly. "She said you were a private investigator and that you would be able to tell me what

I should do, that you always helped people and could be trusted. Then she said..."

Before she could finish, Frank interrupted. "Is my ex-wife connected to any of this?"

He had a passing thought that this was a ruse set up by his ex-wife for some reason. It was the word "trusted" that bounced off the inside of his mind.

"No, I talked to her after the police interviewed me. I didn't tell them everything, I'm scared," she replied.

"I answered all the questions truthfully, but..." She took another long breath, "I have something I should have given them or told them. Can I tell you? Can I trust you?"

When Frank did not answer, she broke the silence.

"Can you tell me who I should go too? What to do? Do you think I...your wife said you always knew what to do in dealing with the police and I know she is a good person."

Frank put his hand up like greeting an Indian in peace.

"Hold it right here," he said. He pushed the phone away from his ear. This was moving too fast. Life had taught him that there were some things not worth knowing unless you got the rules of engagement established. His first rule lately was to get paid. He was not against helping anyone but if this is going to be an investigation case, with a murder in the mix—if he was even going to take the case—he needed to let her know what he wanted for his time before he heard anything else. It wouldn't be the first time that he felt sorry for someone and ended up giving him or her his 30 years of investigation knowledge for nothing.

This young lady had the misfortune to call right after he had opened his mail and seen the second notice and third demand for payment envelopes. He also learned from past experience that if this call wasn't going to go anywhere, it would end sooner when money was mentioned.

"Okay," he said, "first of all, my fee is $150 an hour, plus expenses. I'll need, uh," he went into a fast second level of thought as he added up what he was short for rent, "Make that a thousand up front, in cash; you got that kind of money?"

Frank needed the cash, so if some loony tune wanted his advice he would give it to her and pay on a bill or two. Maybe even send a little to the daughter and son he had not spoken to in months, who had neither forgiven nor forgotten.

"Yes, I have my savings," she said. "Can I completely trust you? I'm still very frightened."

"You can trust me," he dryly replied. Evidently she hadn't got the whole story from his ex-wife or maybe she did if she asked that question. Either way it's okay, he mentally shrugged.

"You got a coffee shop by your house, somewhere we can meet?" he continued.

"Yeah, Denny's on East Camelback," she said. "I can be there in an hour."

"Get the cash and I'll see you there. Until then," he said, "don't talk to anyone else about this, and wear a red sweater or something else red so I'll recognize you, I'll find you, don't worry. I'll see you in one hour. Oh, and don't tell anyone you spoke to me." Frank at this point wanted no connection to her; too many nut jobs running around. They hung up at the same time.

CHAPTER 4

More on Frank the Investigator

Frank always felt better with a little cash in his pocket; greenbacks and self-image were tightly knotted together with him. Though the recent turn of his life had humbled him greatly, it was still a sad fact of his life that he harbored the idea that money usually equaled happiness...or, as so many had said before him, that it was a lot easier to live with sadness and depression if there was some cash in your pocket.

There were those prayerful times when he would be in church and recall the saintly admonishment of giving everything to the poor. He always had a buck or two for those standing on the corner holding a scribbled sign saying they would work for food. The signs always ended with a phrase to supposedly make you feel guilty: "God Bless."

He didn't mind a bit when he thought it would go for booze. Hell, he reasoned, if he were standing on a street corner holding up a sign like that he'd need a drink first, then you can hand him the rake and shovel.

His mother, during his youth, had tried to teach him differently, but had failed her assignment while alive. She would have been proud to know that Frank, as he got older and wiser, finally understood the lessons wasted in his youth and was re-learning the ones he had lost somewhere in the passing years. Those years seemed to have gone by so fast. Frank occasionally, when on those margaritas, had this fatalistic vision of himself after finally finding and living a life of total and complete virtue saying, "I'll be damned, I finally get it," and then dropping dead by the Power so he'd never screw it up again. He knew it was a misguided thought but still he had to admit he had heard of a lot of young people who seemed to have got it all right and boom—dead the next day.

Frank had always told his close friends that if by any chance they hit heaven and were behind him in the judgment line, to get out of that line quickly somehow because God was going to be pretty pissed off after his review of Frank's life. It might be better for them to give Him time to cool down a bit before their name was called.

If he got the chance, he was going to tell God that we needed and could have used a little more help down here. It seemed to Frank that God wasn't watching people in the palm of His hand as much as He should have. But what the hell was God going to think of his opinion? Frank was like Job, wondering where in the hell was Frank when God was putting this altogether? But Frank actually knew if and when he got "there," to keep his mouth shut. He can complain to the others but don't let God know he was still pissed about those flies crawling around those starving baby's faces he saw on TV late at night when he was looking for a good movie to watch. He had to admit, just to himself, that they had got to him and he was sending in the ten bucks a month. When he mailed the first check he put in a note that read, "Please buy some fly spray."

One of his latest and most devout prayers was thanking God for letting him live long enough to be sorry for the sins of his past life. That was the true gift of old age, he thought. The longer you lived the more you seemed to discover how many things you had to be sorry about.

Recently he admitted to himself that he would have given all the money he would ever get his hands on for one more chance to do the past years differently. He knew life didn't work that way and as stupid as he knew he was for thinking so, it was a thought that often crossed through his mind. The hard reality of what money won't buy had grown very clear to him in the last year. It certainly had no power against a broken heart.

He would tell his friends who had a tale of needing money to cure an immediate financial problem that they weren't talking about cancer or some life threatening disease. He would say some guy somewhere just walked out of his doctor's office after being told that he has six months to live, and that guy would love to be able to say to the doctor, well here take this five thousand and have the doctor tell him okay, the cancer is gone now. And that same guy, in a heartbeat, would trade places with them and their good health along with all their money problems.

It was true, Frank knew, you can't fix heartache and you can't send cancer away with any amount of money. There were bigger problems in life than being broke. The sad part, Frank knew, was that only being broke had taught that lesson to Frank, as was the case for most other people.

The red BMW convertible that he currently couldn't afford pulled into the Denny's parking lot. Frank checked himself in the rear view mirror as best as he could before exiting the vehicle. There was likely a spot somewhere on his shirt or pants but he didn't see one. His hair, streaked by age with gray and a splash of Just for Men was a convertible blown-all-over look. But in reality it had looked that way before he put the top down.

He ran his hand across the top of his head attempting to straighten it out, then wiped the corners of his mouth. He looked his 64 years but really didn't feel his age. He never understood how the years came and left so quickly. His mind had not grown up with his body. He still sang out loud with the rock music coming from the radio in his car. It was usually blaring; he also loved classical music, country music, and jazz piano players. He was well-read and could speak on any subject other than quantum physics. He also was one of the few people he knew who had read *War and Peace* all the way through and was able to keep track of all the characters.

He was a complex man. Those that knew him well used the word "unusual" or "different" in their description of Frank O'Hara. He had a photographic memory and seemed to never forget anything, especially things people had once told him and now wanted him to forget.

He was known by clients and his few friends as a funny man, a generous man, a spiritual man, a prayerful man, a restless man. He often found fault when he thought too often and too deep on the subject of a higher supernatural power. He also had difficulty with the idea of a devil out there lurking to steal his soul, and he had given up years ago trying to make sense out of life: the evil he had seen, death itself, or where we went after we drew in our last breath. He still attended Mass on Sundays, and throughout each day often had silent prayers on his lips, even while fighting his own doubts and questions. Frank could sum it all up with one statement: Public Relations.

Frank thought God needed a good PR man, some good advertisement, billboards and some answers to the wars, murders, abused children and hungry people, especially the starving African children with flies crawling on their face. That we need some help down here was a prevailing thought in church when Frank attended and bowed his head in prayer.

He prayed each day, doing his best to keep his own wants and needs out of heavenly petitions. He usually believed that someone was listening, but there were times he wondered. He admitted with some reasoning that there must be some point in all of this...it just can't be as if mankind got abandoned, even if a lot of mankind acted like it.

He questioned many aspects of life, especially the one thought that lately popped up in his mind concerning God, which happened when much of Frank's thinking did: on about the third drink. It was that there weren't any references to God or his Son, Jesus Christ, having a sense of humor. Frank had read the Bible and couldn't find any mention in anyone's writing where Jesus, or anyone else, told a joke or laughed at someone's joke. There wasn't the slightest grin when Peter tripped and fell out of the boat?

It must have been a fall, as prone to mistakes as he often was portrayed. Frank had reasoned Peter was his best example. He had traveled with Christ for three years, seen all those miracles; the blind cured, the deaf able to hear, the lepers healed. Hell, he even saw Lazarus raised from the dead. Yet when Christ was caught and on his way to being judged and crucified, he denied knowing him, not once, but three times. Peter was watching out for his own ass. Yeah, thought Frank, we've all got a lot of Peter in of us.

Jesus Christ, Frank thought, was always portrayed as very serious...kind and merciful, but very serious. He was mad as hell when He tossed the money changers out of the temple, but no mention of a smile or a laugh. There was, though, the gospel story about the wedding feast at Canaan where Jesus, at the request of his mother Mary, turned some jugs of water into wine after the host had the embarrassing calamity of running out of wine. Frank thought that at this point some of the guests were taking their gifts back and heading for the door when alas, water into wine, very good wine. Frank liked that story and irreverently thought that Christ would have been some great guy to run around with back in his younger days. He could even hear himself whispering into Jesus' ear, "Hey someone just took the last Heineken." Frank knew though that God must have had a great sense of humor, even if it wasn't written into the Bible. After all, He made us. And those fishermen he ran around with for three years must have had some good jokes, right?

Generally speaking, Frank had to be reminded to look both ways before crossing the street. A man who had time, or better said, would make time, to listen to anyone's trouble, he hated detail and lost his car keys once a week. He was an exaggeration of many things at different times. Six feet tall and fifteen pounds overweight, nicely dressed but by noon didn't look it. By lunch he had trouble keeping his pants up and was constantly tightening his belt often without the desired result.

It was best not to form a first impression until at least the third time one was forming one. Those who had been on the other side of past cases he worked on soon discovered that it was a mistake to underestimate his ability. He always found the right questions to ask, and—more importantly—got the right answers.

He had a list of contacts throughout the local city and state agencies, developed through his years of learning where to go and what to look for and who could help when seeking information that would win the case, all kept confidential. It had taken all of his 30 years in the business to build the trust necessary for those contacts to work. He was very good at following both the money and paper trail. He had a reputation of being able to find anyone, especially those who didn't want to be found.

Frank held a unique gift in getting people to tell him things they wouldn't tell their priest, rabbi or best friend. He sized up people quickly and he was right on. In his younger investigative years he had been sent to the cold barren shores of Alaska and the sunny shores of Hawaii on various assignments. He had been sent on business trips to London, Vienna, and Tel Aviv looking for and finding the missing witness or the missing papers, which would become trial exhibits and turn the case.

He was as close as one could get to a law degree without having or wanting one. He knew hearsay rules and the rules of evidence. He could, and often did, work comfortably in the gray areas of law. He knew what the attorney wanted and needed, and most of the time got it. They didn't ask how or where. It was known among those that had employed his services that it wasn't a good idea to question Frank about such things. Just pay his bill and know he always kept his mouth shut.

The world was changing in Frank's profession. Most of the PI work being done today lacked the finesse that Frank had spent years developing. Computers now mostly did PI work. Although, Frank didn't understand completely this new tool of his trade; he did appreciate the complexity and the immense capability of storing records, and then with the push of a button having access to these records. Computers now kept a cold uncaring history of most citizens with or without their permission, starting with a simple look at driving records to the vast expanse of past medical treatments. Human interaction in the new PI world had slowly dissolved. Frank didn't like it, but he categorized it with cell phones, Blackberries, and microwave ovens... none of which existed when he got his first case.

For him, some information still required a personal touch, like the so-called gray areas of the case. Information buried, often hidden somewhere between the computer printout and the truth, was the area of PI investigation in which Frank was the best. But he knew the PI world was inevitably passing him by. He was one of the last of his breed. Frank didn't tell many, but he honestly still missed his old office with the electric typewriter. Those days just seemed easier, like when you called your pharmacy or utility company or bank and a real person actually answered. Now they all seemed to have picked up and left with their electric typewriters.

One of those gray areas in his line of work that Frank still felt bad about had occurred a few years back when he was working on a wrongful death case in which the liability was clearly resting on his defense attorney's deep-pocket client. Frank was hired to see if he could get information to knock down the potential money damages that the insurance company was going to have to pay out.

Frank's employers had been offered evidence that the deceased was a needed husband, and great provider. He was a man who would be sadly missed by all, and whose untimely demise was activated by the wrongful deeds of the defendant. His death, according to the plaintiff attorney, caused not only lifetime grief, but would bring financial hardship to the lives of his wife and children.

To defend that damaging information involved attempting to find and develop negative facts about the plaintiff and presenting those findings in the litigation. That presentation would hopefully cause the plaintiff to be interested in settling for less money and not going to a trial where such information had a chance to be divulged. Plaintiff attorneys knew juries could be less sympathetic with their verdict and award when deliberating for a party whose negative lifestyle fell below their acceptable norm.

Plaintiff attorneys didn't want their clients to show tattoos, wear rings in the nose, studs in the tongue, or in any fashion imply that they were "born to raise hell." They hated to use the argument that even though their client might be a no-good bum, he was still entitled to compensation for the wrong done to him. Even if true, it was still often a hard sell to a jury.

It was a potential multi million dollar loss at the point Frank was called and entered the case. Through investigation, which included talking to friends and coworkers of the deceased, Frank learned the dead husband and father had a reputation for drinking too much and Frank started there, following a trail that opened up slowly. More than one casual interviewee mentioned that the plaintiff's long-suffering wife had gone to Al Anon meetings during the last three months of his life for support to cope with the man she married and his alcoholic life. She continued attending these meetings after his death for the mental support she received at these gatherings. Frank began attending the same meeting as if he had a similar problem with a wife, and in a few weeks had struck up numerous conversations in an effort to become friendly with the grief-stricken woman. She casually mentioned one night that she had been planning to divorce her husband and had made an appointment to see an attorney a few weeks before her husband's death.

She had not told his employer yet, as she believed they eventually would discover his "cooking" of the company books. She believed he would be fired, but he was killed first. At one point she asked Frank what she should do. Frank replied that it was a tough decision and he didn't have an answer, ending with a weak piece of advice: "Let your conscience be your guide."

The part of the conversation with her that held less importance to Frank was that her husband had promised to end the affair, stop gambling, and work out some way to pay back the money to his employer. Frank knew by now her wrongful death case was financially going to take a hard hit.

She told Frank over coffee at the end of the last Al Anon meeting he attended that she had never told anyone about her marital trouble but felt relieved to voice her feelings on these issues. She told Frank that he was such a good listener and sympathetic to her plight, and she even apologized at one point for talking so much and thanking Frank for his patience. She admitted to Frank that an attorney she didn't know had contacted her and she agreed after his persuasion to file a wrongful death case. It wasn't something she was initially interested in doing. But the attorney had told her of the possible large amount of money she would receive and how "it was her duty to see such malpractice not happen again to another family."

She still loved him and, as in so many other cases when talking about the dead, buried the truth and talked about the times he was a wonderful caring husband, and the great memories of him with the children. She seemed to bury the reality of her shitty marriage with heaps of sorrow and guilt for not trying harder or doing more, or not being there when he needed her. Generally though, between the platitudes she conveyed the true feelings more than once... that he had been a pain in the ass, had physically hit her on more than one occasion when he was drunk, and that her children were actually happier when he was not around the house. The truth was, she continued, they were frightened of him when he came home drunk, which was several times a week at the end.

He had created huge money debts during his drunken bouts of gambling at the Indian casinos and she was planning to see a bankruptcy attorney, except she had now filed this case against the doctor and hospital and the nurses. She told Frank the details, not knowing that Frank had weeks earlier read all the hospital records.

The litigation filed was against a local hospital that had clear liability for administering not only the wrong dose, but the completely wrong medication when her husband was sent to the emergency room after suffering a seizure at work. He died within minutes of the injection.

Frank was truly sympathetic, and would at times during these talks place his hand over hers with a warm pat saying, "It's okay. It's going to be okay."

The sad and ironic truth of it was that Frank actually helped her and she felt better when she left Frank and the Al Anon meetings. On the drive home she thought that nice man was a gift to her life at this troubled time. He seemed to just listen and had gotten her to talk and bring out feelings she had mentally buried for some time. It was good for her, she thought. He seemed to know just the right things to say, and gave her direction in dealing with her grief and getting on with her life without the burden of failure riding with her, as she continued life as a new widow and single mother of two young children.

Frank had truly been a blessing in her life. She wondered what he did for a living, and was going to ask him, but never saw him again. In fact, she didn't even know his last name.

Of course all this information obtained by Frank was against the rules of civil court procedure and would be denied use in any manner by any judge, as it was covered by a common legal principle called "fruit of the forbidden tree." Nor would Frank's employers ever have authorized him to go the plaintiff, who was represented by counsel, and get her to talk to a nice understanding stranger she met at Al Anon whose number one purpose was to get her to talk about her life and dead husband, simply for the purpose of gathering information to help raise the defendant's side of the legal bar. Frank knew he was way across the line and on his own. He had been there before.

Frank verbally turned in his report behind the closed and locked doors of his law firm client. Nothing was stated ever in writing. Shortly thereafter the woman's deposition was taken, and during questioning the woman who did not lie gradually verified the information about the other woman, the dead husband's gambling problem, and the cashing of stolen checks from his place of employment, as well as her plans of seeing a divorce attorney and the possibility of filing for bankruptcy after she divorced him before he did it for her and died.

The plaintiff attorney had never encountered nor seen such a successful "fishing expedition" by the defense attorneys. The information being "discovered" on record was destroying her case.

Frank later heard that the plaintiff attorneys were astonished when this information began spilling out and into the record. They soon asked to talk settlement, and the insurance company was thrilled to write their check out for far less than they had set aside. After all it was their insured who gave the husband a lethal dose of the wrong medicine according to previous medical testimony. It stated in the record he would have survived the seizure.

Frank's name never appeared in files, nor was his association known to the widow and her attorneys. The attorneys were happy to take 33 percent of the $500,000 settlement paid, though that was only a fraction of what they had originally banked on. They then repaid their costs before sending the rest to the widow and the two young children.

It was all because of Frank joining Al Anon for a few weeks.

Frank thought there was a sense of justice to it, but he had too much heart not to feel like a piece of crap when he thought about those talks with the misty-eyed widow over coffee, who had not the slightest indication that everything she was saying to the nice gentleman was closing the cash register door for her.

Frank cashed the check made out to one of his process serving companies for his fee of eight thousand and flew up to his favorite place: Cannon Beach on the Oregon coast. He walked on the beach for a couple of days trying not to think about how he made his living.

He felt the wind and light mist on his face and had some ridiculous thought that he hoped Heaven, if he ever got there, had something like this place. It was the one area in the world he could always find peace, if just for an hour or two. He made a mental promise during one of those walks on the beach that someday he was going to send that widow some money in an attempt to buy back some of his character...if that was possible?

Neither the insurance company nor their attorneys ever sent Frank a thank you note. But they made a mental note to themselves to use "that guy" again.

You only heard Frank O'Hara's name when you were in trouble and someone to whom you told your trouble said, "Call this guy, he'll tell you what to do."

He had the stomach paunch life tends to give after 60 when one doesn't exercise like the doctors encourage one to; and try as he might he hadn't given up the morning Danish with his coffee. Or, worse, the cigar with the margaritas, which in the past year had become more than a twice-weekly occurrence. His graying hair always looked like it had never seen a brush.

He rarely looked at himself in a mirror. He was always clean, except for the usual spot or two on his shirt and he was always complimented on his after-shave that had been Polo for the last 20 years. He would catch himself stooping when he passed his reflection in a store window and immediately throw his shoulders back. Lately he always tried to walk briskly. He had started his own personal battle with age after the breakup.

It must have been because he was looking old, he would think, although he knew most of the good reasons why, and age wasn't in the top ten. The age factor seemed to be the one he wanted to believe most even though she denied it. The reality of the neglect he had administered on both relationships without thinking was too hard for him to dwell upon. Such thoughts always made him wonder how he could have been so stupid. Those thoughts, when they lingered, were soon followed by a margarita and a cigar...and the bartender who had heard it all before and was pissed he had to listen to it again.

CHAPTER 5

Brenda and the File

He straightened his red and blue striped tie, pulled up his tan pants and walked into the coffee shop. He saw her in the red sweater immediately and walked confidently to her booth. Making sure his shoulders were erect he smiled and said, "Kim?"

She was younger than she sounded on the phone, maybe early thirties, and she filled out the red sweater nicely. He held out his hand. She had long dark hair in a ponytail. Her face, though recently dusted with makeup, revealed the tears as well her beauty and also her fear. Her eyes were a stunning light blue. They would make it difficult for Frank to stay focused. She started to stand as she reached up her hand. Frank motioned for her to sit back down as he squeezed and let go of her right hand. She was wearing black slacks, Frank guessed size six.

Before he sat down completely and spoke he noticed she glanced out the window next to the booth, as if to make sure he wasn't followed. She clutched her hands rubbing her fingers back and forth. Frank casually pushed his hand through his hair and held the fleeting thought that he hoped he looked good...as most men do when sitting across from an attractive woman.

She was holding a large manila legal envelope. He pushed the paper napkin with the place setting to the side, turned over the upside down coffee mug, and said, "Let's start at the top."

His mindset at this point was to get this meeting over and get out of here as soon as possible. As good as she looked, he knew this was not the time or place for anything other than business. Age had finally taught him such a lesson.

The waiter poured the coffee and as she left Kim started speaking almost in a whisper. Her eyes were misted as she told how she had first met Brenda four years ago at a Jazzercise class. "We were instant friends. I mean, we just connected. Started having lunch and then sometimes met after work for a drink. She started confiding in me, and I told her all about me too. It was like a perfect friendship.

"I knew she was seeing this guy, but I'm sure no one else did. I think she was somewhat embarrassed to think she was falling for him. He was totally different from anyone she had ever dated, kind of rough around the edges and uneducated. But he made her laugh.

"He was too smooth and too fast, I thought from what she told me. But to Brenda he was just hiding an insecure child inside...those were her words."

She looked around before continuing, as if the mention of his name was danger. "I'm sure she saw something in him she liked. Like many of us, she thought she could change him. When she talked about him I was always sworn to secrecy. I always agreed, because I just thought it was girl stuff." She wiped her eyes with the napkin.

"Toward the end I started sensing some real fear in her. Not physical fear, so much." She paused and looked again out the window.

"I can't explain it, fear of something unknown... unsaid... but she always denied it. If I mentioned it, she would say, 'Oh, it will be okay,' and apologize for having me worry. But in the last weeks she seemed more tense and upset." Her voice trailed off. She took a sip of her coffee before starting again.

"She never introduced me or any of her other friends to him...it was very hushed. I think I was really the only one who knew, but I'm not sure. If I didn't know better it would be easy to believe she just made him up. Sometimes it just seemed so weird."

"How did she meet him?" Frank asked.

"His name was Dominic." She paused, then continued, "They met at a happy hour bar close to where she worked. She worked for Lewis and Johnson, the big law firm. She was a secretary, but she worked for one of the head attorneys, Mr. Lewis himself."

"She was in the commercial real estate department, or something like that. It was legal work for some land developers. They also represented at least one of the Indian tribes and their casino. She wasn't fond of the work. She and Dominic, his last name was Serrano, began spending a lot of time together. I knew it was getting serious, because I didn't see her as often as before. He was taking up all of her time. When I did speak to her she still managed to keep me in the dark about who he was and what he did. She was extremely evasive about it and grew more protective of their relationship. The day before she was murdered, she called me late, after 10:00. I know, as I go to bed right after the news. She was frantic and said she needed to see me right away and was on her way over. She hung up before I could ask why, and then she was there. I let her in. She was scared. Said she had to give me something and I had to hold it for her. She said she had no one else to trust, no one else to turn too. Mentioned something about taking it from her office and had to get it back, something about a search warrant, and she gave me this envelope. She insisted I tell no one about it—she was very positive about that part— and told me either she or Dominic would pick it up from me the next day. None of it made any sense to me. I did gather that no one from her law office knew she had taken it. Then I heard nothing. I waited for Dominic or Brenda to come pick up the file. It would have been the first time I would meet him, but he never came, and Brenda never came or called. I tried all the next day to reach her at work and then at home...nothing."

She slid the manila envelope towards Frank. "I left four or five messages, and tried later in the day to locate Dominic, but I didn't find a phone number. I called the happy hour bar where they met. She told me he knew everyone there but the bartender said he didn't know anything, and hung up real abruptly."

Again pointing at the envelope, "She told me not to open it but just hide it. She said she couldn't keep it at her house. She was afraid her house might be searched...and she could lose her job...it was all so fast and made no sense. She told me that Dominic and his family were depending on her and he had called and told her to get it out of house right away and give it to someone she could trust. He told her he would explain later, but the police might come to her house. She promised she would get it back the next day. She said she couldn't explain now, but under no circumstances was she to call the police."

She took a Kleenex from her purse and again wiped her eyes. "She said she was so sorry and embarrassed to ask me, and sorry she got involved." She looked out the window again. "I wasn't happy about that either, but she said she would explain everything to me later. She thanked me, gave me a hug and was gone."

She sipped her coffee and then looked down putting her hands over her eyes.

"She left before I could even think of anything to say. Her last words to me were how thankful she was to have me as a friend and repeated not to say anything about it, not to anyone. I thought it was all so weird but at the time she seemed frantic and I didn't question her; I just put the envelope under my bed. I had trouble sleeping and the next morning I started calling her. But, nothing...I never spoke to her again. The police got my messages on her phone and from calling her neighbor. That's how they found me and came to the bank.

"I asked them if she was okay and to have her call me." She looked around, before continuing. "The police asked me a few questions. Why had I called Brenda? Why I wondered if she was okay. "They were interviewing all of Brenda's friends and when I asked why, I was told she had been murdered. I started crying hysterically. I couldn't believe it. Sometimes I still don't. I was so upset they broke off the interview. They said to call them if I thought of anything, and someone would get back to me.

"I didn't have time or even think to say anything about the envelope or Dominic. Then, after they left, something told me to keep quiet about it. Brenda was so positive about her last instruction to me. I know it makes no sense at all."

She looked away and stared out the window again then quickly looked up and faced Frank. "I never went to sleep. When I left my apartment I made sure I wasn't followed. When I was told she had been murdered it stunned me and I just...closed up, and now I don't know why I didn't say anything about it. But I didn't."

"Am I in big trouble?" She looked Frank in the eyes wanting the answer she needed to hear.

"Don't know," he said. "What's in the envelope?" He knew by now she had opened it.

"I did open it. It is just a bunch of legal documents and a disc...it doesn't mean a thing to me, but I do recognize some of the names. Mr. Lewis and some others I've heard or read about. Politicians, and something about casinos in Cuba, and drugs. I was so upset I didn't pay much attention. It had numbers beside the names, like percentages, and a mention of a big meeting in Costa Rica. It didn't make a lot of sense to me other than it sounded and looked illegal. I don't know why Brenda would have it or ever give it to me?

"I was going to call the police this morning and tell them about it when—and this is where it really frightened me—last night, around midnight, I got a phone call. I didn't answer it, and the entire message left on my answering machine was about giving the envelope back that Brenda gave me. They knew I had it. They said they were friends of

Dominic. And I was to leave it outside my door under the doormat and it would be picked up. They said they were watching me. The voice said they hoped it was still sealed and told me to forget I ever saw it...said it might cause me some harm, and if I wondered why, I should ask how Brenda died...and hung up. I tried to immediately trace the call, but it went to a pay phone.

"The voice was so firm and repeated not to tell anyone, that they would know if I did and I could have a problem if it wasn't there. It scared me, really scared me. I decided to call the police as soon as I got to work but I still wasn't sure if I should leave it. I couldn't sleep.

"I left for work real early, 4 AM, and went to an all-night McDonald's. I took the envelope and locked it in my trunk. I was so scared, I was hoping a policeman would come by and I could grab him and tell him. None came, so I went to work at eight. I guess you know the rest."

Frank looked straight into her blue eyes. "Lady, not to be overly blunt...but I still have no idea what the hell any of this means."

"Will you help me? Please?" She grabbed his hand. Her plea and her hand on his hooked Frank, though he didn't like it.

"Yeah, I'm going to do some checking around for you, but we do need to turn this envelope over to homicide. I have a very good friend there. I'll contact him this morning and set something up for you. You might need to go into protective custody or it might be all a bunch of nothing."

Kim was quick with her reply, "These people are serious, and Brenda even told me not to trust the police.

Can you be sure? I know it all sounds incredible and stupid. You will go with me to the police?"

Frank was stunned at both her story and how his ex-wife still referred him a case. The guilt in his stomach rolled over once more. He had heard lots of strange stories in his 30-year career and this one was quickly screaming toward the "don't touch this" list.

"I also should also mention that in one of my last conversations with Brenda before the night she came over with the file to hide, she said that Dominic was in some kind of trouble, something to do with his family. She said she was helping him and if anyone knew how she was helping him it could really hurt her and Dominic.

"She said that Dominic was being pushed to get some real estate information and he needed her to help him for his family. That's about it, that's all I can remember. Except I don't know how anyone got my phone number, I'm not even listed."

Frank took a few seconds before responding. He took a sip of coffee and decided mentally that if her story was true, she was in serious need of help. She was right about this being big trouble—maybe too big for him.

A second brain wave was sending him another message: Or is it totally all bullshit? Regardless of which brain message told him what to think of her story, both levels agreed that there was no question she thought it was real.

"When did that last conversation with Brenda take place?"

"The same day, at lunch, before she came to my house that night."

She again pushed toward his side of the table the thick envelope with $1,200 in cash from her savings account paper-clipped to the outside. He was finishing counting it when she asked again, "Please help me, what should I do?"

Frank was impressed. She had given him more than he asked for. He grabbed the bill for the coffee from the side of the table, and taking the envelope with her cash in his other hand he stood and said, "I'll take a look at this and see what I can do," picking up the file, "and I will need to make a couple of calls."

He gave her two of his business cards, and had her write two phone numbers on the back of the second one where she could get a message. "The second number is my sister in Colorado." She handed him the card back.

"I'll call you within 24 hours."

"Thank you." She took his hand still sitting at the table. "Your ex-wife was right. I know you will help me."

Frank turned and felt the sudden rush of pressure erupt in his brain....followed by a fleeting thought of handing her money back and wishing her good luck. But he didn't. She stood up with him, still holding his hand and thanking him. They left for the parking lot together.

CHAPTER 6

What's a PI?

Frank had been a private investigator for 30 years, and often wondered what the hell he was doing in such a business... more now than when he was new at this profession, if it could even be labeled as such. It was true, they really couldn't teach a class in private investigation. Sometimes on TV a commercial would say they did. You either had a knack for it or you didn't. The "knack," which Frank personally understood and accepted, was his ability to operate his mind on two levels at the same time. It was much like a piano player playing with the left hand going much faster than the right hand. It was two different sets of instructions being sent to two different places at the same time by one brain. His brain could flip back and forth at times and someone could ask him a question in the middle of a thought that he didn't answer. But when they broke the silence and said, "Frank did you hear me? Are you paying attention?" Frank could easily repeat the question and answer what was just asked, even while in reality he was thinking entirely of something else through the whole process. Only he knew this.

His career was much like a roller coaster: often high and fast in earlier times and now in his older years often low and slow. Lately he had been stuck at the gate, waiting for a passenger. The good-looking girl in the red sweater and blue eyes sitting across from him this day looked like the only one wanting to ride with him.

One might very well be thought of as having ADD or be manic or some other weird mental thing if one was successful as a PI. It seemed to be an essential element that no one had ever studied. He had heard from a psychologist one time that there were close mental ties between cops and criminals, but at some point the cops turned one corner and the criminals went straight ahead. To his knowledge no one had done a study on PI's. Such a study wasn't a high priority in the scientific world. The gift of his brain being able to be at two places at the same time was invaluable on a case when interviewing a witness. So was processing discovered information, instantly placing it in his brain locker, and moving on with his investigation interview, knowing he could go back and open that locker when needed. He rarely ever carried a note pad and pen. It was a gift from God, for which Frank had, in the past years, began to thank Him while apologizing for other wrong things he had done.

Frank was uncomfortable when a stranger asked him what he did for a living. His usual reply was that he was high priced gopher, looking for people and records for attorneys. He found most people had their opinions of PIs, formed by the years of television shows featuring such characters. He knew it wasn't like that at all. He didn't carry a gun and the last time he followed some errant husband for a worried wife was many years ago—and he wouldn't touch a case like that again. Frank knew the technology had passed him a few years back. Now you just put a GPS system held by a magnet under the guy's car and went home to the comfort of a computer and all the information about where the guy went and how long he stayed was right in front of you at your cozy desk. No need to follow them anymore.

He had also stopped taking child custody cases. They were unhappy circumstances from start to finish. Neither the mother nor father, or most importantly, the child, came out winners. He had seen such cases destroy families, with deeply pitted parties who all loved the children in question but were willing to destroy each other for the right to have them.

He had spent the last years taking lots of photos of wrecked automobiles, interviewing people who saw the accident, and hunting for some who did see, but for unknown reasons couldn't be easily found. Fortunately, computers had made it difficult for people to hide; there was always now a trail left. It might take longer for some but sooner rather than later a computer record of some kind would bring the lead and eventually the find.

Most cops, Frank heard, referred to PI's as a "cop wannabes" who couldn't make the grade to be the real thing. For Frank, it was the last occupation he would ever be interested in doing. He didn't like conformity, and could never wear a uniform or answer to some figurehead in charge of him. The biggest drawback would be having to explain why he was late with his paperwork. And then asking for more time to find the citation book he had misplaced again, not to mention the police car keys.

Frank as a PI was trying to live a life with character and ethics while still being an honest guy who generally got paid for lying to people. As a PI, others trusted him with their darkest secrets. He had little trouble providing information to others for them to take action, but it was getting tougher on his brain and his soul. Of the people who were part of a case he was working on, half didn't like him. Only lawyers had that same percentage.

The business was getting harder on him as he got older. In truth, he had no way of knowing it but he and the professional hit man were both thinking the same thing: how to get a little place on the beach and leave their current life and occupation behind. The only difference was that Frank didn't have any secret bank accounts and knew he would never be able to afford such a place.

He was daydreaming in one of his biggest fantasies to meet Paris Hilton someday in a remote bar and offer to buy her a drink...and she would be somehow, in some way, attracted to him and want to take him home to her place on the beach where she would shower him with tender care. She would say lovingly that his hazel eyes reminded her of sunflowers, that she loved to rub her fingers through his gray hair, and that she thought his little stomach paunch was cute. Outside of that fantasy, it was keep working and hope they would keep raising social security.

He knew in clearer thinking times he was the only one giving a fat-ass thought about him or his future. He had pissed off most of his friends by the divorce and the younger woman. He could not yet bring himself to say her name anymore. Those few friends who remained on his side of the ledger knew better than to ever bring her up in any conversation. But at this point in his life he was still too proud to get on his knees to his family and ask for forgiveness or help or to be welcomed back. Every time he got that thought, he would think and even say out loud, "Screw them." But he always knew he was wrong.

He frequently found himself alone, and was realizing lately that he more often than not enjoyed the solitude. He played the piano, but strictly for himself. In the middle of the night when sleep was hiding from him would go to the piano and play some of the best blues no one would ever hear but him. It was a way to express the feelings that roamed back and forth on a road from his brain to his heart.

He took the card Kim had written the two numbers on and slid it into his shirt pocket. He thought of the last instructions he had given her in the parking lot.

"I'll do something; in the meantime keep your mouth closed. Let's assume Brenda's advice is right on. Don't mention anything to anyone, even about speaking to me."

There were two reasons for that last bit of advice. One, he had learned long ago that you needed some secrecy in this line of work just on general terms. Second, if her story was even remotely true, he wasn't getting a bullet to his head by having this envelope no matter what the hell it means to someone else.

Frank said he would call after he examined the documents and made some calls to some people he knew. Actually he had no idea what the hell he was going to do first, but that's how he always started a case.

In the meantime he suggested that she stay with a friend or better yet go to a hotel and register under a different name. Lay low, don't talk to anyone. Not even your mother or priest. He again mentioned they would have to contact the police...there was no way around that.

She said she understood, and would be waiting for his call. She thanked him again and drove away. His eyes followed her out of the parking lot until she made the turn onto Camelback Road.

He didn't know completely why but that primeval gut instinct that tells us to be careful because there could be a snake in the grass kicked in and he caught himself looking around as he got into his car. He put the file in the passenger seat and then pressed the button and put up the top. He decided to drive to his office and see just what was in this envelope and maybe find out why someone might have died just for having it. He would have to ask Norma to come in. He called her at home.

CHAPTER 7

It's Off to Work

"Hey I got a little dough. You can have some of it toward your pay, but can you come in for little bit?" Frank talked in that sincere manner, hoping to sway someone who usually could not be swayed.

"What do you need?" Norma replied, just a little annoyed.

"I need you to make some calls and do some checking for me. Hell, to be honest, I don't know what I'm looking for...some real estate records maybe. Not much, come on now you know me, I wouldn't call if I didn't really need you."

Norma had worked for him for 28 (or was it 30?) years and knew he hated detail work. He had no patience for meticulous research. But he knew what he wanted and could tell her where to go to start looking for it.

She hadn't been in the office for three days. He told her to stay home and play with her grandkids for a couple of days but she knew it was because he couldn't pay her. She had been with him in the flush money times, but in the past year he seemed to have lost interest in both his business and the money it normally generated. She knew the last year had been tough, even changed him.

When she really got irritated she would tell him to "get over it...she's gone." Yet she knew there was no better person you wanted on your side. If she were ever in trouble, Frank would be her first phone call.

She sometimes wondered why she liked him, as a good friend far better than a boss. There was no question he was often frustrating to work for. But she did. There were days she wanted to get up and walk out the office door, but she knew he wouldn't make it without her. He had depended on her far too long. He wouldn't even know where the checkbook was or who owed him or whom he should be ducking. Since his divorce, break up, and loss of revenue she had become his anchor in his chaotic and often depressed life...whether she wanted to be or not.

He was a person all his own; it was love of a best friend. There wasn't a thing she didn't know about him, from top to bottom. It amazed her to learn on so many occasions that he was going to do exactly what she thought he would before he did it. It was a "gift" that she sometimes wished she didn't have.

She had learned long ago that he was a guy that had spent most of his life touching wet paint signs. He would walk in the office every morning with a Danish and Starbucks coffee, and she would hand him a napkin and tell him to wipe the crumbs from the corner of his mouth and quit wearing white shirts.

It was the same routine every day. What was also routine was that he was the first person she and most of her friends would call the minute something was going wrong in their life. From a fight with their spouse to a behavior meeting with their son's school teacher, they would say, "He'll know what to do."

She also hoped no one would ever ask to see their files. Frank kept most of the files in the storage locker in the back of his brain.

When he or a client actually decided they needed to see some report he had pulled from somewhere it always started a frantic search through the papers on his desk and office floor to make sure all the pages were there. One of the hardest parts of her job was keeping Frank organized.

But he had some strange gift of knowing just the right words to say if you were having trouble in your life, and usually everyone felt much better after talking to him. He offered a perception that might not solve the problem at hand, but the listener left feeling they could either handle it or live with it. Knowing the right words to say even when not solving the problem at hand comforted the afflicted. It was another blessing from God that Frank did not give much thought to or even acknowledge. Norma always thought he would have made a good priest, at least before he got kicked out for saying out loud "Oh my God, no," when hearing a confession.

She knew Frank did not have the patience to sit in a closed box listening to the sins of others. It was strictly a time thing with Frank—ten minutes, twelve at the most—and Norma reasoned he would exit the confessional box and suggest that everyone in line meet him at Fernando's Bar and Grill. He'd get a big table and a pitcher of beer and chips, and have them all talk things out together like some group therapy session. Then everyone would ask God for forgiveness.

The best part of him, she thought, was he always had time to talk to anyone. From the panhandler on the street who usually got his last dollar, to one of his slow-paying attorneys whose wife had run off with another woman and was having trouble paying his bill.

"Yeah" she said." Give me time to put my face on," as she pulled out her makeup kit and made a mental note to pick up another bottle of "spot remover" on the way to the office. She was certain that Frank had by now lost the last bottle she gave him, and knew there would be a coffee drip on his shirt. "I'll see you in an hour."

CHAPTER 8

The Start of It All

Legalized Indian gaming had its start in 1988 when Congress formally recognized, with limitations, the right of Native American tribes to conduct gaming operations within reservation land. The same congressional act required the tribes to negotiate with the state regarding which games are to be played, but also ensured that tribal government would be the sole owners and operators of their gambling establishments. As with past treaties with "red brothers," the beneficial U.S. government saw this act as a way of promoting economic development for the tribes, who had a high poverty level, social issues with alcohol and drugs, poor health clinics, and low high school graduation rates.

Most state governments were not pleased with this development. While the tribes with this new gambling revenue involved did build hospitals and medical clinics, improve reservation schools, and add tribal police departments, there also was no question that some of the money was flowing elsewhere and the states wanted to share in this new Indian land gold rush.

That involvement and the sharing of wealth between the tribes and the state government had created new wars between whites and Indians in just how this money would be shared. Pacts between state government and the tribal gaming officials were constantly being renegotiated by the states, especially where gambling revenue for the tribes was consistently on the rise. What initially started as Indian bingo parlors had grown to room after room of slot machines, poker parlors and blackjack tables.

State law enforcement bodies had, from inception, voiced concern over organized crime getting involved and infiltrating the casinos, but the biggest concern was making sure that the state got its share of gaming taxable income...no matter who was involved.

Problems surfaced from the start, from cheating and skimming to the typical social problems associated with gambling. There was also more than one case of dishonest tribal members involved with non-Indian elements of the criminal world in taking illegal and non-taxed money from the counting rooms. It was an area of gaming that, unlike Nevada and Atlantic City casinos, seemed to be creating new rules. Wording in pacts with states was changing faster than the federal and state regulators could routinely arrange for their own vested interests, although they never quit trying.

The continually changing laws seemed vague. Background checks on non-Indian involvement became skimpy at best. Bribes to public officials were rampant. One indisputable fact was that the Indians were getting rich in those tribes that had gambling, with the unforeseen result that migration of Indians from the reservation had slowed to a trickle. The payout to tribal members had finally made the reservation land given in a treaty years ago some of the most valuable real estate in existence, and a profitable place for the Indians to stay put, knowing every registered tribal member got a share of the gambling revenue. There was more than one case of a white man trying hard to convince tribal census takers that his great-grandmother was 50 percent Indian and a long-forgotten tribal member whose gambling share should be handed to her dubious offspring.

A side benefit of this venture included the shopping centers, resort-style hotels, convention centers, and golf courses sprouting up next to the casinos. What was once land that seemed to have little use was now every developer's dream.

Corruption had been a cousin of legalized gambling from its inception, and tribal casinos were not immune. The first cases of taint across the Indian nations gained birth with the Washington lobbyists. It filtered down to the local politicians and finally organized crime had found some doors they could open. No one knew better how to get their hands on casino money than the boys of organized crime. They didn't need much help from the Department of the Interior, which had Indian tribes still under government rule. Holding Indian reservations "In Trust," organized crime and their legitimate companies sold the tribes the slot machines, booked the entertainment and soon opened the doors to the actual management of the money room. Unlike the casinos in Nevada and New Jersey, there weren't strict regulations on just how cold those slot machines could be set.

A Senate Indian Affairs Committee released a report to the public in 2009 that did not fuel much interest in reading when made public, even though it revealed a glaring insight into improprieties between certain lobbyists and what they termed the "multi million dollar scam," and tales of betrayal in casino-rich Indian tribes.

The Senate report only gave organized crime a paragraph in which it mentioned that they "could be involved." The report was a lot of political bark with promises of future action. Unfortunately the grease of corruption continued to oil the wheels of the committee and promptly slowed down its forward progress and any good its report might have done. Little or no change was noticed...or more importantly, effected.

Frank was about to get an unwanted lesson on how deep the corruption had grown, starting the day he pulled into his office parking lot with the legal papers given to him by a frightened lady in a red sweater. There would be a lot to learn. On the day he took Kim's case, there were 23 casinos in operation on tribal land in Arizona alone.

CHAPTER 9

Dominic Wasn't Swimming

Two young boys were throwing rocks into the swift-moving water of the canal. Canals were the veins of the land for people living in Arizona, though most didn't give them much of a glance. If you weren't into farming, you got used to the idea that water was just there—how it got there didn't much matter. Most gave little or no thought to where it came from when they turned on the faucet to brush their teeth.

The fact that the dwellers of metropolitan Phoenix got their water through a series of man-made lakes and dams, filled with snow runoff from the northern mountains and whatever water their legislators were able to take from the Colorado River, was not an issue. The Colorado River bore a magnificent waterway. By the time it ran its course supplying much of its water in feeding otherwise arid land on both sides, it dwindled from a river to a stream to a marsh before finally trickling into the Mexican Gulf of California.

Arizona had long ago enacted legislation stating that the powerful utility companies who owned and operated the canal water system were protected by law from litigation when some unfortunate soul jumped or fell in and drowned in the swift moving water. It was necessary legislation for the simple fact that it was extremely impractical to fence the miles of canal banks of such a vital element for survival in what is essentially a desert. As the farm owner would say, "No water, no Phoenix, Arizona."

Where the water went and how it was used was the bigger reason that those questions were an unpopular and often-silent issue in political circles. Necessary state law was too often thought to favor those with the most money. Developers and their need for water were often having blockades put in their paths by local and county governments. You had to know which wheels to grease for that golf course with its tiny ponds and lakes, and the water to keep it green.

Some new upstart politicians had begun to turn a critical eye on such use of valuable water. Some of them did not change their election promise to guard Arizona's gold but many others forgot such principle when the lobbyists found their pockets and got the spigot turned on.

Canals were maintained and only on occasion drained when repair or clean-up warranted. Finding a decomposed body floating on top was not an everyday occurrence, but it wasn't a rarity either.

The older of the two boys saw it first. He squinted into the blaring Arizona sun which was doubly bright from the reflection off the water. It looked like a life-sized rag doll.

He picked up a rock and tossed it but missed what was left of the rotting corpse of Dominic Serrano.

The water had done its damage, and the chains that initially held it under the water had let loose of their grip when the skin began to peel away and the gases that formed in the body bloated inside the decaying skin, forcing Dominic's remains to the surface.

"That's a man," Timmy yelled. The other boy who was a year younger, without saying a word thought it best to start running the other way.

"Wait, we gotta tell somebody," Timmy continued. He ran off the canal bank and into the street waving his hands. It took only a second for the first car to stop, and in less than five minutes the Phoenix police were on their way. It was called in as "a party swimming in the canal," which was against the law and for which a ticket could be issued.

Dominic Serrano, before death and floating in the canal, had been on the wrong side of the law for years. Sometimes no one knew, and other times he was second-page news, with a paragraph barely glanced at by most Phoenix morning newspaper readers. Like many young men in his line of work he was born into it. It wasn't that he didn't have a choice, but for a 17-year-old making $500 a week dealing marijuana to his high school classmates with his old man looking the other way, it was hard to make other career decisions. He was, simply put, raised a crook... and in his thirties he was a full-fledged criminal.

Three months earlier when Dominic first saw Brenda Dawson it was at a downtown bar known for drawing the single office girls after work. Where single office girls went, the boys were sure to follow. He was dressed in his usual four-button suit with a starched white shirt, and French cuffs with studs containing the initials DS outlined in small but effective diamonds. Any street cop would have (and had) pick him out as a wise guy wannabe, just by his dress. He was usually loud and cocky, and always flashing a roll of folded hundreds held by a Tiffany silver money clip. He was a small-time local hood who would love for all who knew him to think of him as a "connected" guy. He would not discourage the talk among his friends that someday Dominic was going to be a "made man." In reality, that dubious honor could never be, for Dominic was only half Italian. His father, unfortunately for him, was from south of the border down Mexico way.

"The big boys are going to hear about him and he'll be running the state of Arizona," his friends would say. But for now he was just a local car thief fence who dealt a drug sale here and there, and helped disburse burglary items that had been removed from some of the nicer homes of north Phoenix. He had a loan shark business financed by the local sports bookie, whose late-paying clients were a nice moneymaker for Dominic.

His dark hair was always combed back. He wasn't as tall as he thought he should be, but you had to look closely to notice that the heels and soles of his Italian leather shoes were custom made to an inch and a quarter.

The bar was crowded with the after-work happy hour patrons. Brenda passed by his seat at the bar and he liked what he saw. His glance went right from her long red hair to her backside—and that part of Brenda James stood out nicely in the beige blouse and brown tweed short skirt. Her long hair was brushed neatly to one side and held by a brown hair clip to keep it out of her face. His eyes followed her all the way through the crowd until she joined a booth with some other young ladies from her office.

She was not a regular patron but on occasion joined her coworker when pushed to do so, usually if she had absolutely nothing better to do, which was the case this particular Friday night. It would have been wiser for her longevity in life if she had made other plans that night.

Dominic took a fast sip from the Pernod on ice, set it on the bar and walked through the standing crowd right up to the table where Brenda Ann James and her friends were sitting. He looked right at her and said "Can I talk to you for just a second?" It was a move and verse he had found successful before.

The table went quiet—Brenda didn't know how to answer. Dominic continued, before anything could be said, "Just for a second—at the bar." He held out his well-manicured hand. She might not have moved if the friend sitting next to her didn't give her a nudge unseen under the table.

"It's okay, really it's okay." Dominic reached for her hand saying, "Just for a second." He slowly and gently pulled her hand as she slid out from behind the table and with her hand in his he led her to his spot at the bar. "Can I get you a drink?"

She was still very unsure of what he was doing. Why was she letting this happen? Had it not been for the comfort of the other office workers enjoying happy hour around her, she would have left.

"No thank you," she said. "I only have a moment, what do you want?" She looked nervously back to the table of friends who were all smiling at her and what they perceived to be her good luck this night.

He sipped the Pernod and looked right into her green eyes. "You," he said with a smile. "I don't know who you are, but you are without doubt the most gorgeous thing I have ever seen. I know you might hear that a lot, but I took one look and had to meet you. Had I not, I would have never forgiven myself. Now you can turn around and walk back to that table, or you can give me five minutes of your time and let me get to know you just a little, so that the next time we meet I can do this again and you might enjoy it. In fact, I know you will. So how about that drink?"

Brenda was flustered, yet flattered. But before her next word, he took her hand and said. "Let me guess, I can tell from your touch you are a red wine drinker, uh, let's see, yes, a very good Merlot."

He motioned to the bartender who knew him well from the big tips he always left and the beautiful women he always seemed to be talking to...like right now.

"Bring my new friend here the best Merlot you have. Now my name is Dominic Serrano and you will hopefully have lots of time to get to know me, but let's start with you. What name did your father give to his beautiful daughter?"

It was the start of the end for both of them. She would, within three months, literally never know what hit her. And he would know too well why and how his hands and the last breath of his life had been taken during his late night toss in the canal.

CHAPTER 10

A New Case for Detective John

What was left of Dominic was placed in a body bag. One of the shoes was still somehow dangling from a swollen foot, held barely on by a black shoelace. One of the ambulance attendants commented about the heel on sole of the shoe, "It's kind of big, ain't it?"

There was no identification on the body, and both hands were missing. The body was in bad shape and the sweet sickening smell of death permeated the air. The attendants were gagging as they were loading it into the ambulance. They could tell only that it was male but no visible cause of death could be seen. "Nice cuff links," the attendant said to no one listening. He didn't think to mention there were no hands below them.

The ambulance with Dominic's wet, stinking and lifeless body inside a black, plastic zippered body bag headed for the Maricopa County Medical Examiners in downtown Phoenix where the following day a doctor at the morgue would say into his recorder that Dominic had a "gunshot entrance wound to the back of his head, execution style."

There was no exit wound. He would probe inside the open skull through the discolored sponge of Dominic's brain before locating the projectile of blunted lead just behind the right eye socket. "22 cal," he dictated again into the microphone above his head. The body had been wrapped in chains and although not functioning totally may still have been alive when put in the canal, as there was evidence of breathing—water in his lungs—when the body hit the water. He later wrote in his report that the body had been in the water for at least one week.

Of further interest was that both hands had been physically cut off. The doc thought and wrote in his autopsy report that the hands of Dominic Serrano were likely still in the canal. He further wrote that it appeared they were removed intentionally. He photographed the body, then scraped some tissue sample from the wrist stumps into an evidence bag. Under cause of death he noted homicide, "Gunshot to the back of the skull. Possible mutilation of the body while still alive."

He ordered DNA tests on tissue collected. There was no ID on the body or in the clothing removed from the body and placed into an evidence bag.

It took four days before the lab got the DNA results and they were able, through their database, to put a name, age, and background on the body. It was a 31-year-old male, five feet, eight inches in length, 170 pounds, with black hair and brown eyes. Name: Dominic Anthony Serrano. He had a rap sheet which, along with the autopsy report, was sent to Homicide. The body was placed in refrigeration.

The body found on the canal hit the morning newspaper but only in the second local section under the caption, "Murder victim recovered from canal." There was no mention of the cause of death or that the body had its hands cut off. The homicide section of the Phoenix police had purposely held those facts back.

Had it not been for the fortunate fact that Dominic's DNA was on file from a previous arrest, it may well have been a difficult ID for the boys in the lab.

When the two young executioners who had been sent to Arizona from Philly for the specific intent to cut Dominic's hands off (after attempting to find out what he had done with the files he had obtained from the law office, before sending him swimming in chains with a little lead in his head) read that omission in the news article they were a bit perturbed. After all when you cut the hands off, you did it so others would know. Orders from the big boys were important to follow, especially if you were trying to move up in the organization like Sal and Vinnie had. Or, more importantly, you didn't want your hands chopped off for failing to complete the assignment. "Hell," the bigger of the two commented to his traveling partner, "that ain't easy cuttin' them hands off, stuffing that rag in his mouth to stop the squealing son of a bitch."

"Yeah, well we got bigger problems than that if they don't get that envelope back. I knew the Rolodex that Sal got from that broad's house would help us. Just be glad they gave the girlfriend to Sal and Vinnie. Heard Vinnie hit 'er in the head with a hammer. That had to be a messy one. 'Til we started on his other hand I was starting to believe him. 'Stop please, I don't know where it is.'" The bigger of the two was mocking Dominic's last words. "The bastard finally gave in when you started sawing off his other hand.

Asshole must have thought he could still be her guy with just one hand. Maybe he was hoping she would end up with just one breast." They both laughed. "He must have shit after he told us and gave you the key to her place, and you still went on cutting and then we took him swimming. I think the poor prick actually believed you when you told him you'd stop as soon as he talked and gave us the key."

"Good liar, ain't I?" came the proud reply. "He didn't know it just confirmed the number in the Rolodex for us."

"Yeah" the other agreed. "Asshole bleeding all over. Ya know, I was thinking we should've used a hatchet."

They laughed, again. "Getting that piece of shit knife you had through the bones was not easy, took forever." The big guy smiled at his partner. "Yeah, you prick, next time we gotta do hands, bring a hatchet."

"Forget about it," he answered, "The sons-a-bitches didn't even put it in the paper. You told the boys we did it right? Damn, don't want them thinking we didn't do it."

"Yeah, they know we did just like they wanted, I gave the information to Sal. He and Vinnie will handle it now. We're done, let's get the hell of here. This place is like living in a furnace...how the hell do Sal and Vinnie live in this oven? They won't have far to go when they head for hell."

They left for the airport, with their mission completed. It was now up to Sal and Vinnie. The organization wanted there to be no doubt to others who might be involved that they were viciously angry. They believed Dominic was not operating alone and wanted a message left for whoever else was involved.

CHAPTER 11

Detective John Fordham

Dominic, with his rap sheet going back to juvenile court, was known among the police as a small-time hood. He was thought to be connected to the local drug scene. He was also known to have dealt in stolen property, and been arrested more than once. But for all the arrests filed, there wasn't much on him.

He always had the best defense attorneys in town show up before the paperwork was printed, always made bail, and within months the legal wheels went into motion and the charges were dropped for one reason or the other. The Phoenix cops were no different from their comrades in other large cities. They hated criminal defense attorneys unless they needed one and Dominic's were at the top of the list.

Detective John Fordham was assigned the new murder case. He had been there when they did the autopsy on Dominic. "What do you suppose they did with his hands? I never saw that before, but I've heard about it happening. It means someone was sending a message about this guy.

It's like taking back a handshake in an extreme measure." One day earlier John Fordham had been working on the murder case of Brenda James. At this point he did not know there was a connection between the body he saw lying on the autopsy table without its hands and the murder of Ms. James. That information would come the next morning from an unexpected source.

Forty-one year old Detective Fordham was always at his office early, and was a neat freak. There were no loose papers on his desk, and (like the clothes on his back and the shined shoes on his feet) his work area was spotless and all the parts were in the right place. A lot of his fellow officers didn't like him, because he was too much of a company man. "Why so many hours, John? Slow down." was a continual refrain coming from the cubicles around his spotless desk.

Per his personal schedule he was usually at his desk 30 minutes early. The latest murder file regarding the body pulled from the canal was set on top of the thicker file of Brenda James. It struck him how brutal both of these murders were. Her parents cremated Brenda James as soon as the morgue and police released her body, and a Catholic Church memorial service was held within a day.

Detective Fordham attended both as a courtesy to the family and to take a close look at the attendees, and if the opportunity presented itself he wasn't beyond having an informal interview with one of the mourners in his quest to find the heartless ass who crushed this beautiful young girl's head.

No one, it seemed, had much interest in claiming the remains of Dominic Serrano. His body, minus hands, was still at the morgue.

He set down the James file and picked up Serrano's. The autopsy photos were on top. He mentally said the hell with this, and just as quickly set it down and picked up the back file with the recent suicide DRs, or department reports.

Like all homicide detectives, he also had to handle suicide cases. It was part of the job he didn't like. They usually left notes. In his four years of investigating and working homicide, he had never completely detached from the suicide cases. He had heard someone say it was a permanent solution to a passing problem. He kept copies of the notes they left and would find himself re-reading them months after the file was closed. In his self-analysis he wondered about his morbid curiosity in keeping and reading the last words of desperate people. In some strange connected way it made him aware of his own mortality, at least more so than the murder victims who had little choice in their demise.

Suicide succeeded in taking away a life that maybe, if someone had said the right words, would have taken a different turn a mere half hour earlier...who knows?

He wondered, when they stepped off the chair with the rope around their neck and began gasping for breath, if their free hands tried to pull the homemade noose from their neck, or when their second foot stepped off the building ledge, sending them to death on the ground 34 stories below, if their next thought was, "Oh shit, what have I done now?"

Prior to being transferred and upgraded to a sergeant in homicide, Detective Fordham had been in the sex crime unit. A stressful job, in two years it damn near killed him and did kill a 15-year marriage. Detective Fordham had found alcohol to be his best escape after too many interviews of pedophile victims and the emotional drain of working in child pornography, which demanded viewing evidence photos of all young ages of rape victims; many with their eyes blackened and puffed out from the beating administered before some piece of shit ripped their panties off and forced their ugly penis into a too-small vagina. His thoughts formed by the graphic photos were starting to be with him long after he left the station. He was one drunk short of entering a room and saying, "Hi, I'm John, and I'm an alcoholic," to a bunch of strangers.

He had become a cynic of the human race, and lost his faith and his wife for reasons he didn't really know or couldn't verbalize. He became an obsessive neat freak. The therapist he had started seeing told him it was his way of trying to save himself by rising as far as he could from the trash infiltrating his mind on a daily basis. He personally thought she was wrong. But one Sunday morning when he exploded in the middle of a family breakfast because his three-year old son had spilled his orange juice on the white table cloth, and his wife grabbed her first-born and ran screaming from the house yelling "You're crazy, stop, please," he knew she might be right. Two days later she served him with divorce papers. When Detective John was handed the divorce papers he noticed coffee stains on the process server shirt and shoes. He thought immediately that his therapist was right.

When John went to work the following day he walked in and demanded a transfer. "I'm out of sex crimes or I'm out of here." That afternoon he was transferred to homicide.

He knew it was a big change from sex crimes. It was a move made too late to save his marriage but not too late to save his life.

He liked to do his own reports rather than dictate them for someone else to type. He was in the middle of finishing the first of the two suicides from the past week and had set Dominic's and Brenda's files to the side to wait for the remaining field reports to come in when his desk phone rang.

"Fordham here."

"John, it's your old friend," the voice on the other end replied. "Been awhile, but I need a small favor."

He recognized the voice. "Frank, how the hell you been? You've been hiding on me...I was beginning to think you owed me money."

"No, been keeping to myself. The divorce damn near wiped me out and I'm still nursing a broken heart from the other one. Can't seem to drink enough to cure it, so I just sit home and watch the weather channel and listen to Eva Cassidy CDs 'til the beer and wine run out."

Frank continued, "I got a case that came into my office this morning. Not sure what I'm doing with it. I just wondered if you guys had anything on it. It's for a friend of that murder victim...uh, her name," Frank took a second to pull her name up from his brain locker. "Young girl, Brenda James. I heard from my client she got her head knocked in. I'm just trying to get her a little information. Calm her down a bit. My client is pretty upset. They were good friends."

"Whoa Frank," Fordham interrupted, "that's not your usual file, what the hell happened to automobile accidents and suing the insurance companies? This is a bad one. What's your part in this?"

Frank hesitated as the second level of his brain kicked in.

"I just got a call from some friend of my ex-wife, to be straight with you. I don't know what the hell my interest is, but was hoping you might be able to tell me something and then I'll know."

He didn't want to say much more than that. For now, he felt for $1,200 he needed to give his client whatever he could learn that might help before sending her and the envelope to the police, especially considering the alleged threat she received.

Fordham was a good friend as well as a good cop. He was younger than Frank, but they had met a few years back when Fordham was a street cop and handled a couple of fatal accidents that Frank worked for a plaintiff attorney. They didn't see each other for long periods but through the past years had established a social as well as working relationship. They would sometimes meet for lunch and, in happier times for Frank, have an infrequent cold beer and cigar after work. When they parted they always said, "We should do this more often." But then would go weeks, or even months, without talking.

Frank learned years ago that a PI was only as good as his contacts and Fordham was a good one. Frank also knew not to abuse the working relationship. That was the unstated rule that was never was crossed. They had built a block wall of trust that neither wanted to crumble. It was confidential, never to be used lightly. Their trust and respect for each other was long-standing and strong. When he needed some fast information that Fordham could pull,

Frank asked. But it was a two-way street between them. Frank had connections at the phone company and could get unlisted numbers and phone records within an hour of asking. Fordham had to get a warrant for that kind of information, so when he or someone in the department needed it fast—and not by a warrant—he called Frank.

"What can you tell me Frank? What do you know and what do you need to know? You know I don't go out too far unless you're up front here. I got retirement funds to protect."

"Well, so far not much, just trying to help this young girl out. Nice-looking by the way."

"Come on Frank, you're not trying to impress some skirt are you?"

"No, no, she had a hell of a story, seemed she was a friend of the victim. For all I know it might be all her imagination. She has a problem that I'm going to try and help her with for now. Not my kind of case in my old years. Your department, I think, spoke to her at her work. Her girlfriend was murdered." Fordham said nothing as Frank continued.

"I would really like to find the victim's boyfriend, just to talk to him. The name is familiar but I don't know from where. Does Dominic Serrano ring a bell with you? I got a feeling you boys might have a file on him. I would like to find him just to check out a few things. Or if you've interviewed him let me take a peek at the department reports. I got a small retainer and want to give her something for her money. You get me an address, maybe a copy of his rap sheet and a little background on this guy and I'll owe you one. Hell, I'll buy you two beers and two Havanas."

When Fordham heard the name, he reached under the Brenda James file and pulled the DR files marked Serrano. He was again looking at the crime photos and autopsy report as Frank continued with his "Can you do me a favor?" pitch.

"Just want to ask him a couple of questions, that's all. Hell, you know I'll give you anything I get if it helps. It seems her friend, Brenda James, might have been his main squeeze...or that's what she thought. But she didn't tell anyone about him, a secret lover deal. My client thinks she might have been embarrassed about liking him and wanted to keep it from her friends and family. So I'd like to just check him out and ask him a question or two. Not stepping on your turf or trying to solve a murder...just giving my client some info."

He paused. "Can you give me a little help here, friend? I'm not sure, but she might have a couple of personal items she wants to return to him."

Frank mentally started crossing his fingers with that last statement.

Fordham took a couple of seconds and set down the photos and then picked up the autopsy report from the file.

"Well Frank, you know a good medium? Because you're going to need one if you want to talk to this guy... and if you should get him to show up, don't expect to shake hands."

"What are you saying, John?"

"This guy was pulled from the canal two days ago. And he wasn't in for a swim. Wrapped in chains, both hands cut off and a piece of lead in the back of his skull to make sure he stayed down for a spell. That information is strictly for you, and I'm serious about that Frank. I just got the case and have only briefly looked at what we have. It's not much. I was at the autopsy. Has a rap sheet with nothing big ever sticking. Local bar boy, dressed fancy, basically liked to look connected, talked like it, but a new breed, the old Godfathers would have slapped him around for 'no respect,' you know what I mean? He beat every arrest, drug deal, stolen merchandise. He was small-time but had some money to put in lawyer pockets.

"It's a new case, new file; I don't even have a next of kin interviewed yet. Body was taken to the morgue and no one has even claimed it. To add to that mystery, not even a missing person call. Doc says he was floating in the canal for a few days before the chains slipped off enough to get him to the top, that's about it. Some boys from the department are out talking to his old lawyers, checking out addresses. Nothing back in the file. Don't tell anyone this either, Frank, but around here he's one of those names we're glad to finally get rid of.

"Oh except, Doc thinks there is a big chance his hands were cut off before they sent him swimming. We're keeping that quiet for now. That last part is for you only, and if I get shit on by telling you any of this I will personally pour those beers over your sad-ass face and put my cigar out on the top of your head. No shit Frank, that info stays with you."

"John, you know me, I haven't heard a word you said."

Fordham continued, accepting Frank's reassurance. "I've received no pressure on this. I was in the act of cleaning up some paperwork before I even read the initial DRs."

Frank was a little stunned at this information. Maybe he thought, he should tell his new client that the boyfriend took a swim and didn't come up. Hell, that had to be worth something. He could give her $200 back and call it even. His first level of thinking came back: the envelope.

"Yeah well, thanks John, I guess he won't be telling much on his dead girlfriend. But you know, if he killed her and was in deep remorse, I think he would have needed one of his hands to put the gun behind his head and pull the trigger. Both of them murdered in the same weekend... something here John, something here," he paused. "You got some work to do my friend. I'll give my client a little of this. Tell her to call you if she has more. And hey, thanks, let's get together soon."

"Not so fast Frank, what's the personal items story and what's your client's name?" Frank knew his police friend had the same gifts he had, and did not miss his statement. He knew he couldn't lie, nor did he want to tell John the rest of his client's story yet. That had to come from her, and soon.

"Detective, we have worked close and been friends a long time. I need some trust from you, and more important, a little time. My client has asked for a little hiding space and I'm giving it to her. I can assure you—and I have never been anything but straight with you since we met—that I'm quite certain her only involvement is that she knew the victim. She has some real fear going for her own safety. I'll get back with you, my word on that, but I need a little time from you. It's for her safety. Only for her."

Fordham didn't like the arrangement being pitched, but he still carried the long-built trust for his friend. "Frank you have a very small time frame. I'll arrest your ass and haul you in, and believe that Frank. You got minutes and hours, not days." The silence on both ends was unexpected. "You understand that completely?"

Frank replied, "Understood and appreciated."

He didn't know himself why he didn't say anything about the envelope or the disk inside it. He thought, what the hell has this client gotten herself—and now me—tangled in? I don't even know if the envelope is connected to any of this. No need to mention it. He was uncomfortable with that decision. He didn't like holding back, especially from a friend as well as a homicide detective.

"Thanks again John, you'll hear from me soon." He started to close the conversation down, but Fordham wasn't done.

His reply was firm and to the point. He was too much of a cop. "Frank, you give me all you got on this, don't pull shit from me."

"Hey, I will, I will...you know me, I got to find an auto accident where the doctor with six kids gets hit from behind by the drunk Exxon Truck driver with the previous DUI. I'll get back to my client. I'm going to tell her to call you, okay?"

Fordham, with pencil in hand, tried again. "What's her name Frank?"

"Let me talk to her first John. She's a little hyper and frightened right now. Give me a little slack for a day, John. I'm going to let her know the boyfriend is dead, but I won't say any more than that. I'll call you back within 24 hours and you will get all that I have."

Fordham was still processing the information from Frank's call, and answered back with an abruptness Frank didn't normally hear from his cop friend.

"Alright, call me back. Twenty-four hours or I get a warrant out with your name in capital letters. No slack or time to give you Frank, you get back to me. I'm not messing with you Frank. These are two brutal murders and you are hiding a potential witness...our friendship ends if she isn't walking in my office by nine tomorrow. Oh, and make sure she has those 'personal items' with her."

He hung up without saying good bye. He was writing on his pad. The murder of Brenda James is tied to Dominic Serrano. The hell with the suicide reports. He yelled out to his assistant across the office cubicle. "Get me everything we have on the Brenda James murder now. Get me all the reports and anything else on the body we pulled from the canal." He picked up his phone and dialed his homicide partner who had worked a drive-by shooting in south Phoenix in the early hours of the morning. "Pete get your ass out of bed and get in here. Looks like we got a connected double homicide. My gut feeling is it was professional."

CHAPTER 12

The File Seven Days Earlier

Seven days earlier Sid Lewis could not locate a particular secret file he maintained daily regarding financial transactions with the tribe and its casino revenue. He had the only key to the locked safe inside his private office where this single legal file was rigorously guarded and maintained by Sid Lewis and only Sid Lewis.

But this day it was not there.

This file contained the usual innocuous original land purchase reports, but also agreements of sales, contracts with distribution and percentages of fund payouts, and most importantly all the investors in the gambling and resort construction contracts. Plus all the extremely secret names of the local politicians and state officials who had been bribed, as well as pertinent personal information about each partner...except for Lewis.

At Lewis' specific request when this particular file was forming five years ago, there were no copies and only one disk, which he kept in a separate envelope. He even had the hard drive from the computer that was used to create the file taken out only weeks earlier and destroyed. The extreme measure was necessary after the Cuba casino deal was initiated. No one had access to the file or was allowed to touch it except Sid Lewis. He had not seen the file now for two days.

His will contained the unusual provision that his personal representative was to burn the entire file without opening, should he have a fatal encounter. Which he knew, unfortunately, was a possibility after a call he received this morning from someone in Philadelphia who wanted to meet with him. This same party mentioned, before Sid hung up on him, that the meeting concerned his arrangement with the local tribal casinos, and their interest in purchasing controlling interest and buying out the partners. It was a very disturbing phone call, to put it mildly.

Lewis knew how highly sensitive and secret it was, let alone revealing of a huge conflict of interest. He and his firm personally represented two of the local tribes. It contained records of illegal transactions regarding investments in tribal gambling operations in Arizona. The latest file entries revealed the strong possibility of this hushed illegal investment group expanding not into another Arizona Indian casino, but a casino in another country, just a few miles off the coast of Florida. Cuba.

It all started five years earlier during his legal representation of one of the local tribes when he learned that they were filing several lengthy forms to borrow money to build and open a large hotel next to their growing gambling casino. The loan request was prepared for a local savings and loan. There were several hurdles to jump in order to get the loan completed, from the approval of the state gambling commission all the way to Washington and the U.S. Department of Interior, which was the ultimate governing power of reservation land, treaty or no treaty (a fact that Sitting Bull and the Sioux learned in 1876 before annihilating General Custer). The U.S. government taking back the Black Hills in South Dakota, which was given to the Sioux, was a violation of a treaty dating back to the 1880's with the Sioux Tribe.

Sid Lewis had the lawyer's intuition of finding the best side of a presented problem by going outside the box, and this one had been handed to him from Anthony By Water, the Chief. He preferred to be called Tribal President rather than Chief, and casually voiced, during a closed-door meeting with Lewis, that he wished there was "an easier way to get the damn money," adding, "too much damn paperwork."

Sid Lewis, via his legal representation of the tribe, was well informed of the enormous profit being taken by the tribe through its casinos on Indian land surrounding Maricopa County, Arizona. He also knew there was no legal way for him, other than his over the top legal fees, to share in such profits. That was, until Chief By Water's statement that he wished there was an easier, softer way.

The day after this meeting, Sid called the chief and informed him he had found a corporation with plenty of money for their expansion project that needed very little paperwork; just some assurance they would be paid back. The interest rate was very favorable as well. It would only be between the tribe and this corporation. In fact, By Water could just sign the agreement as president or chief. It didn't even need a formal tribal vote. No state government, no federal government. Best of all, no state or federal Gaming Commission.

The chief was very much interested...and after all, this was the tribe's highest-paid attorney offering this deal. Within days Lewis had the chief in his office, explaining the very favorable wording of the agreement which stated, in essence, that the tribe would not actually have to ever pay back money it did not have on hand. The corporation lending the tribe $8.5 million would only take a monthly measured share of the profits from the casinos operating on tribal land. The amount of payback would be based upon a percentage of what the tribe took in. Simple, sweet, and hassle-free. But before the chief signed, Lewis mentioned that the corporation would need to be nominally in charge of the accounting procedures necessary to determine the amount of each payment. "Not a big problem," Lewis cheerfully volunteered, "I'll have some of my people come out to set it up." And then to close the sale, as a good used car salesman would, he added, "You know this corporation will lend the tribe money whenever you need it. Your credit is excellent." Dropping his voice to whisper, he said, "Chief, I would like to make a personal donation to you for your excellent work in saving me from all that damn government paperwork." They both laughed as the tribal president signed in his capacity all the papers Lewis placed in front of him, not concerned at all that he didn't read one line of the document. After all, Lewis and his firm had always taken care of him, even lending all the assistance necessary when the tribe had to elect a new president every four years...assistance that always assured By Water remained chief.

After the chief signed, Lewis handed him two checks. One for $8.5 million and one for ten thousand dollars made out to Chief By Water. When the chief was leaving his office Lewis reminded him that it would be best for this to never be discussed, for the better of all. He pinched the ten thousand dollar check in By Waters' hand. "In fact, let's say this never happened."

The Chief answered, "As far as the tribe is concerned, the savings and loan folks came through just as we'd hoped."

Putting the check into his wallet with a smile, he shook Lewis' hand and said, "You and I have always worked well together." And with that, like the crooked Indian agents of old, Lewis and his group had their hands in the chief's, and more importantly the tribe casino's, pocket and the chief didn't appear to mind a bit. Lewis knew from past representation that By Water and his tribal council were easily controlled.

That was the starting point. Over the following years, inch-by-inch, Lewis and his investors went silently into the operation of two casinos in broad daylight. In the next five years the original small monthly accounting procedure went to a weekly, and then a daily share of the nickels and dimes and quarters all through a corporation based in the Cayman Islands. Unfortunately, the tribe's "loan" in those five years using the accounting of Lewis' firm had only decreased a mere million. Lewis and his offshore corporation were in the casino's counting room and life was good.

Illegal transactions were, in reality, the small part of the file. It went much deeper than that. It contained the names of all parties bribed, a police officer, political donations needed and set aside for future favors, and in some cases personal information on members of this group of investors such as the names of their current and past mistresses, should (Lewis disliked this term) extortion ever become necessary to protect him from the other members.

It was the kind of file that would have more than rivaled any other file in the fraud department of the FBI building in Washington, DC. If the FBI even had a hint such a group existed they would have been on it faster than the hunt for any terrorist, with the Internal Revenue Service close on their heels. It would be information placed in front of a Congressional Committee and on CNN within days of its discovery. The criminal and RICO (Racketeer Influenced and Corrupt Organizations Act) charges would just be a matter of time.

The item that would draw the most questions would be the private phone numbers of the Cuban Embassy in Mexico City and the Mexican Cuban Ambassador, Felix Guerrero, as well as detailed copies of large checks sent to Mr. Guerrero through a third party in Costa Rica, listed as charitable donations to certain Cuban charities. This had all been illegal since an embargo enacted on Cuba nine presidents earlier under President John Kennedy. As a strict rule all documents concerning the tribe were confidential. Any and all correspondence between the Lewis Law Firm and the local tribe were "guarded" and never discussed outside of Sid Lewis' office. One had to be extremely trusted by Lewis to be anywhere near the general casino files, but this particular missing file was created solely by and for the use and protection of Sid Lewis only. No one else ever saw it or (he thought) knew of its existence.

Unknown to him was that both his secretary and his paralegal, Brenda James, did know of its existence but not a word of its contents. Like most secrets, it had been maintained for too many years not to be discovered without even looking for it. Lewis would, without thinking, leave his office only briefly and Brenda would go into his office to leave a paper for his signature and innocently see it open on his desk. They also knew he kept it locked up and understood without being told that this was a "hands off" file.

Lewis had first maintained it for protection and a record of money invested and money made, as any astute businessman would have done. But as the scheme grew and started trampling on the legalities and common rules of law and the IRS, he slowly realized he was now maintaining the file for his own protection. He often wondered, when he was being realistic, how the hell he ever let this thing get so out of control.

The initial agreement with the investors was all established to be limited and secret, and any meetings were conducted on a golf course with winks and nods when a vote was needed. He had decided early on that the same wink and nod would never be used against him, and thus initiated this personal file which would take many of his cronies off to the jails before they ever got interested in Sid Lewis. It would start with both a U.S. Congressman and a Senator, and then local state government elected officials being investigated before anyone would come knocking on his doors. He had estimated correctly that he had enough dirt to obtain a favorable plea bargain by turning others in if and when the trail headed to his office door. He would already have been disbarred, but what the hell, he said to himself, he never really practiced law anymore anyway. His money was handled like W.C. Fields had done before him: in banks across the country with names only he knew.

This missing file contained not only financial data but also a sub-file including names of county commissioners who were paid for their votes as well as utility executives on the state commission who controlled water rights and had approved all that illegally obtained water for those casino golf courses and man-made lakes that 95 percent of state residents would never see, let alone tee up to play.

It also had the name and unlisted cell phone number of a police lieutenant who John Fordham said good morning to each morning when he arrived at work, Lieutenant Phil Barnes, who had strongly supported John's move to homicide, and to whom John was very appreciative. Lt. Barnes had been on Lewis' "under the table" payroll for two years before Detective John's move to homicide, and was money well invested.

The file also listed all the names of who could be paid when their votes were needed or when they were asked to look the other way with regard to liquor and building code licenses for the Las Vegas style resorts financed by Lewis' corporation on tribal land. Most of the corporation members were not aware their names were even in such a file. Had they been aware they would be gravely unhappy and worry through many sleepless nights. Not the least of those would be the Cuban Ambassador in Mexico City because of his endorsement of checks from Lewis and his investor friends that were going right into Raoul Castro's own secret bank account...which his brother, Fidel, knew nothing about.

This missing file was also designed and planned by Lewis in the remote case a problem might arise as to the distribution of money if one of the investors questioned his handling techniques. In addition, Lewis knew what needed to be erased or moved from the tribe's general file if an inquiry by the IRS or Department of Interior should ever request any documents. Fake and altered copies could be produced and handed over to them.

If one of the investors had a complaint and asked for a meeting with Lewis, such a meeting would be behind locked office doors where the complaining party would be presented with what he had signed and agreed to, as well as a personal file they didn't know existed. It would be the only time they would see the file that detailed every misstep ever taken in their life. All parties believed such a meeting would never be necessary, but Sid Lewis' legal experience had long ago taught him that "never" is not a legal term and "cover your own ass" is.

All other documents regarding the gambling adventure by Lewis and his group were well-maintained and would withstand a brief audit or exam by an outside agency, should the tribe ever request one...that is, if the auditors stayed focused on what was given them to examine, which Lewis believed he could control.

The monthly payout to the members for their loan was currently running near 25 percent. Everyone involved with Mr. Lewis was very happy and more than willing to take a risk, especially since they were assured by Lewis that any actual risk was extremely remote and could easily be "taken care off." That risk involved the filing by members of false income tax returns.

But now the file was missing from a locked safe in his office. The file contained information ethically damaging to his firm and to him personally as the tribe's Attorney of Record. And the fact never mentioned by him to the other parties was that the financial arrangements discussed and in place were illegal from their inception and could send someone to prison. In fact, not just someone. All of them. The file was a time bomb and once opened would rattle the Hallowed Halls of Congress and every gossip rag newspaper even before the mistresses' names were printed.

The file documented in detail the initial loan as well as the current investment for a multi-million dollar transaction to build a new casino and golf course. The local construction was underway on the reservation just north of the Phoenix city limits to build a resort-type casino complete with water canals and an eight-acre lake in this Arizona dessert. This was a fact that the farming communities west of Phoenix would be very angry about if they knew, especially since a state directive had recently restricted the amount of water available to them.

Certain controlling members of the tribe had agreed to give a larger chunk of the profits from this new loan operation to Lewis and the group he was heading. By Water and his braves would never know the majority of their money was being skimmed from the top even before the tribe got its share. It still put enough money in their pockets to the point that they seldom, if ever, gave a thought about whether it was a fair share. It was a share they were more than happy with. They thought a little for me, a little for you, and then a little more for me. Lewis liked the way they thought. Too bad they had to pay taxes on their share.

But the biggest developing plot for Sid Lewis and his already rich, immoral partners was a new venture to open a casino in Cuba. Casinos had flourished in Cuba back in the 1950's under organized crime families before Castro came to power and shut them down as corrupt signatures of capitalism, which he stated inherently "robbed the poor." Now Castro was old and sick, and unknown to him, his brother Raoul (who he had named to succeed him), was not totally against the idea of returning Cuba to its former reputation as the "Las Vegas of the islands." The money, jobs, tourism, and especially the consulting fees and interest in gambling revenue paid to him, loomed large in his favorable interest in bringing such a reverse of Cuba's current government policy. Of course, nothing could be done as long as Fidel was alive. It was now simply a matter of time, waiting for age to invoke its natural right. And there was the little issue of Uncle Sam frowning heavily on such an undertaking by a group of rich Phoenix businessmen.

Lewis was currently using local tribal casino money to pay three Washington lobbyists to get the embargo restrictions on Cuba lifted. Under the harmless and merciful guise of uniting exiles with their families, he was working slowly and silently toward opening the gambling enterprise, all legally, to be operated under the Cuban government.

This new Viva La Cuba Corporation that Lewis had created would not be issuing any 1099s. All the money would be washed nice and clean when it passed into the investors' hands. Investors who, by government and state law, were prohibited from having any interest or involvement in a casino on tribal land, or operating and profiting from gambling casinos sixty miles offshore from Florida with a dictator as the newest partner. This partner was told in one of several secret meetings with Lewis in Costa Rica that casinos "will turn a crumbling economy around and make Cuba a thriving nation again."

"Thanks to your help and investment...it's welcoming to know there are some smart people like you in the United States willing to help Cuba, not smash us down," Raoul Castro had said to Mr. Lewis after the handshake as he boarded his hired private jet for his return trip home.

Fidel Castro had no idea of his brother's nefarious involvement in such a plan, all planted in his ear by Lewis and his rich cartel, and delivered by a contact from the Mexican Embassy in Costa Rica. Lewis could only imagine the reaction of the public when it was learned that a local group of businessmen had become very rich through investing in Indian casinos and were now going to rebuild and operate a casino in Cuba. Yes, thought Lewis, that is why America is so great. There is so much room at the top and how you get there isn't that important. The old Mafia families had nothing on these good old Phoenix boys when it came to opening a casino in Cuba. At least not yet.

But for now, until Fidel died, there were only the local tribal casinos.

It had started as a sweetheart deal that only comes to crooked investors once in a lifetime, and was covered with payouts to non-Indian untitled parties, with hidden costs. Illegal skimming from the casino were problems for the Lewis law firm that would (as Mr. Lewis said in the last unofficial meeting on the seventh tee of the Tomahawk

Golf Club) "be simple bumps in the road that can be smoothed out when we come to them."

Distributing millions in unreported cash would, without the right touch handling it, be more like a cave-in, and then a bomb, but Lewis and his partners felt comfortable that it would be a smooth ride. And, without question, a most profitable one.

Until the file went missing.

Lewis had already established fake charities in various names, with his investment partners on the boards and controlling how the money would come in the front door and go out the back windows. Many an unwed mother would see those baby wipes and diapers promised them by the local "Christians for Unwanted Babies." But even more would not when most of the money donated returned to the donor, after being properly deducted.

Until the secret file went missing.

Sid Lewis, storming in and out of his office, not only looked angry and worried but was. "Go through it again," he yelled, "maybe it got put into the wrong folder, damn it, it can't have just disappeared, find it now. Tear down the damn building if you have to, but find that file."

Helen Pursey had worked at the firm and for Mr. Lewis for fifteen years. This is not my fault she thought. I told him we needed to save the disk but he wanted everything destroyed but originals. Now it came back to bite him in the butt. There was a vague smile across her face. She had worked for attorneys too long and had grown through the later years to enjoy their worry about screwing something up. Most lawyers she had found through her years of working in law firms had a superior attitude and the penchant of doing things at the last possible moment, a process that caused undue grief among their secretaries who had to stay late to bail their asses out. Worst of all was the sad fact that the secretaries were seldom thanked for their hard work, unless one counted the frozen turkey they got each year three days before Christmas.

Returning to her desk, she remembered that Brenda James, his paralegal, would have been the last one who might know where the documents were, but she did not come to work this day. "I have no idea where to start," she mumbled to herself. She pulled out the first stretch binder and began to look through each page. There were fifteen volumes labeled Tribal Documents, files containing little more than the week-to-week memos in the routine legal representation for the tribe. The file Sid Lewis was concerned about was a separate entity. As far as she knew, no one saw it but Mr. Lewis. It was always locked in his personal safe inside his office. She felt fairly certain she wasn't even to have known of its existence. She had more than once entered his office on routine matters and caught a glimpse of him going through it and then quickly covering it up nonchalantly.

The first file she pulled out was "Land Purchase/ Condemnation." She began to go through each page. This will take time she thought. She did notice however that Mr. Lewis' file cabinet was still locked and only he had the key. She figured he probably took it out in one of his manic legal episodes and forgot to put it back, so now it was misfiled somewhere.

Sid Lewis continued to pace the floor in his office and started going through his drawers and looking anywhere his eyes landed. "Where the hell is it?" He could not find the key to where it was normally kept. He started throwing everything out of his desk drawers, out of control, his mind spinning. The possible problems with losing this file were growing in his head, so misfiled was his last and only positive hope. After hours of looking and yelling at his staff, he closed his office door, laid both the key to his office and the empty key ring to the safe on his desk and slumped back in his stuffed leather chair. He knew he was wishfully waiting for either he or someone in his firm to find the key and file and all the stress would immediately evaporate from his mind. But in reality, he knew a bomb had started ticking and his ass was about to be blown off. He knew someone had taken it. He was not a careless man. The key was stolen, the file and disk gone, and he had little doubt whoever had it would not keep it as secret as he intended.

The federal government would take more than a harsh view. The IRS would be frothing at the mouth. His job and reputation were gone. And those were the minor problems. He knew it went deeper from there. That's the agenda for the first day, he thought as he again started to tear through his drawers.

He did not hear himself talking out loud. "If it got into the wrong hands and someone understood the contents," that thought made him jump, "got to find it, damn it, got to find it." He began going over in his mind the last time he had seen it, hoping it was something as simple as being put in the wrong place. He was breathing heavily, with his pulse racing, and the sweat was on its way down his gray sideburns.

CHAPTER 13

Kim and Frank

Kim was relieved to hear Frank's voice. She had been growing frantic, after trying several times to reach him on his cell phone.

"Frank O'Hara here, I got some info for you."

"Thank God," she said, "I've been so worried," she answered.

Frank didn't hesitate to explain the delay in calling her. "First of all, Dominic is dead. Murdered, so let's hope they continued their relationship in the afterlife. There's going to be big investigation by the police. Her secret love affair is going to be out for all to read about as soon as some reporter finds the two murders connected, and I think the chances are high that they will.

"I can't get much from the police and I didn't mention the file to them. I had my office run the info through assessors' and recorders' offices, and whatever else to see what it all might be connected to. There's not much on public record. Basically, it all concerns the tribe and building a gambling casino, hotel, and golf course, and then operating it with a generous percentage going to the tribal council and the rest to some well-known local investors. It also has some, for lack of a better word, nice gossip items that a few wives in our local society won't be happy with. Also, get this, there's a police lieutenant who is on a monthly payroll. There are lots of financial items. I'm no accountant, but my hunch is the IRS would send a crew in here tomorrow if they knew about it. I would need an expert, hell, a group of them, to figure this out. There's stuff on deals for slot machine manufactures, building water canals to golf courses, and...get this...a mention of opening a big hotel and casino twenty miles from nowhere, all vacant desert Indian reservation. As we speak it seems lots of water for the golf course is already being diverted from the farmers to the west, who are going to need more rain than normal after the resort gets built. That's a lot of Colorado River water to keep a golf course green and the swimming pools full. Hell, they even got plans for an eight-acre lake.

"It's all under many corporations and LLCs, and parent companies operating under agreements between each other. Payments made...no that's too nice...*bribery* payments to some of our elected local and national officials. And last, but not least, it seems these boys have some idea to open a casino in Cuba. I wouldn't have believed that, but hell, I didn't believe it when someone told me they were going to bring the London Bridge to Arizona.

"It's a jumbled web of legalese but it appears in what available records we could check that the tribe was going to lease, or maybe already has, some of their land to this group, which is a stretch, as it reservation land. Why the tribe would give it away along with the rights to build a rather large subdivision with a golf course and resort hotel next to the casino back to a group of non-Indian investors, headed by Brenda's law firm, is a big question. Not only is it illegal, but the strange thing is it stays in the tribe's name. Some questions here, it looks like only two of the tribe's council members are in on it going from names on the docs showing money paid to them. And not one mention of the water rights.

"Personally, based on my experience it beats the hell out of me why anyone would keep a file like this... it's nothing but trouble. I can pretty much guarantee you we have the only original copy of it. But I will also bet a copy or two have been made by now. This was never meant for public viewing. And I have little doubt now why two people that we know of were killed because of it. By the way, there are telephone numbers to someone in the Cuban Embassy in Mexico City. Who knows, maybe they were buying or selling sugar cane too. Oh, and get this...it looks like Mr. Lewis himself met Fidel's brother in Costa Rica. Why the hell your dead friend had this and gave it to you is a mystery I'd love to have the answer to. These are definitely the originals. As far as I know the local boys listed aren't supposed to be in the gambling business. This deal gives a big payoff from the proceeds, and I'm not sure how the hell that works. It seems some of our locals want to play rich Mafia Casino Guys...I wonder if their wives know it." Frank was always a bit sarcastic. "Not to mention, some state legislators and the Department of Gambling. I would bet my next social security check that there are some fat rich hands in the tribe's pocketbook."

Gambling profits were meant to be for the tribe only, as a government gift back to the tribes for taking all that nice land centuries ago, and was thought to be well-regulated by the state and the government in general. "I haven't even gotten to the part about a casino in Cuba. Hell, you need at least three honest attorneys to go through this. I only know two. I started reading those documents and the memos all going the same direction, big deal, lots of dough. That's where I get puzzled. When people die from a blow to the head as hard as your friend received, and her seedy boyfriend is found in a canal missing his hands, that has the earmark of being a little scarier than what anyone around here fools with and is far larger in scope then those crooked bastards at the Lewis law firm. We're talking big money here, but with no record of it...and as far as the county records go, it still is reservation land. Why Brenda gave this to you to hide...that a big question. But she had to steal it from her boss."

"No," Kim immediately interrupted, "she would never do that."

Frank, again sarcastic: "Well then, the envelope with its disk flew into her hands and she wanted to share the reward money with you."

"You don't know Brenda, I mean she just wouldn't take something like this. She had no use for it, and I have no idea why she would have it. She was into music and books and her sister's kids. That was her life, I know. What do you think it all means, Frank?"

Frank spoke slowly. "When people die like that, someone wanted to make no mistake it would be known how they died. For lack of a better term, let's call it message killing. There are some big players in this. And you may not want to know."

"Oh Frank, let me just throw them away. That's what Brenda should have done. Just toss it all in the trash. I want to be left alone, with no part of this."

"Well right now it isn't that simple. Remember, someone got your unlisted number and your name is tied to Brenda and the little package she was holding, which was given to you to hold. They have your address and other information by now, things that can't be tossed in the trash. Not to mention you...or now we...have a duty to turn it over to the police.

"I think your friend Brenda took this from work for reasons only she knew. Dominic, I found out, was somewhat of two-bit crook, but he's connected to this in some way. He had to be...it's too coincidental for him and his secret lover to be killed so close together. And by the way, he was missing his hands. The big time boys, the old Godfathers would have hands cut off, usually when someone shook hands on a deal and then reneged. It was a nice subtle way of showing what happens when your handshake turns out not to be good. The Godfathers don't like that. I think they believed your friend Brenda was also involved and wanted a message to be sent to anyone else who knew about or had the file. That's why she was eliminated in such a brutal fashion."

"Frank who do you think Dominic was killed by? Who are the Godfathers?"

"The Godfathers are the heads of organized crime families. We don't hear about them much anymore, but the common word is Mafia. Conventional wisdom is the FBI has put them all out of business in the past few years with a lot of help from the RICO laws. The last of the Godfathers supposedly went out with the arrest and final conviction of John Gotti. He died of cancer in a super max prison in Colorado. You ever hear of him?" Frank asked, already knowing the answer.

"No, was he a Godfather? Mafia?"

"You're on the nose," Frank answered.

"The Mafia," she replied, "that makes no sense in Phoenix."

"Not in Phoenix, but it makes sense where there are gambling casinos. I mean if Sid Lewis and a bunch of fat rich Phoenix boys could find a way in this, and if the word got out that there was a chance of them opening a casino in Cuba, some good old boys from back east in silk suits and Gucci shoes would come a-runnin'. I'm not sure of any of this, but until I have a better hunch, it's where my mind is for now...stuck there until some better logic comes along."

Frank paused before continuing.

"I have a good friend who is a homicide cop. I've already spoken to him. Your name was not mentioned, but you need to call him today. Use my name; he's expecting your call. I don't have any more ideas at this point."

"No," she said, her voice grew loud. "I can't trust anyone; I'm not ready to talk to the police or anyone about this yet, especially after what you just told me. My name will get out, especially when they know what I have. I called my neighbor to let her know I would be gone. I know you told me not to, but she is elderly and would worry if she didn't see me. She found my front door had been kicked in, and the inside of my house was ransacked, a total mess.

"I told her not to call the police, and that an angry boyfriend did it. I told her I didn't want him to get into trouble, so she said she wouldn't. In fact, I am leaving here and my sister is giving me money to go east. I'm very frightened. Brenda said not to tell anyone, not even the police. Maybe she knew if I did, I could be next. Oh what has she gotten me into? Just give the file to them, your police friend, I just want this to end and I'll just disappear. You can help me still, can't you? Just take the file into your police friend?"

Frank, more sympathetic than usual, but still unnerved by her proposed plan, answered slowly. "Okay, I understand, but I need to do some thinking here. I'm holding a file four inches thick with some sensitive information that's connected to illegal investments in tribal gambling, some other very nice building proposals, and lots of money to someone, and without having the slightest inclination why. Then add in the fact that your girlfriend Brenda, along with her ne'er do well boyfriend, have stopped breathing, likely because of this file, AND the person who gave it to me is somewhere hiding out in Colorado and now telling me she is moving somewhere else and wants me to call the police." He paused. "You ever hear the old saying, 'Something wrong with this picture'? Oh and let's not forget Cuba," Frank ended, waiting for a reply.

She didn't answer, Frank continued.

"I'm real close—and believe me, I need the money—to getting your twelve hundred bucks back to you and putting this file by your busted-up front door and pretending I never met you. But I'm getting bad feelings about this. I believe you are in danger, but I also think I will be too if it ever gets out that I have the file...not to mention the fact that I'm holding evidence that might be an integral part of a murder investigation, which, in case you aren't versed in that act, is a felony. And although I'm damn near ready to get out of the business, this will rush it a bit 'cause I can kiss my PI license goodbye, and then my ass, as I'm hauled off to jail. We need to make a decision here, right now, as I see it, and we aren't sure of the ramifications of any this. In fact, remote as it seems now, there might a simple explanation and these papers might have nothing to do with Brenda's murder, Dominic's murder, or the Mafia. So before you do any traveling," he emphasized YOU, "fly back here and take this file to the police. I'll go just another step with you. I think we might contact the law firm, in fact the man who signed these memos and letters, Sid Lewis himself, and see what he has to say. I have just enough time to do that before I, along with you, go see my police friend. We're just about out of time with him; he'll be issuing a warrant for me today. At this point the file isn't doing Brenda James or her deceased friend any good.

"Your friend worked at the firm. My mom didn't raise a stupid son, and I'd bet she took these papers for a reason. Now we're holding them without even knowing what the hell is going on. I can't stretch my time limit with Detective Fordham much longer; he's going to be out looking for me and you, and I don't want that to happen. He's a friend, but he's a cop first and he'd turn his mother in before he would violate his cop oath. His next job could have been an IRS agent. I have a suspicion that a call to Mr. Lewis may get us some fast answers and might offer you a bit of protection. In the meantime, I'm going to let Fordham know you'll be calling him for an appointment. If it'll help your nerves, I'll tell him to be extra nice to you as you just had a root canal...but make sure you call him. He is a very good cop friend of mine, so be ready not to go hiding, or you leave me in a pile of shit...you understand? I will help him track you down. It might get me out of jail quicker.

"Of course, before you take everything in and I talk to Lewis, we make copies of it, and keep two sets. One set will be ready to be mailed to the paper with a little note of our own, stating the connection and untimely death of two people...you okay with this? In poolroom conversation it would be known as covering our eight ball... you understand?"

"I do...I do," she said in a hush, then added, "Just don't let anyone know where I am for now."

"Don't worry about that. Now I'll get these wheels turning; you call me on my cell phone only. If I don't answer, don't leave a message and don't talk to anyone about this or me, or what we are doing. Not your sister, no one, got it? You call me back by noon and I should have some information for you. And by the way, see if you can put together another $500 for me, we don't have much time on this. I'll try to buy some time. You get a flight in here ASAP. Tonight, not tomorrow. While you get buckled up and in the air, I'm going to make a call to the crooked Mr. Lewis. Let me know your flight info, and I'll pick you up at the airport."

He felt bad about asking for more money but this damn case was growing bigger by the hour, and he needed to call Detective Fordham. He knew his pitch for more time was not going to be well received, but he also knew that he had a hell of a lot more information that would make his homicide friend a little more receptive. His last words to her before hanging up were, "Here's his number, call Fordham in exactly two hours; that will give me time to talk to him first." He gave her Fordham's direct line. "Two hours, don't forget…and tell him I'm bringing you in to see him tomorrow morning first thing. Oh, make sure you tell him Frank said you will have some documents he's going to enjoy reading."

"I will, I promise."

CHAPTER 14

The Romance of Death

Dominic went slower than usual with Brenda. He had the bar boy intuition and knew this was not going to be a quick roll in the hay. She was different. He might have overwhelmed her initially at the first meeting, but the second and third times together were strictly at the bar and it wasn't until the sharing of their third drink that she offered her home phone number.

After that things started moving, although he was polite and sensed she would still rebuff any moves made toward a bedroom. He was rather flattered that she liked him. She was obviously educated, plus had a good job, and a history of hard work. More than once she mentioned that she was a church attendee. She had recently broken up with guy she had been dating for three years. She let Dominic know that she wasn't ready to get serious, at least for now. She still hoped to marry someday and have children. She was gorgeous, and Dominic found himself being a good listener once he got past the fact that this was not going to be about sex and the single girl. He began to listen and share conversation with her. That was new to him, even if much of what he said was pure bullshit.

He discovered—amazing even himself—that he was drawn to her intelligence. And for the first time in his life, it was becoming a little bit about the person rather than what he could get from the person. He knew he was stepping way up in class, and even admitted when thinking about the relationship he had started that it probably wasn't going to end well. "But hell," he said to himself. "I'm here today... so until something better happens, enjoy the ride."

He didn't know it at the time, but he had unwittingly found, without understanding it, that a little value had entered his life. The bottom line was that this was a girl you took home to meet your momma. A girl you married. It was value he knew he didn't deserve, or would ever understand.

Their first real date was dinner and a movie, some chick flick that he would never have seen under any other circumstances. It was a throwaway line when he told her he enjoyed it. He took her home and she invited him in. He had never been inside her place before. She offered him a Diet Coke and sat next to him on the couch, but not close. She had previously turned on the music and he knew it was classical, but that was as near as he got. She said, "Rachmaninoff. He is one of my favorite composers, this is the second piano concerto, and I always think that if God wrote music this is what it would sound like." Her long red hair fell off to the side. "Thank you for a very nice night."

Dominic had the first sense that this night he might get his first kiss from her. She talked about work. How busy she was on a land project that involved an Indian casino that she really didn't understand. It was very hush-hush, but very boring. She talked about her niece who she was taking Saturday afternoon to see Disney on Ice. And she talked about maybe having Dominic, if he wanted, over after the show as her niece was staying all night and she was going to make spaghetti and meatballs. Dominic was thrilled with the invitation.

He hadn't told her a lot about what he did. He told her initially that he worked with a couple of the car dealers in both sales and as an adviser on products and merchandising. He didn't go into the part that some of the cars and parts were moved overnight across the Mexican border for the final illegal transaction.

The one thing common among most good girls like Brenda was that they also had a marvelous naivety to them. She didn't ask a lot of questions about Dominic's business, and based on his manners towards her had no suspicion that Dominic was anything but a very handsome straight-up guy who she noticed tipped well and seemed to be attracted to her. She had no inclination she was swimming with a shark who was so thrilled with the dinner in front of him that he had started thinking he might not be a shark after all.

He was right about the kiss. She said it was time for him to go as she had to be at work early, and she got up and walked him to the front door. He turned toward her, and as she came close he put both arms around her and kissed her. Her mouth stayed closed but she had put her arms around him. It was quick, but it was a kiss.

Dominic had never been so pleased by a kiss in his life. She pulled back and said, "Time for you to go." And he was out the door.

He was smiling all the way to his car. He had just started a relationship with the girl of his dreams, as long as she didn't learn who and what he really was. For now it was going very well, and for a guy who lived for the rush of the minute with not much thought of consequences it was perfect.

He didn't know it but it also was the start of a clock that gave Brenda and him just a little under two months left to live and enjoy each other. He would bring a tragic end to such a good and beautiful young life, right after losing his life with a lot more pain.

Dominic's business dealings sometimes did cross paths with those who were not just mob wannabes, but were the real thing. Like all men of reasonable intelligence, gangsters liked to get out of the cold of New York and Chicago and Philadelphia, and some headed to sunny Arizona when the snow started falling back east. They were always vultures and never snow birds, as Arizona residents referred to winter visitors.

As the adage goes, "Water seeks its own level." And mobsters, as well as mobster wannabes, hang at mobster hangouts. It was inevitable that Dominic would be in the right place at the right time when someone needed a service. He was always looking for ways to get in with the right people. The organization had keen intelligence, and had long been aware of Lewis and his corporation, from tips and conversation picked up on the streets of Phoenix and vendors to the casinos. They also knew through some of their own union vendors who sold accounting software, plastic money chips, and slot machine maintenance to Lewis and his crooked investors. They controlled the talent agencies that booked the entertainment, all controlled by various unions, and which had always been run by companies owned and operated by various gangsters from one generation to the next.

They also heard one of their "friends" was dating a gorgeous girl from Lewis' law office who worked as Lewis' paralegal and didn't particularly like him. It wasn't hard to find out, as Dominic had bragged to everyone about "this great piece of class ass he was stalking who worked in this big law office," that the office represented the tribe and that his new girl worked for the main man.

Pete "The Nose" Martello was part of the Philadelphia family of Sam Benito. They were big into drugs and prostitution, and most recently were very interested in finding entry into Indian gambling casinos. They had ears everywhere and an extremely impressive intelligence network. Most of this new breed had their sons in good colleges, and the business degrees and accounting knowledge fit nicely with their cousins and nephews who had law degrees from well-known east coast universities. The family business was being handled very well, and for the most part very cleanly, as far as the books went.

Donnie, the current son of Sam Benito, was a recent graduate of University of Virginia Law School and not as well-versed in the family history as his parents and grandparents, but came to accept their connections to gambling and real estate ventures, jukebox supply, and slot machine lease and repair. The various unions, crime connections, prostitution, and narcotics were part of a past when their families were discriminated against and had to be illegal in some of the operations just to stay competitive in order to support their families. Bribing the police was a big part of it.

But today he believed it was cleaned up and he was lucky to be coming from such successful families who, just a century ago, had emigrated from Italy and arrived in the U.S. with nothing but the clothes on their body. He knew that occasionally there had to be some unfortunate and questionable transactions, but believed the days of breaking legs for perceived wrongs had long passed. Most were honored to keep the family name and he thought more than once of the honor given to him to make his family name respected again and not just part of a sad and bad history of Italian Americans.

He quietly respected the John Gottis of today, but had too much education to admit that any operation of the old Mafia life from their grandparents' time still existed. In truth, most of their knowledge of the Mafia had been shown him on the big screen by Francis Ford Coppola and his motion picture "Godfather" trilogy, based on the bestselling book of Mario Puzo. There was never even the slightest mention of any "Philly Organization." He was not too blind to realize there was some dark history—he had seen too many men of questionable character come and go in closed-door meetings with his father—but that's where it stopped.

Indian casinos were the logical place for the families to go after Vegas was cleaned up with the casinos taken over by the large corporations who marketed it as being the next best place after Disneyland to bring mom and the kids. The organized crime influence in Vegas had come to an end in the 80's when the federal government decided enough was enough, and the government RICO acts made a life of crime that had always been dangerous now awfully expensive.

But the solution to their large problem was handed to them when the federal government opened the doors for Indian tribes to own and operate their own casinos on reservation land. The mob bosses knew the best place to clean up those bags of drug money, prostitution funds, illegal union dues and non-taxable gambling profits was a casino.

To the Organizations, one Indian tribe was as good as another. In fact, in many ways, it was better than Vegas could have ever been. The hardest part was over once one of their holding companies and fancy-named corporations got in the front door and then to the office door and the accounting office.

The tribes made money. The boys in Philly made money. The state and federal government got their tax payments. Everyone was smiling. But you had to keep finding Indian casinos and it damn near seemed to the boys back east that there was one opening every month—hell there were more casinos on Indian land in the U.S. then there ever were in Nevada. If only they could keep finding ways to get into the counting rooms...which, they had heard through union gambling suppliers, Lewis and his boys had found in Arizona.

The tribes were novices about running such operations and when companies like Kachina Freedom Accounting and Management Service, and Always American Indian Financial and Consulting, contacted them in other states right around the time they got approval to get gaming licenses, they were more than willing to listen. How and where to buy, maintain and set percentages on the slots, get the right state lobbyist out for lunch and golf, how to count money, pay the taxes and give the state and government their lowest possible cut. How to hire inside people. Eventually the companies basically told the tribal council, "You nice people go home and just enjoy the profits that are heading your way. Build a medical clinic or two, and a new school. Buy some new fire trucks and police vehicles. It looks good. We will take care of everything else."

They had not the slightest idea that Kachina Corporation, Always American Indian Finance, and Kokopelli Management Service, represented by those well-dressed and sophisticated people, were employees of holding companies removed from Sam Benito and the Philly mob. Lewis and his wealthy group should have known that the boys in Philly would eventually learn of those rich Phoenix boys playing in their sandbox. Philadelphia wasn't interested in taking in new partners, and Lewis and his friends were about to be told that fact in a brutal fashion.

Pete Martello was sitting in one of the darkened back booths of the Chock and Hen Club in downtown Phoenix, AZ. The bartender showed Dominic to the booth. He had no illusions about who he was meeting—it gave him a notch of self-importance to think Pete Martello had asked for him.

'What would you like to drink, Dominic?"

"Pernod on the rocks, sir." Pete motioned to the bartender who was still standing by the booth to bring Dominic what he wanted.

"I understand you are dating a secretary from Lewis Law Firm, that right?"

"Yes sir," Dominic replied. "Nice girl, we've been dating for about two months. She could be the one, you know what I mean?"

"That's nice...very nice. I'll get you both dinner some night." Pete grabbed Dominic's hand. "Sam in Philly needs a favor and he never forgets a favor done. Understand?"

"Yes sir, Dominic replied. "Anything for Sam."

"We need you to get some information...and of course we will pay for it, it would be much appreciated by Sam...he is thinking about a little investment, but you know, doesn't want to take a big risk and lose his position, you know, so when we heard you knew somebody from this firm, it gave a little comfort, know what I mean? See, Sam heard this law firm," Pete leaned over closer to Dominic, "this law firm is doing part of the deal and he needs to know everything is like he's been told...you understand?"

Dominic nodded his head yes.

Pete continued, "You know we don't want nothing to cause trouble. Just some information that your lady friend might pick up for us, you understand?"

Dominic continued nodding affirmatively.

"She might—you know on some free time or something, just get us some names and let us know a little bit about the deal, you know like if it was her old man who was putting in the money, she would want to watch out for him. Sam kind of needs someone like that, you understand."

"Yes, understand," Dominic smiled.

"You think you can handle this Dominic? Your girl will help Sam? You keep this to yourself, but her law firm has got its hands a little dirty in the local casinos here, and Sam is not real happy about that. It's kind of like Sam has a shoe store and this law firm opened another shoe store right across the street...you understand? Sam would like to know how dirty their hands are...but we want it kept quiet."

"Yes sir," Dominic replied.

"I mean if it's something you can't do you tell me now," Pete said, squeezing Dominic's hand.

"I can do it, no trouble."

"Good Dominic, that's good. Now I'm going to give you some things you might have your friend look for, and you see what you can do and get back to me, okay"

"Yeah. Right away."

Pete then slid over a folded piece of paper saying as he did, "We'll see that you and your girl," Pete smiled, "if she wants to take you, get a nice vacation from us with a little shopping money. You tell your girl what we're looking for and tear this up. Eat it, you understand?"

Dominic said, "Yeah, we can do that."

Pete then said, "Here's a little something for your trouble. You take your girl out and get her some good pasta," and put five crisp 100 dollar bills into Dominic's hand.

"You see she gets some good shopping money, you understand." He then motioned for Dominic to leave and Dominic knew how to follow orders, especially one given by a connected member of the Philly mob.

To wonder how anyone connected knew he was seeing a girl from the Lewis Law Firm never entered his mind.

CHAPTER 15

Frank's on the Case

Frank was in his office reading through the notes and copies Norma had obtained from the county assessor's office. He had left two phone messages for Fordham who had not yet returned his calls.

The fact that it was nine PM Thursday night and he was alone didn't register as long as he was working at something. He was a lonely man, more than he realized. He had made the tragic mistake of falling in love with a younger woman who had spent one too many Saturday nights and New Year's Eves alone.

The reality of it all was that he found her to be everything he had ever wanted in a woman. She came along at a time in his life when he had learned that a great figure, fancy clothes, and sex were not as important as he once thought. There were the intangible things mixed in with the obvious attractions. Like someone who was interesting to talk to, listened to your day's events, and was understanding of your faults. Someone who laughed at your silly jokes that most others didn't get, and made you feel young and needed again, as though you were the best thing she ever knew.

In the middle of the night when he got up to take a piss—a frequent routine over age 60—when he came back to bed she never said a word, but then her foot came over and touched his and she let him know by that touch that life was good and she was his woman.

There were some advantages to being with an older man like Frank. He didn't carry jealousy issues and was not bothered when she needed space, asked for or not. Often she reminded him to comb his hair and told him when he forgot to pull up his zipper, but he had always been like that.

Overall he had developed patience with her and his demands were few. The experiences of life had softened him and he was very appreciative of just being loved by someone he greatly admired for who she was and the adversity in her life she had overcome. Most might have found her plain and not at all what they thought Frank would have fallen for, but in his older years he had discovered in her an inner beauty that he recognized the first time he laid eyes on her, and that view had never changed.

She was messy and had a habit of flinging her clothes anywhere they landed when she changed outfits. She often went to bed with the pan of soup still on the turned off stove with the spoon in it, and she had a dog that shed unmercifully. But he had decided, at this stage in his life, he could live with all of her imperfections even if she couldn't accept his. There was no trade off. He loved her, simply stated, unconditionally, shedding dog and all. He just quit wearing anything black when he went to see her.

He knew the end was his fault. He didn't get free soon enough to care for her as she should. And when he did it was too late. He regretted the fact that he literally killed her feelings for him, but he now realized there could be no other ending. It was true that time heals a broken heart. He had written her a few letters after she left his life, conveying as best he could how sorry he was. She never responded.

The few close friends he kept in contact with had all told him that time would take care of it and that he should get on with his life, but he hadn't been totally able to do that. He had little interest in finding another relationship. It would not be possible until her memory dimmed to black, whenever that time came.

He heard through a friend of hers that she got married in Georgia, of all places. He was also told the guy had some money in his pockets, and had purchased a house in Scottsdale. At this point Frank was just happy for her. She had a good head on her shoulders and would do okay. She had come, as Frank remembered from a line in an old movie, "a long way baby."

He was his own best therapist when he reminded himself to be glad for the time he did have with her. It was something most men would never taste at his age. He remembered an old joke he had heard once when a friend told another friend he was dating a woman 30 years younger than him and his friend replied, "Are you crazy? Do you realize that in ten years, when you're 65, she will only be 35?"

The 65-year-old friend replied, "Ten years, hell. I'm just hoping it goes another weekend."

For now, there was this case, which he knew from instinct could be dangerous. He thought of Kim Dawson hiding in Colorado or wherever the hell she was now. She was someone he would have been interested in at another time. Long dark hair, stunning blue eyes, very intelligent, and a great figure accented with a posterior that stood out and looked as inviting to touch as the driver's seat in a new BMW. No question, she was attractive and she was smart, but Frank still lacked the ability to put such traits in the correct order.

She was probably about 20 years behind him. The thought of loving again, especially with a younger woman was too remote. But he knew he could easily like her if he could get past the feeling of lost love. Still, he had to remember, she was now his client and he forced himself to make that his main thought when he started thinking other thoughts about her. Frank was still a PI and that fact by its very nature kept his mind on her problem more than on her.

He didn't know why the hell he was letting himself get into her problem but he also knew she did need help and he was not the kind of man, no matter how much the danger alarm went off in his mind, to not help someone who he knew needed help. It didn't hurt his quest that he had to acknowledge mentally she was beautiful...and it's much easier to stop and fix a flat tire for a gorgeous woman.

He had a few dates with a girl he met at church, but then at dinner one night she informed him (for reasons he never quite figured out) that she had been having sex with her ex-husband every night for ten years, and then over-divulged that she had been told she was very good at oral sex. She also told him once that she had to go see a doctor when she was sick, and was mortified that her bra and thong underwear didn't match. He had trouble relating to that as a priority, unless she was after the doctor. She had some strange ways, no doubt.

Frank knew that he had passed her generation when the first thought he had, after processing what to him were unwelcome facts, was that she should never put such information on eHarmony.com, as it would definitely attract the wrong people. But, he also reasoned, it was good information if you were applying for a job as a hooker. Frank still sometimes saw her at church, but the memory of that information had now tainted his thoughts of her. This was a girl you took to Vegas for a weekend, and Frank was no longer attracted or interested in just a piece of ass. Those years were in the memory bank of his brain, and he now realized they had been spent in utterly selfish ways. He figured the best he could ever do now was maybe a half-hour from start to finish twice a day—and that was with Viagra, Cialis and whatever else he could get from his doctor. That left 23 hours each day, which meant there had better be something else in a relationship or he'd lose a lot of money playing blackjack in Vegas all alone.

He picked up the file Kim had given him and decided to see what he could find on some of the people mentioned either by memo or letter on the papers Brenda James had taken from her law office. Frank found the file with its spreadsheets not only swirling in his mind but above his knowledge of what the hell most of it meant. He knew he needed expert help from the one guy who could put together a computer background online on Mickey Mouse and tell if he had cheated on Minnie, stolen from Donald Duck or forged Goofy's name. Mike Ferdinand.

Most people had no idea of the information that was floating around in cyber space that could be accessed by the magical clicks of the mouse, starting with a social security number...which wasn't a necessity to get started. It was all there, how much money you made, how much taxes you paid, property you owned or had ever owned, the car you drove and the car you turned in to buy the new car. How much you owed and to whom, from traffic tickets all the way through an entire divorce file. Phone records, both residential and cell, mostly from people who had sent such information to cyberspace on their own and never had it come back. Corporations you were part of, plus any and all litigation ever listed with your name. Who you voted for, who your doctor was, what drugs you took, and prescriptions issued. What your neighbors could or would say about you and your family. Cold and factual information you might have lied about or tried to hide by not mentioning it in some application you filled out, from your personal finances to what you paid for or sold your house for. Where your passport stated you traveled, the names and addresses of your kids and family, your neighbor's phone, and most of the telephone numbers to residences on the same street.

You didn't need a lot to get started. Mike Ferdinand needed just a name. Middle initials and birth dates weren't necessary.

Frank remembered when he was in the military and he was given the code of conduct and how you gave only your name, rank, and serial number if you were captured;

that same code applied in the civilian world. You only had to have the smallest detail that one would think was of no importance that would crack open the gate to get bigger and better information.

Frank often told the story of how he would use the local drugstore's phone, saying he needed to call home because he "forgot something," then would dial the mother of someone he was trying to find who had been in hiding for some time. Knowing they had caller ID, when they answered he would say he was from the drugstore and he had some developed film with this phone number and they were cleaning out the film drawers of pictures developed and held in the bin box for two years with this number and name, and rather than throw it away he would just be happy to send it free of charge if he just had an address. And she would say, "Oh that's my son," while she gave Frank an address and phone number, laughing about how "he must have forgotten they were there."

Frank told others there are certain lures you use for certain fish, and when needed, this lure had a high catch rate. Another lure was to tell them you were on the high school reunion board after establishing the year and school they attended, and had tried to find them by mail, and did they possibly have a good address or phone as they were wanted to participate in a school skit. It also usually always caught the fish.

Frank had told most of his friends never to give out information on the phone, emphasize the word *never*. Also, never open the door to strangers, even if they look like police or say they are police. Call the police and ask for dispatch to make sure the police should be there, and then even if it checks out don't let them in without them showing and reading a warrant. Same with parties who say they are with the local utility service or cable company...if you didn't call, the red flag must be raised.

When interviewed by the police, remember that police can lie with impunity. That's why the answer to the Miranda rights should always be, "I want an attorney," and no questions should be answered. Frank had worked on two cases where the party arrested was innocent, but because he did not follow such advice, got convicted and served twelve years in one case before his conviction was overturned. One was on death row in Arizona for ten years before he was finally set free as the innocent man he had been all along. A friend instrumental in the case wrote a book about it and mentioned Frank's name between the pages more than once.

On another occasion Frank had needed to get some information about some assets of a defendant party in a personal injury case where the insurance company had indicated it was willing to pay policy limits, but unfortunately for the plaintiff the amount was not near enough to cover his injury. Frank was hired to see if the defendant, a well-known college professor, had any assets the plaintiff could obtain to assist in covering his damages. Frank, using one of his many PI cons, called the defendant's employer and was told that he was on vacation in Europe. Frank waited a couple of weeks and called the professor's residence in the middle of the day. His wife answered.

"Hi," Frank said, "I am with the State Department and we are just following up with random selections from passport information to do a survey, and of course this is all confidential. Your name will not be used—do you mind if I ask you a few questions about your recent trip for our government survey?"

"Oh no, sure," she replied. "To assist the State Department would be an honor."

So Frank began asking her where they went and how long they stayed and if they had any trouble with their passport or any complaints, and then he slowly worked into, "Do you own any property or land other than your residence?" He followed that with some additional innocuous questions about which countries they had visited, which banks they used, whether they had any boats or RV's, her husband's salary range, any income from other investments and any resort homes?

"Yes," she said. "We love our cabin at Big Bear Lake!"

By the time Frank had finished, he had a complete financial background on the defendant, all given freely by the spouse who informed her husband upon his arrival home later that day about the nice gentleman who called from the passport department doing a survey, and the interesting questions he asked. "He said I was very helpful."

When the husband finally got the blood back into his head after going over the questions his wife was asked and answered, and what his wife could remember saying, he furiously begin making notes to start getting assets out of his name the next day. That is, if it wasn't too late...but it was. He was going to be forced by the harsh legal rights of the forever paralyzed motorcycle rider who he had hit when his RV failed to stop at a red light to sell the cabin and throw the money into the pot along with the policy limits of his insurance company.

Frank finally closed his eyes lying on the office couch. When he opened them it was morning. He called Mike Ferdinand.

CHAPTER 16

The Computer Geek

Mike Ferdinand picked up on the first ring. Frank did not start with a big explanation. "I got a project for you."

Mike Ferdinand was retired from a large worldwide banking firm where he had designed and overseen the installation of the entire computer system for their branch banks all over the world, including Singapore and Australia. He once even gave the Chinese government some help. People had long ago tired of asking him what he did for a living, as no one ever understood his answer. He was above most mortals in intellect and why the hell he was a friend of Frank's, Frank never knew. Frank would with smile thinking of what his mother had said about birds of a feather flocking together. He could only surmise that Mike Ferdinand was a bird of a very different feather to be in Frank's circle of friends.

Ferdinand liked to work, and he liked puzzles. Real puzzles out of the paper, and the puzzles that came from Frank's work, who he had known since grade school. When Ferdinand retired ten years earlier, he had a mind that would not stay idle. So one day when Frank told him he was having trouble finding some information on a case he was working on, Ferdinand went home to his computer office, dialed up the Internet and within the day called Frank with everything he needed.

Frank was stunned. He even had the guy's cell phone and a record of all the calls made. Frank, whose computer skill was somewhere between electric typewriters and Windows 93, knew then that his old friend would be part of his working life from that project on.

"Listen, I need some background on some individuals, corporations, land purchases and whatever the hell you can come up with. I can't say why yet, because I don't know. But it may well be connected to a couple of murders. Like everything else, I don't have a big budget on this, but it is exactly the kind of work you like. So put a smile on your face when you think about billing me."

Ferdinand replied, "What kind of time frame am I on?"

"Needed it one week ago and we might have saved two lives...other than that, your usual all-nighter. I will see you in the morning at the office."

"Frank it's my anniversary. I have to take her out to dinner. You ever heard the loud clap of thunder? It's a little louder than that when her thighs close, which is what I'll be hearing if I miss dinner."

"OK, get into my office day after tomorrow, I don't want your ear drums to blow out."

Frank hadn't smoked in fifteen years except for the occasional Cuban cigar, when Fordham would hand him one with a stein of Sam Adams or an ice cold Heineken.

He wanted that cigar now and made a mental note to call Fordham again. John had still not returned his calls. But first, the call to Mr. Lewis. He cleared his throat and dialed up the Lewis Law Firm.

CHAPTER 17

Mr. Sid Lewis

Sid Lewis had been considered a distinguished member of the Arizona Bar for 45 years. When he started his profession Phoenix was a small town with no freeways, and most lawyers made deals in the hallway with a shake of the hand, meeting for drinks at the Adams Hotel bar as soon as their clients left the courtroom for home.

It was a different time now. The rules of evidence and discovery in those earlier days made few enemies among the legal community. Oh how things in the legal world had changed. In the current legal climate of the present law firms, those polite indications of friendly adversaries representing the interests of their client had dissolved into a truly cutthroat mentality that only the toughest of this new breed survive. Lawyers were finally deserving of the jokes so often told, making fun of billable hours and why there are no skid marks on the road in front of the dead lawyer. There were exceptions, Frank knew, but the majority of this new breed of attorneys was not immune to crossing any and all lines when no one was looking.

The pressure to succeed, piled on top of the pressure to keep the giant insurance companies happy, was immense. Turning in those endless time sheets all added to the burnout and callousness slowly but inevitably ingrained in their profession. Complaints to the State Bar of Arizona were on the rise.

This all ultimately became evident to those new young attorneys fresh out of law school who had taken an oath to serve the blind eyes of justice within a few years of graduation. Statistics showed that close to 80 percent of attorneys would not have chosen the legal career if given another chance. Life becomes harder if you don't like what you're doing for your paycheck. The new, and constantly changing, rules of evidence and required paperwork had long ago erased the handshake lawyers made when making an agreement outside the courtroom.

Sid was wishing he would have retired four years ago when his wife wanted him to, before he ever got the hell into the Indian casino deal. Hell, he didn't need any more money, and was morally against gambling since his oldest son had been a gambler and finally through the grace of God had found and joined Gamblers Anonymous. This came after one day of losing everything but his sperm, which in one of his broker times he tried to sell to a sperm bank, and was crushed to learn that his was of no value. So he took his hand out of his pants and walked slowly outside to ask the first stranger he came to for bus change. Since then he had been in and out of street shelters, doing his best to straighten up. He failed once or twice each year, but overall was taking his life slowly in the right direction.

Sid Lewis found himself in a web of greed which was now about to cut his balls off with some dull scissors...a thought he wished he could accommodate if it would bring that file back and place it in the locked safe. He knew that easy money always had a bad smell, but he had ignored it. The casino deal had grown from a small legal folder to accordion-bound memos that were more often than not legal mumbo jumbo to make reasonable what Sid Lewis knew was not legal, let alone reasonable. He was now in so deep that he couldn't get out. He had brought in most of his wealthy friends who jumped at the chance to get what was "under the table," tax free, gambling money profits in hushed talk, paid at the country club. The return on their investment would be more than 25 percent in the first two years and went up from there.

David Duncan, lobbyist for the Fort Kachina Indian tribe, had enjoyed deeply his one and only account for the past five years. He thought of himself as "doing very well." And the tribe, since their association with him, found themselves doing very well. He was one of those Sid Lewis cohorts who loved getting his weekly check. Gambling had opened doors that General Crook had closed 150 years before. Most Arizona residents had no idea that the Fort Kachina Indian Casino was actually built not far from where the original cavalry outpost with the same name was standing 150 years earlier.

From those original Fort Kachina doors 150 years past, U.S. troopers rode out and fought and killed Indians. Today those doors opened and let the descendants of those troopers back in. The Indian descendants of the ones those troopers had chased and killed smiled while they took their white brothers' ten and twenty dollar quarter rolls after they had placed them in what might be the most tightly set slot machines in existence. It took a lot of quarters before the "Wheel of Fortune" spin ended on the player's side of the spinning machine.

Frank had learned from his quick study that Indian gambling had brought revenues to the tribe beyond his first, second, and third guesses. Most citizens of Arizona had little conception of the money flowing through the casinos.

The white establishment had made treaties in the last century with the tribes and soon—though not planned— white society introduced its alcohol to its red brothers— who immediately developed one of the highest rates of alcohol abuse and subsequent suicide and domestic violence reports as a society in the United States. But it didn't stop there. Prior to the white invaders the Indians were thin, athletic people who were healthy as a whole, and whose diet and way of living worked for them. They ate lean meat and lots of vegetables, due to the simple fact that they had to depend on food they caught or grew which made them a dietician's dream for healthy living. Since the forced association of white ideals and culture, they now found their daily food to be lots of carbohydrates, sugar, calories, and fat purchased in fast food restaurants and modern supermarkets, as well as the local convenience store that rotated its goodies to sell the older Twinkies first. So this once thin, robust tribe now found itself being overweight, out of breath, and having one of the highest rates of obese people with diabetes and heart disease among any group of people living in the States. Not to mention the continuing problem with alcohol and domestic violence.

But, Frank sarcastically thought, the tribe in its own fashion had found some retribution from their association with the "white men" and that was the vice of gambling, that pie-in-the-sky mentality that permeates most of white society, that one can get rich if just the right numbers come up on the machine with the next quarter inserted. Just find about any reservation in the states and chances are good you will find a gambling casino. Enter that reservation and find the glitter of the casino promising you laughter and fun and bring your money and your troubles might be over in an instant. But most folks who lived off the reservation went home a lot poorer than when they came.

Indians with casinos, though, had never been wealthier. They built medical clinics and schools, and expanded the fire and police departments—but above all they added to their pockets. Allotments to tribal members in some years totaled more than 35 thousand a member, and in really good years the tribal elders would sometimes vote to pay the taxes due on the allotment. It was hard, though, to get an 18-year-old tribal male or female, with their Nike outfits and shoes and new pickup truck, interested in going to work or school when they were getting tens of thousands in tax-free money annually just for being an Indian living on the reservation.

But that was nothing compared to the greenbacks Sid Lewis and his people quietly took in right from under their tribal noses.

Chief Anthony By Water had been the elected head of the Ft. Kachina tribe for four years. He drove a new

Hummer, had cowboy boots made from alligator skin, and smoked the best cigars. His wife drove a new Cadillac and didn't miss a sale at Nordstrom. Like the majority of his tribe he had diabetes, which went with his large stomach and poor diet. He did little to combat his poor health.

By Water officially received a salary of $63,500 a year for leading his tribe to the Promised Land of Casino. But the money flowed way beyond that in the Chief's world. He was seldom without a roll of hundreds held together by a rubber band. He would peel them off and flip them out when paying for anything. And the tips he left were highly appreciated. No one in the tribe really questioned the chief and that roll of hundreds. "Hell, we're all doing good," they would say. "I'm happy. Don't anyone rock the boat," was the common attitude among his red blood brothers.

A prevailing thought that many others have shared is that when things are going too well, something bad is going to happen, and the tribal members worried among themselves that the white man might catch on and quit playing bingo, slots, and blackjack. Life is good they said to each other. If the chief needed to take a little extra money home, he deserved it. Life is good.

When the tribe first voted to get into the gaming business they had already been contacted by Duncan. He and By Water became good friends the moment they met because, like Frank's mom used to say, water seeks its own level. Duncan had advised By Water on the talking points needed for the tribal council voting members to hear at the council meetings, to assure they would not pass up such a positive way to bring much needed finances to the tribe coffers.

Duncan, with Sid Lewis and his rich friends, put the package together with By Water within a week, pushing through all federal forms. And soon the Wheel of Fortune machines were spinning and putting money into the tribe pocket, as well as those hidden "white boy" investors. Duncan's big job was to keep the state legislators looking the other way after their tax check was delivered. He was good at it.

And the best part was Duncan showed the chief that they could technically just print up some more chips when they needed cash, and no one needed to know. That the tribe was devaluing the betting tokens with all those new chips with no real cash behind them did not seem to matter. In other banking worlds it would be known as the biggest float of money going on. Need some fast dough—print up a couple of thousand dollar chips. It was much like a "Ponzi" scheme. They only had to depend on the count catching up through the law of betting averages, and those extra chips would all even out as long as the betters continued to lose, which the statistical numbers to-date had been correct on. By Water, with Lewis' group's approval, didn't do daily accounting. Every other day had become the norm, which gave lots of room for the bookkeepers and money counters to balance out.

Duncan and By Water felt that this was better than running the U.S. government who, on occasion, had printed up some extra cash at those mints when they needed it. Besides, in their gracious logic, occasionally when they did not need so much they would take some of the chips back out of play, to even up the balance sheet. They had their own mint and basically their own currency. Just like the U.S. treasury.

The only problem that no one saw was one that had just surfaced. Some large financial company from back east, which evidently was in the casino business for other tribes in some other states, was seeking an appointment and had sent a couple of what Duncan and the chief thought were salesmen who wanted to pitch a topic of running the casino for them. Duncan and the chief laughed over a Heineken when the chief, referring to the news sales pitch they thought they were going to hear, said "Hell, there ain't any more room in this teepee. Whoever these guys are, they don't know how we do things here."

It wasn't until a made member of the Philadelphia mob approached them one sunny Arizona day that they learned they were, unfortunately, going to have partners, and frankly speaking, there wasn't shit they could do about it. In fact, there indeed wasn't any more room in the teepee... for them.

CHAPTER 18

The Contents

Mike Ferdinand called Frank. He had left his wife after dinner and headed for Frank's office where he spent the entire night into the early morning hours going through the file Frank had left for him. "Frank this is big time shit... worst I have ever seen...the IRS is going to close all its offices just to work on this case. Some people are going to prison and I hope like hell you are not one of them. How the hell did you come across this...and is it for real?"

"Yeah it's for real. It's a long story. Came from a new client, but it doesn't belong to her either. I'm in the process of turning it over to cop friend of mine...what do you get from it?"

"Well to skip over the cheating and the phony tax returns, there's illegal investing in Indian gambling casinos and meeting with the brother of a foreign government dictator. Those are just for starters."

Frank interrupted him. "Listen, I gathered some of that...can you index it all out for me and put it in some order so the cops can figure it out easily? Put it together and highlight the important stuff."

"Frank it's all important, but I know what you need. I'll hide it in your usual hiding place in the office you can pick it up in a few hours. To be honest with you, I could spend a lot more time on this."

"There is no time. I have got to turn it over right away. Just do what you can...and by the way, happy anniversary. And thanks."

"You're welcome...my bill is in the mail and hope you are not this Lewis guy's buddy 'cause he gathered enough dirt on his friends that none of them will be able to make their first communion."

"I could have figured that. Not a nice guy, huh?"

Eddie Passerelli was well-dressed and there was no reason to think he was connected. He had made an appointment to meet By Water at the casino. By Water thought he was one of the Kachina American Financial assistants who had set up the operation and was just making a courtesy call. Passerelli walked into the office took a seat without being invited to sit down and his first words were not friendly.

"Say Chief, I heard you, or should I say the tribe, is going to build a big resort.

By Water's mind jumped. "Where did you hear that?"

"Not only heard that. I heard you and your friend Duncan been doing some Indian business with that crooked son of a bitch lawyer, Lewis. I did not believe it when I first heard it; I was going to call the IRS and ask those boys if they had any info on it, but shit," he said, with a snide smile, "I thought why not just ask the chief? If it's true, my boss back in Philadelphia is going to want to be a part of it, so I guess you could call me your new best friend and partner."

By Water, still stunned, did not initially have words to respond. Lewis had told him no one would know that it was written. He immediately denied having "any idea of what the hell you're talking about."

Passerelli continued with his snide smile, as he pushed the door to By Water's office shut. "You know I don't like playing word games, and my boss likes it even less. I'm not shitting you when I tell you that about a year ago my boss asked a guy a question that he knew had the answer. That guy denied it and my boss stuck a stick of dynamite up that guy's wife's ass and lit the fuse. The guy started screaming for him to take it out, that he would tell him. But hell, it was too late, the fuse had burned too far and that guy's wife and her last meal were all over the parking lot. Trust me; I got meatloaf on one of my new shoes.

"Now, you want to tell me again that you don't know what I'm talking about?"

By Water, recognizing real danger stammered, "Yes there was some talk about something like that, but Lewis, our lawyer, took care of it and I really don't have any information...really," he repeated. "Really. I was just acting on the tribe's behalf. That kind of business is well over my position. I don't know anyone else Lewis has spoken to. I can give you Mr. Lewis' private number." The chief was nervously going through his wallet.

"Got it," Passerelli said. "What I do need is for you is to tell Lewis to let all the partners know there is a change in ownership. And start packing up your things...this is your last day here. I wouldn't want to see another stick of dynamite with your wife's name on it." Passerelli put his cigarette out on top of the chief's desk

By Water left immediately without responding to the rest of the threatening remarks. He would, however, remember all of them when he met Duncan, which is where he immediately headed.

This visit was only the beginning of trouble for Mr. Sid Lewis and his group of investors who were very much in on a deal with Mr. Duncan and Chief By Water to build a hotel golf course and a brand new casino on the eastern edge of the reservation. And who had met with a dictator's brother to initiate plans to build a Las Vegas style casino in Cuba, which the Philadelphia boys back east hadn't been informed of until they heard through another source about a secret Lewis "file."

Before his untimely death, Dominic told his killers as much as he knew, at first doing his best to protect Brenda. But finally, through his pain and the view of his right hand on his garage floor, he gave Brenda's address and house key and the key to Lewis' private safe and the name of who he believed her best friend was, in hopes of keeping his other hand.

He also gave them the copy of the stolen file he had made before giving the original back to Brenda to return to Mr. Lewis' locked safe on Monday. Sam Benito, when he got word of the file and what it contained, was extremely interested in all of it...but especially the Cuban connection.

CHAPTER 19

Frank Meets Lewis

His secretary informed Mr. Lewis that there was a call for him from someone named Frank O'Hara. She told him that Mr. O'Hara said it was important and personal concerning some legal papers he had found.

Sid Lewis closed his office door and picked up his phone, "Sid Lewis."

"Mr. Lewis, I need this call to remain very confidential and I am sure after you understand its importance you will agree."

"Okay, let me hear it."

"Well to cut to the chase, I have some original papers and letters, memos regarding your law firm and its representation as stated in these confidential memos concerning the operation and evidently...for lack of a better word...partnership in gambling casinos. It seems a strong possibility to me that the other two individuals who had some type of interest in these legal papers have left earth, and they didn't take these files with them. I am not sure if they were worth dying for, but it seems someone thought they were.

"Your employee and her lover, or at least good friend, had them in their possession. Frankly, he was a small time local bad boy. I don't why they had them or what they wanted them for and thought you might give me some idea to the answer of that question. My experience tells me these files are more than 'hot' and I would bet my BMW they've already been copied and are in someone someone's briefcase."

Lewis stopped listening, then started yelling into the phone. "Who the hell are you?"

Frank continued. "I don't have a particular interest in these, but I have a client that is extremely worried for her safety, so before I make my next call I thought I would contact you first to see if you had a good suggestion of what I should do with them. Other than meeting you in a dark alley to give them back to you, which I don't think would be a good idea for me. To be honest, my next stop is the police and a friend of mine in homicide."

"Who the hell are you?"

"Frank O'Hara, and trust me when I tell you that how or why I have them, is not important. This is not blackmail and before I go to the police to turn them in I thought I would make the unlikely assumption that there is a simple explanation. I can tell my client, who, by the way, did not want them in the first place. Now, should we continue or just end the conversation now? I'm not in the mood to continue if you keep your hard-ass lawyer act up. I have an appointment with a homicide cop in an hour."

Mr. Lewis, stunned, surprised and frightened, but not showing it, said, "Do you mind telling me how you got those papers?" His voice was low, but angry.

"Not yet, I think you need to give me some information first. Remember, I'm calling you." Frank knew he had the upper hand.

Lewis nervously put a cigarette in his mouth and struck a match. He inhaled deeply, coughed, and then said in his unmistakably lawyer voice, "You understand I have clients and I am not permitted to disclose such privileged information. But I am willing to give you a reward...cash... for the quick return, no questions asked." He was hoping for a quick solution. "You're the one the police would be interested in. Say, five thousand if you can drop them off at the reception desk by three. I will leave cash for you with instructions to hand it over when we get the documents. Of course, you will not make copies, I trust you're a reasonable man and must have integrity to have made this call. I hope I'm correct in that assumption."

Frank replied quickly, "Not a bad start. But sorry, I'm not interested in the money at this point. I first want to know why someone thought two people should die for these. After all, one of them was your employee. The police tell me she didn't finish a book she was reading, because someone put a hammer or a golf club in the back of her head. That's the first question on the table."

Mr. Lewis' response was again loud and angry. "You don't get to question me about this. I know nothing of that, and am certainly not involved in anyone's death. Those papers were confidential, and now I know they were stolen from my office. If it wasn't for my concern about protecting the interest of the investors and the confidential nature of these negotiations...which are entirely legal...I wouldn't give a damn about them or you. I should be the one to call the police and inform them, since you have, by this call, confirmed that you are in possession of stolen documents. I am not going to be threatened by any assertion or association of any kind to murder. You understand that, whoever the hell you are?"

"I'll give you the number of an honest cop," Frank said." And you let him know I have them and I will be happy to turn the papers over to him. And by the way, you aren't going to buy me for a lousy five grand. I just wanted some simple explanation. So if this way you want to go, get a pad and take this number. His name is Detective Fordham. I'll let him know you'll be calling. Oh, and don't forget to mention you're a friend of Fidel's brother...it might help keep your bond down."

Lewis interrupted, sensing he was losing control just like a witness on the stand. He needed to regroup. He changed his tone.

"Hold on, hold on. This is a delicate matter, and I don't want to see it in the press. If it is connected to a murder, which I don't believe, then of course I will cooperate with the police. But I find it dubious that a hotel with a golf course has any connection to the murder of my employee."

"And a casino in Cuba," Frank interjected. "And at least one on tribal land, with big tax-free payouts going to you and some nefarious group you represent."

Mike Ferdinand had briefed him well before the call.

Lewis quickly replied, "Can you meet me in person before we go any farther with this? I think we could talk and decide what to do; a solution that would work for both your client and my clients. Hasty decisions are usually bad decisions. I am still interested in how they got into your possession, but let's talk about that later. First can we meet soon, just you and me?"

Frank replied. "There's a Starbucks down the street from your office, be there in fifteen minutes. Just you. I will find you. Order me a tall latte and a cheese Danish." Frank hung up.

CHAPTER 20

The Meeting

By Water walked into Duncan's office by the state capitol building. He had an unhappy face, "You know what the hell is going on?"

Duncan was surprised. "What are you talking about?"

"Some nice young man," he said sarcastically, "came to see me this morning, just walked right into my office. He started off with a story about putting dynamite up some wife's ass and blowing her the hell up. It went downhill from there.

"They knew a lot about the deal with the Lewis group, said it was not a nice way to treat a partner. Hell, they are not our partners unless you were dealing behind my back. One of the sons-a-bitches put his cigarette out on my desk top...they told me they weren't going to keep us, yeah us, as partners anymore. Told me I had 24 hours to get out. The exact words were, 'pack my teepee and be gone by five.' Said he was looking to see if we had any papers with the other partners, because they needed to ask them to leave too.

"I tried to talk, but he pushed me back into my chair and told me, just listen. He told me I could keep the money in my pocket but the days of pulling chips was over. He said not to worry, as they weren't going to tell the council about how I've been cheating them. Said I could keep the money in my pocket but I was resigning my participation in the casino effective immediately. Laid these resignation papers on my desk," showing them to Duncan, "and said they would be back in the morning when I was cleaning out my office to pick them up. This is serious...he was threatening. I tried to call security after he left and the dumb shits said they didn't see anyone. We need to call Lewis."

Duncan for the first time in a long time was speechless; it took seconds for him to talk. "I have no idea what you're talking about. Is this a joke?"

"Joke, my ass, we got a big problem. They know about you and me and Lewis and the new casino...and God knows what else. They had inside information."

Duncan stood up." You know I keep nothing from you. What did they say about the casino? How the hell could they toss you out? They have no interest. Damn Lewis and his group double-crossing us or something. No one knew about this deal, no one." He picked up the intercom, and his assistant answered. "Get Sid Lewis on the line now. I don't care if he's in the toilet...tell him to call me now."

The chief, feeling like Duncan was onto the problem, finally sat down.

"Sounds like these are some rough dudes, I don't know, maybe they got us confused with someone else. What am I supposed to do? I thought about calling the police, but if they know we been taking money, that could come out and that's all I need."

Duncan picked up the phone and called a friend of his at the Corporation Commission. "Hey, you know the tribe has that consulting company called Always American Indian Financial, or is it Kachina, something like that, they run the Casino? Can you get me everything you got filed on them and anything else you can find out? We're going to fire their ass but I want to know who the hell to talk to. Yeah, the chief is going to fire them. We'll be filing a change today...keep that to yourself." He hung up, smugly satisfied that he was taking care of things.

The chief walked up to where he was inches from Duncan's face. "No my friend, your ass is with me on this. You're going to be with me when we fire them. I've already met them and I am not looking forward to meeting them again, to tell them they are fired. In fact, we're doing it by phone or Western Union...and before we make that call, we get our wives out of town."

Duncan said, "OK, but let's call in extra security and we will be ready for those jerks whoever they are. Keep quiet about this, we don't need this kind of information out in the news, understand? I'm calling Lewis right now."

The chief stood up, "Yeah, I'm going to stop by my house and get a gun. You be at my house by four, and write down what you're going to say. I'm going to bet there is someone from Kachina American Financial, or whatever the hell it is called, in my office. Just tell whoever answers to get their ass out; we're still running our own operation."

CHAPTER 21

Starbucks

Frank was standing across the street from Starbucks to make sure Lewis came alone. He thought of Kim; he had been thinking of her a lot lately with her long black hair, soft blue eyes and great mind. A perfect combination, as if God had a hand in putting her together himself. And the physical attributes were just the start; from the short time he had sat across from her he knew she would be easy to spend time with. Frank had learned in his business to make quick judgments and he was usually right on. For a client she was nice indeed...he just wished it hadn't grown into the hell of a mess that he was afraid he now was now a big part of.

He knew that he would enjoy spending time with her—if she even had the slightest interest—but for now she was a client, and that's how it had to be. He also reminded himself that her best friend had a hammer or other object put through her skull and had definitely made the wrong choice for a boyfriend. The PI part of him made a mental note to move a little slow with this case and when it was over, with Kim...if he could move in that direction at all. Romance would have to wait but it was a nice thought. He missed the buying of flowers and the small-talk phone calls that go with new love and romance.

He recognized Lewis from a photo in the Arizona bar book. After watching him enter the coffee shop, Frank crossed the street to do the same thing. He went inside and walked up to the table.

CHAPTER 22

Back to Dominic

Dominic had ordered wine for both of them and as the waiter left he reached over and took Brenda's hand. "You look lovely tonight," he said.

"Thank you...you are very kind. I never thought we ever would be having so much fun. I did not think I would find anything like this so soon, you've been very healing. I do enjoy your company and I appreciate you being patient with me. I'm still too old-fashioned by today's standards."

Dominic kissed her hand saying, "You also have been very healing in my life, and there is much I want to tell you. Being patient is easy with you. My Italian heritage is proud of me and all the saints are applauding in heaven. They are singing "How chaste he is."

She laughed, more of a giggle, "In time," she said, "in time. Anticipation is very much part of the chase, isn't it?"

Dominic was torn. He liked her very much. But he knew he was giving and presenting to her a false person. A person who would potentially walk out without saying good-bye. He was still so much a part of the hustle side of life and living in the fast lane where money came easy and illegally. He had lived all his life that way. He paid no taxes. In fact, he had never filed.

He had a complete set of false identification, including a social security number he used when it became necessary. It belonged to a man who was living in a nursing home. He had used the number for so many years and so many times that when anyone went to check it, all but one of the notations went to Dominic and only one to the real owner—who had no need for credit and legally didn't have to file taxes.

He had spent many nights with too many ladies, mostly strippers, and was well known in all the topless gentlemen clubs for putting the dollar bills under the G-string, with the promise there was lots more after "she got off work." He had no illusion of how he made money, didn't even think of it as a "bad" or "good" thing. His sense of right or wrong had been dulled before he became old enough to vote, which was something else he never did. There were never any thoughts of marriage or children, and if such a thought ever came it was quickly dismissed as remote and unnecessary. Until he met Brenda.

She represented everything he thought he could never have. Respectability in the honest world. Motherhood, spirituality. A future he had never thought about before. He was overwhelmed by her, and his "wise guys" friends and bar acquaintances had noticed the change. He was not seen around town as much, and after he turned down two stolen car transactions, eyebrows were starting to raise. His wise guy friends talked. "What the hell has got into Dominic?"

"That idiot's in love. Who would ever have thought he'd get pussy-whipped?"

Truth was that Dominic had hardly kissed her, let alone made love to her. He was satisfied just kissing her at the door when he took her home. She was desirable, there was no question in Dominic's mind but she also represented the porcelain doll that would shatter if you squeezed too hard or dropped it.

Dominic was, for the first time in his life, totally and completely falling for a woman who had no idea who or what he was. And for the first time in his life he had the smallest of thoughts that he had made a mistake being who he was and what he did, because he knew he would never be able to cross over to her world. And he knew that when she discovered his, their relationship would shatter. He didn't want his world to touch hers. But it was going to be necessary. He was going to ask that porcelain doll to take a step in manure. The urge for fast money was still too strong for an emotion called love. Selfish motive was always going to rule and dominate Dominic.

After Pete "The Nose" approached him, he started formulating a plan that would somehow convince this new love of his life to get the information Pete had requested from her law firm. He had justified it in his mind as being not such a hard thing for her to do. He particularly liked the idea that she should think of her grandfather as putting his life savings into a deal. If he shouldn't, she would want him to know, right?

Still when it came to bring the request to her he found it harder than he realized. Brenda had surrounded him with enough virtue to know that he shouldn't be getting her involved. But when it came to making a decision between the new love of his life or the old love of his life, he regrettably chose the latter. After all, how in the world would he ever forgive himself for blowing a chance to do something for the Godfather of the Philadelphia mob? Those chances didn't come every day to a guy like him. He never got to the next thought in his brain, which by some inkling might have led him to the conclusion that girls like Brenda are a rare item in this harsh world.

Brenda had informed him earlier in the day that it was their anniversary, they had been seeing each other for two months now and talking a least twice, if not more, times via cell phone each day. He thought it might be a good time to he see just how good his chances were, not for sex, but for seeing if he could get Pete's request filled. He picked her up promptly at six and with a small kiss on the cheek handed her bouquet of red roses, saying," I have reservations at a very fancy place for such a special day."

Impressed once again, she smiled and said, "Thank you Dominic, what a nice surprise," followed by a gentle kiss on his cheek.

Tipping the maître d' his usual twenty, they were taken to a secluded table. Dominic ordered the best wine as well as the dinner. After a couple of sips and a toast to their first two months, he reached for her hand across the table. It was now or never, he thought.

"Honey, I need to get some information for an older relative of mine. A family member is thinking about making an investment. You know, to supplement his income. He loves Arizona. He asked me for some advice, and I know you once mentioned to me how you are working on a land deal, I think you said it is with the Indian reservation. Anyway, this family member—oh by the way, he sent his warm regards for you and insisted on giving me some money to take you shopping—uh, anyway he just wants to know what I can tell him about the casino real estate deal your firm is doing. You know, you mentioned to me you were working on it. It's his life savings and anything you can do, well my family would be so appreciative. You know, it's like someone giving you a stock tip, you understand?"

Brenda wasn't sure exactly what he was asking. "What can I do? What is it he wants?"

"Well, he is thinking about investing in the casino deal, as I understand it. I happened to mention that you were doing some work on that yourself, only on the business end, and he was hoping I might get him some information. You know, so he won't worry about it being on the up and up and a good deal, that's all. Just keeping an old man happy."

Brenda set her glass down and replied, "Well I don't know if I could do that. You know, law offices have a rule that you don't talk about clients and what they are doing. Couldn't he just call Mr. Lewis himself and ask? I mean, I think that would be okay."

"No, no," Dominic said, "I didn't know it would be such a hard question for you." He had just unknowingly shown her a glimpse of his other side with his frown. She could tell he didn't like her answer. He also could tell he had startled her.

"You know I don't want you to do something you don't want to do. It's just that I'm with a big family and we all take care of each other, and when one of us has a friend that can help out another friend we go to bat for them, that's all. I just wanted to see if you could get him some reassurance. He's a proud man, he doesn't want to call up just anyone. I'm family and I just mentioned you might know something that I could pass on. It will make me look really bad to my family when I tell them you won't do it. He said to give you this, so take it anyway." Dominic had trained himself long ago that after the first no, you offer the money. "I don't want to hurt him by telling him you wouldn't even take his money. Dominic handed her three one hundred dollar bills. "He said you should go shopping. You're my girl, and that is the way he treats people who are friends of his family. I told him you might be the one. I guess he thought we were pretty close and you wouldn't mind helping out, but it's okay." He turned away. "Keep the money anyway."

There was a long pause as she stared down at the table. She brushed her auburn hair back from her eyes. Any man would have seen the uncomfortable fear in her eyes.

"Dominic you know by now how much I care for you. What information does he want?" She pushed the $300 back to him.

"Well, who is on the other end, for the tribe, what kind of money is involved, I guess in general he just wants to know who the big guns are, excuse me, the main characters in the operation. It would mean a lot to him and to me, and no one will ever know. You could just let me look at the file and I'll get him copies and you can just put the file back, maybe this weekend or surely by Monday. I promise you," he continued, "no one will ever know." He took her hand again. "No other copies will be made, I assure you by my love for you; there will be complete confidentially. You can trust me on this."

"I don't know Dominic, that is asking a lot. I could get fired. Lewis keeps all of those files locked up. He doesn't even know any of us even know what's in them, let alone where he keeps them."

Dominic still holding her hand across the table, looking in her eyes softly replied. "I won't let that happen to you. No one needs to know. I know it's asking a lot, but just get me the file and I will pull what he wants, make copies and you put it right back, end of story. You told me you are in and out of his office all the time, so it would be very natural for you."

She was visibly upset with his request. "I'm really uncomfortable. It seems wrong and I wish you wouldn't have asked me."

Dominic lowering his voice "It doesn't seem like anything more than information that will be in the papers as soon as the other people find out about it. My grandfather just wants some inside information. He doesn't want to lose his life savings...think of it as your grandfather and me having information that could help him. You know I wouldn't think twice about helping you."

The last statement weakened Brenda's resolve.

"Oh Dominic, just the thought frightens me, but I will see, that's all I can say. Please don't ask me anymore about this." For her the anniversary date was now like a balloon losing its air. "You're asking a lot." She didn't look up. "I don't even know where to look."

Dominic smiled. "You really are terrific," he said. "My family will be in debt to you. Dinner again tomorrow, at the finest Italian restaurant in town. Here take this money. I have faith in you, you will find it. I'll look it over, you put it right back, bada bing, that's it. Come on, a toast to my girl."

He raised the champagne glass. Brenda didn't respond. He pushed the three one hundred bills to her again, as if he was closing a stolen car stereo deal.

"No, I will not take money...it's demeaning to me," pushing the money again back to Dominic. "If it's a favor for your grandfather, then he doesn't have to pay me. You should know I'm not like that."

Brenda went in to work early the following morning. It was Saturday and she knew she would be alone. She had keys to enter the law office. Still, she was nervous and felt like she was committing some type of mortal sin. She took the first key and opened Lewis' desk. She searched for the key to the locked safe against the wall, opened the locked safe, and pulled out the file containing the partnership agreements and other documents, including the disk in a double-sealed envelope. She had no idea that this file was prepared by Lewis himself and totally secret. Its contents were known only by Lewis.

Brenda had typed most of the agreements and prepared the documents for mailing under Mr. Lewis' direction, but she didn't recognize these particular documents. She knew that most of the information Dominic requested would be in the sealed documents. It was several pages, too much for her to remember or write down, so she hurriedly went to the copy room, removed the stables and was just starting to run them through the copier, when she was startled to hear her name.

"Brenda, what are you doing here, you know we don't get overtime." It was Pamela Tanaka who worked down the hall from Brenda. She was standing outside the copy room door and was smiling. Brenda was startled when she turned and saw her.

"Oh, I am just finishing up something I should have completed yesterday, but I'm done and heading home right now. As she talked she turned her back to Pamela and placed the file and disk in her large purse and zipped it shut. She was sure Pamela had not seen her do it. "Well, I'm out of here, hope you don't have to stay too long."

"No, not me, I have a luncheon date," Pamela said. "I'm right behind you." Brenda rushed back and closed the safe, taking the keys with her so she could open it when she put the file back Monday morning, and headed for the elevator.

She took the elevator to the bottom floor and exited the building. She couldn't believe what she had done. But the weight in her purse let her know the truth. She had the file. She wished she didn't. She thought, Dominic is going to have to make the copies after all; She was uncomfortable with that thought. As she walked there was an inner voice telling her to turn around and take it back. She ignored the warning, like most sinners do and kept on walking. "I'll just go in very early Monday and put them back."

Her Catholic upbringing, taught to her by both her parents and schooling, had implanted the commandments in her mind, and she spent the rest of the morning hours with the words "thou shalt not steal" playing over and over in her head.

Her only justification, she kept telling herself, was that she was doing it for an old man she didn't know, and protecting him. He was Dominic's family, his godfather he had said. Surely God would not be as angry as she was only trying to help Dominic. That and Dominic's words that he would get it right back to her so she could replace it immediately Monday gave her the only moments of peace.

That evening when Dominic came to pick her up she answered the door with the file in her hand. "Here," she said, giving it to him. "I feel like a thief, I have never done anything like this before, ever. If you didn't mean so much to me..." her voice trailed off. "Make your copies and bring it right back. I need to get it back where it belongs early Monday morning. That's a must. Please do what you promised."

He grabbed her and pulled her close. "No, no," he said, "you are just giving a little boost to my godfather. This is nothing that bad, no big deal, believe me. Well it is a big deal, but let me look at this and copy what I need, and you can get it right back. No one is the wiser. Trust me, it's okay, now come on let's get some good pasta and I have a little more shopping money for you."

"No," she said. "Take it, copy what you need and get it right back to me. Remember, it's got to be back by Monday morning. I don't feel like going out. I just want to stay home."

"Brenda, you can trust me." He took the file from her hand. "Now let's go to dinner and have some wine. I'll have this back to you tomorrow." He took her hand and led her to his car. "I'll not be happy unless you come." She wasn't smiling, but she got into the car and then abruptly said no and exited the vehicle. "I'm not much in the mood for this. Bring it back soon; it will put me in a much better frame of mind."

CHAPTER 23

Frank Meets Lewis

Frank pulled out a chair and sat down. He looked Sid Lewis right in the eyes. "First of all," he said, "I have no doubt that two people so far have lost their lives because of these papers. One was a former employee of your prestigious law firm and the other was her boyfriend. One is in the ground at this point and the other waits at the morgue for someone to get him...which seems each day to become a little more remote.

"Make no mistake, I made a copy of the contents of that file and if anything should happen to me, a memo concerning their death, along with the copy, is in an envelope waiting to be mailed to the newspaper, who I think will be pleased with such a hot story. Casino gambling, big law firm, stolen legal papers, two deaths, three if I happen to join them. Oh, let's not forget meeting Fidel's brother. So I'm not going to beat around the bush. What the hell is going on? You can count me as a client, so we both will keep it confidential. But I'm damn sure another copy besides mine is in someone's hands...bet on it."

Lewis was taken back at Frank s harsh approach, and caught completely off guard by this development. He was unsure how to respond. Years of legal maneuvering had taught him to choose his words carefully and not to give too much information, but of course sound as if you were. He coughed to buy time, then looked back at Frank and said, "I feel like I am being blackmailed. Those documents were confidential, and again I tell you there was nothing illegal about them. Sensitive yes, but I have no idea who or what had enough interest in them to steal them from my office.

"They are also sensitive to the people involved. People who, for various reasons, wanted to hide assets from whoever, family and wives, to shield legal income from taxes. They chose to remain unknown. That is the sole reason that it could be construed as being on the shady side, if there is a shady side, of this deal, but shady isn't illegal. And there is nothing in this deal worth dying for. And with that in mind, how do you surmise Brenda's death was connected to this?"

Frank answered, still looking Lewis right in the eyes, "In a nutshell, she gave the papers to my client. I am not saying she took them. She was killed before she could return to pick them up and I'd like to hope planning to put them back where she got them. Whoever killed her wrongfully believed she was part of the larger picture, which I don't believe she was. Why? I don't know. And I have no idea how much of your story is true. You haven't told me much I wouldn't have figured out on my own."

Lewis instantly responded before Frank finished speaking. "I am not going into more right now, but you hopefully can appreciate the situation and I can get your help getting them back, before bringing more trouble to both of us."

Frank now cut him off. "Of some interest to you is that Brenda's boyfriend, or at least he was some close connection, took a swim in the canal with a bullet in his head and some chains wrapped around him. Not a safe way to jump into the water. He had some help. No one kills like that unless they are leaving a message for someone. The only people I know who leave messages like that consider such an act as part of their business. Not a good sign, I think, for you or me."

The old attorney was starting to show some signs of agitation, his voice grew louder. "I never met her boyfriend. I sure as hell wouldn't have been involved in anything that would have killed one of our firm's paralegals. Or anyone else, for that matter. This was a business deal. Granted, I was somewhat growing dismayed with some of the characters involved and—I shouldn't be talking to you about these things—but suffice it to say that things began to happen in this deal that were either ironic coincidences or had a force behind them I didn't understand. I'm telling you this because you seem to be holding the better hand at the time but I trust you will indeed keep this confidential for the time being." Lewis was taking a gamble by talking to Frank, but at the moment he saw no other option.

"It all started out as just a simple land contract with all the usual clauses and sub-clauses and first part of the second part." He was purposely leaving out the skimming of gambling funds and the non-reporting of such income to the IRS.

"But by the time it was over, it had grown from two local residents of Maricopa County Board of Supervisors and members of the tribal council to a rather substantial group of, let's say, some of my wealthier friends and clients. Then about two weeks ago," he paused, "funny but now when I think back it was right after Brenda's murder, I get a call from Duncan, the lobbyist for the tribe and the chief. By Water is his name. I couldn't find the file by then.

"He was telling me that they were being told by someone who came to By Water's office to get out of the deal and sign all their interest over. They thought I was behind it. I convinced them I knew nothing of it, but what this operating company wanted was for us...me along with the current partners...to cut our interest and basically give it to them. I was stunned. It was simply them telling us what they wanted. They seemed to have everyone's name, the percentages, everything. Nothing in writing, and they told the chief and Duncan they were out. I mean it was bullshit. No one had contacted me.

"For that to happen, all the others would have to agree and get their money back. We are talking about a substantial investment. They said all majority interest was going to, I think, Kachina America Financial Corporation... something like that. They had connections with some of the other Indian casinos around the country. Their people basically set up the procedures and managed the operation for the tribes; you know, they hired some of the tribe members to work in the cages. Sell drinks, wait on tables, Overall they were the operation behind it, but usually they kept their own money out, worked on a contract, year to year I think, but no complaints that we could tell. My office did some checking after that phone call and everything was sketchy at best, but nothing jumped out to say they weren't legit.

"In this case I was told by Duncan and By Water that Kachina American Financial, or whatever the hell they called themselves, were going to be operator owners, with 75 percent of the deal and profits. That's where the other members had to cut our interest, so that they could get the 75 percent. The other 25 percent was to go to the tribe, which they said was a better deal than they were now getting. They had all the agreements changed, down to each detail as though it was that way from the start.

"A couple of the senior members balked but within a day had changed their minds and said it was okay with them. Never gave a reason for the fast change of heart; just walked away from their investment. But they hung up fast, and hand delivered by messenger their resignation. Wouldn't take my return calls. I mean, you're talking about wealthy people who for no known or stated reason were turning down a substantial profitable business deal with a phone call and letter to me."

Frank sipped his coffee. "Well that answers who else has a copy doesn't it? How many investors? There was plenty of collateral and plenty of credit floating around for some banking money. Hell, anyone would have wanted in. All you had to get was the state and government approval, who I doubt would have smiled after they saw how it was set up. Frankly speaking...and I don't like using my name this way...you and your friends sound like some high class crooks. Again how many, and how much...and what did the tribe get?"

Lewis felt he had nothing more to lose at this point and he hoped the knowledge he was sharing would help him. "There were 25 of us at 100 grand each to start in the original casino deal. Then a year later and another 100 grand each, the tribe was putting in the rest to build a resort. It was a big development, with a golf course and hotel. The casino was going to be big with Vegas type acts. We were planning on being open in two years.

"It's beyond anything that has ever been around here. The investors had no ownership but it was a loan deal, strictly to the tribe, at 15 percent interest for the first five payments, to be made in the first three years. Then there were an additional twenty payments over the next two years at 25 percent each." Lewis had neatly skirted the skimming and the monthly unrecorded payments, as well as the money put into the hands of the state water people and the county officials who were looking the other way on some of the building and liquor permits, which most tribes couldn't get, and the huge diversion of Colorado river water to keep that grass green in the middle of the desert and that lake full.

"Tell me Mr. Lewis, after that loan was paid, did you continue to share in the profits?"

Lewis nodded, "Yes to some extent. Why is this important? Who the hell are you to be asking these questions?"

"I guess I'm someone who has a hell of a lot of bad information on you, and is also trying to help out a girl who knows nothing about this and is wondering what my next step to help her will be. You answered enough. We haven't even touched on the Cuba deal." Frank shook his head "I'd get a good attorney...surely you know one." Frank started to stand up.

"Wait a minute." Lewis said, "this all started after that file was stolen. I looked days for it...tore my office apart...I will be losing control of this deal just like the tribe. Hear me out.

"As soon as these new partners came in, Kachina American Financial or whatever the hell they called themselves, our firm's involvement came to a halt. I was looking for the file for the purpose of seeing what we could do legally about getting our money back, with some interest. I mean, I'm sure you understand, there were parts of this thing we couldn't even bring up. I mean, you can't call a car in as stolen when you stole it yourself earlier. You understand, Mr. O'Hara, parts of it were technically like that.

"It just stopped abruptly, I tried calling By Water, the head of the council, back and he wouldn't return my calls. Then I checked with the one of the investors who changed his mind rather abruptly and he said he couldn't talk to me. Hung up after saying he gave up his interest, 100 grand just like that. I tried to find out where the money went. It was like it never existed, gone. When I finally asked my office for the file that was always locked up, I was told it was missing.

"I initially thought it was just misfiled. All that was left was a bunch of useless paperwork, initial proposals, interoffice memos. The heart of it was gone, one file among all the rest. I was making calls to the investors, but nothing, no one returned my call. That file you have is a time bomb that will blow up a lot of nice Phoenix people...and put others in jail."

Frank was not moved. "Should have done something about that two weeks ago, and a nice girl would still be alive and working for you." He walked out of Starbucks. Lewis caught him by the arm on the sidewalk.

"I have told you everything I know; more than I should have, so can you get me that file back? You look like a good man, Mr. O'Hara. Consider it for humanitarian reasons... we all have families, and we had nothing to do with that girl's death."

Frank pushed Lewis arm off his. "Yes you did, you prick. Not directly, but she's gone from this world because of your shit dealings...and I'm guessing you've got bigger boys than the police coming after you."

It was then that a junior member of the firm came up and interrupted.

"Mr. Lewis, we have been trying to reach you. Something has happened, can you get back up to the office immediately?"

Lewis walked over to the side with the young associate, where they talked in low, urgent voices. Lewis seemed obviously distraught. He turned quickly and walked back to Frank. "A new bad development, I am afraid, Scott Jennings, that investor I told you about, the one who wouldn't talk to me...he was found dead in the front seat of his car. I have to leave but I will call you, give me a number where I can reach you. We'll talk more about getting you to give those documents back. I now need your help Mr. O'Hara, just like your client who sent you to me...and I will pay."

Frank gave Lewis his card with his private number and said, "I'm not sure I want to keep them and I sure as hell will not work for you. If I were you, go get right with the police and other agencies real quick. The police will have the file by the end of the day." Frank walked away with Lewis still trying to stop him.

An hour earlier Scott Jenkins was angry. He had just finished playing golf, rather poorly and was not in the best of moods. He was putting his clubs in the trunk of his car when the tall gentleman walked up and gave him a message he did not like. He had already kicked them out of his office and hung up the phone in their last attempt to speak to him.

His response was immediate. What right did someone have to tell him where to put his money? He had worked hard all of his life, and the casino deal was too good to pass up. He looked right into the eyes of the man standing in front of him and said. "You can tell whoever sent you to go to hell. I have been pressured by the best of them and I am not giving up one iota of my percentage on the return. You're telling me I have no interest at all; that is bullshit. I'll talk to Lewis about this. Hell, I'll go to the police, or the governor, who is a friend of mine. I'll go to whoever the hell else I have to, and I will find out who you people are and what you're up to." He turned and got into his car and started to turn the ignition.

Sal Fortunato shook his head and said, "My friend, that was a wrong answer." He looked around the deserted parking lot, walked closer to Mr. Jenkins, and pulled the 22-caliber pistol from his coat pocket, which had a silencer at the end of the barrel. He pointed the gun at the back of Jennings head and pulled the trigger. The bullet entered the back of the head and went out through the left eye socket.

Jennings' head fell briefly onto the steering wheel and then slid off to the side and came to rest with his head on the passenger seat side of the Mercedes.

Blood was gushing from the hole in his head. Fortunato walked around to the other side of the car and reached his arm through the window. He put the barrel directly next to the ear that was facing up and pulled the trigger again. There would be no doubt that Jennings had said his last words on earth. He and his wife would not use the tickets to the Phoenix symphony that were in his pocket for the performance that night.

A young girl, walking with earphones blaring music from her iPod, saw the tall man walk briskly away from the car. By the time she got to where he had been standing, he was long out of sight. She looked into the car as she passed by and saw the body and the blood, then screamed. Others came to her aid, saw what she saw, and called the police.

Detective Fordham's cell phone rang right during his first bite of an early dinner date with the call about a body in a car. Saying, "I'm on my way," he kissed his date on the forehead and said, "Gotta go." It didn't bother him that he was leaving his date and his steak dinner to go see a body bleed out in the front seat of a car. It was his job, and he loved it.

She was upset, as always. They'd had a lot of dates ruined in the past year of their relationship. "Can't you give it to someone else?"

"I wish I could," he said not really meaning it. "I'll call you at home." He threw a fifty dollar bill on the table. "This should cover it. If not I'll make it up with some loving when I get home, keep the bed warm." He turned and headed for his unmarked car in the parking lot. Before he started his car he figured mentally it would take him 16 minutes to get to the scene.

He knew good cops were like that; they had computers in their heads for details no one else gave much thought too. He still looked at license plates when he pulled up behind another car at a stoplight, even when he wasn't on duty. Mothers and policemen were always on duty. He also noted two missed calls from Frank, and made a mental note to let Frank know he was out of time. That thought pissed him off.

CHAPTER 24
Good-bye John

Detective John Fordham ran his life like a Swiss clock. He was out of his garage every morning at 6:15. His briefcase was always next to him on the front seat of his police vehicle, which was washed almost daily on his way home from work. He was always one hour early to his office. This was the day after Scott Jennings' murder, and he was hoping for a meeting with Frank and his client the next day. Maybe he could at least close those murder cases. Not a practical thought, he reasoned, but a hopeful one. Frank had never been anything but up front with him and he expected no less this morning. This particular day was starting much the same. The garage door opened and John drove slowly out. It was not completely light outside and Frank was somewhat startled to see a party who appeared dressed in a rain outfit walking towards his car. It was even more unusual because it wasn't raining. The party even had plastic covers on his feet and a plastic cover over his head. The party called out, "Hey John, it's me, Lieutenant Barnes."

John recognized Barnes even with the strange outfit on. "Man, what the hell are you doing?" John asked.

"I'm going on a stake-out that I need to talk to you about, and I need to borrow your gun. It's a long story, but I changed cars and in putting this stupid outfit on I forgot mine, and I knew I could catch you before you left. I know, it's against regulations, I'll sign for it and take the heat if anything comes down. You can consider it an order. I'm assigned to the Feds on nabbing this bank robber, they called me for backup last night."

John was extremely hesitant, and the part about it being an order by his lieutenant placed him in a position he didn't like or understand, but he reluctantly agreed. He reached in his briefcase, took out his loaded Glock, and handed it to Barnes. Barnes took the pistol from John and said, "I'll write this up this morning as soon as I get back to the office. You meeting that PI friend tomorrow morning? I'd like to be in on that." John was not sure how Barnes knew about the meeting, but replied, "Hopefully, and he's bringing in some documents on those murders, plus some client of his who was a friend of one of the victims and has some info."

Lt. Barnes said, "I'll be there, got to go now." He then, in one quick motion, took the safety off the Glock and placed it next to John's head. Before John even realized what was happening, the gun went off. Barnes hurriedly placed the gun in John's hand, making sure John's prints were on it and placing his index finger on the trigger, and then let the gun fall to the floor. The sound of the shot had awakened other neighbors and lights were going on as Barnes pulled away in his dark vehicle parked across the street. He was sure no one had seen him. He stopped in an alley a mile away and with a shovel buried his rain gear outfit, along with his shoes and head covering, four feet deep to the side of the alley. He poured bleach over all of them before covering them back up, and placed a large rock over the small hole. They wouldn't be found. He then drove to the police office, smiling and saying to everyone as he walked in, "Good morning, let me know when John gets in. Tell him I need to see him right away."

Frank wasn't sure what his next move should be. He drove back to his office and decided he should at least bring his client up to date. He also needed to call Fordham and give him what he had learned from Lewis and the file. He was surprised Fordham wasn't on his ass by now, as it was well past the window of time Fordham had given him. He used his cell phone and dialed up Fordham, but got his voice message again so he called the station and was informed that Fordham wasn't in yet. Frank left his number. He wished he had made Kim call Fordham directly earlier but damn it, he didn't. "Why haven't you called me?" he yelled out loud as if Fordham could hear him, and again thinking of Kim, "and damn it you too, my client, wherever the hell you are."

He found himself thinking more and more of her. His heart hadn't healed completely from the last woman he loved but maybe a new voice and some pretty eyes would be like soothing Aloe Vera for the heart.

A though in answer to his thoughts, his phone rang. Caller ID showed it was from out of state. It was Kim. "I've been praying you would answer. I was worried about you," she said.

He liked that thought. "Thanks for the worry but I'm okay. I met with Lewis, and he claims no knowledge of

Brenda's murder or her taking the file, and even gives a story that he has been forced out in this deal. It seems he got word that another one of the investors has joined Brenda and Dominic, and not by choice. That file has been read by a few people at this point... but who? Now that's the big question. Trust me, no one in on this wants it out. And apparently there's been another murder."

She gasped, "No...oh no," and then let out a soft sigh.

"Don't get upset. I know that's hard information to hear. Listen closely: there is a big price and big players somewhere with this whole operation. I am going to meet with my cop friend and give him as much as I can on this, with or without you, but it would be much better if you were with me. I'm picking up a copy that a friend of mine has gone through and made it a lot easier to follow, I hope. We're going to pick it up at my office and take it in with us. This is getting way over our heads, with the third murder that I think is directly connected to this story. You need to get back here and come see my police friend with me. I have to come fully clean with him, NOW. You can trust him and he'll get you protected. I promise you on that. You with me?"

"Yes, yes, but I'm scared."

Frank responded immediately. "I'm now in it, you are in it. We don't have the slightest idea who else is in it with us. It seems that your dead friend Brenda had no idea how much of a price she was going to pay when she took that file, and I am at this point pretty sure it was her."

"But why?" Kim asked, "Brenda was a responsible, no-nonsense girl; she had to have a very good reason to do something like that."

Frank answered, "Or a very stupid one. I'm going to try and figure out what that reason was. In the meantime, don't answer any knocks on your door, don't phone anyone, answer only if you identify my cell number. Don't get lost without letting me know. And did you make a plane reservation?"

"Yes, but the soonest I can get to Phoenix is seven tonight. All the flights were booked."

"Then I guess that's all we can do. I'll pick you up at the airport. Let's hope the police aren't waiting with me. Let me know when you arrive...and by the way, I worry about you too."

"Thank you," she said, "I'll see you at the airport."

Frank called Detective Fordham and left another message asking to talk to him soon, and saying he had something that might help in the murder investigation. He needed to see him personally and didn't want to discuss it by phone. It was unusual for him to have such a hard time getting in touch with Fordham. He knew he was late in bringing his client and her file in to John, but she was flying in tonight and he would have her and the file at his office early tomorrow morning. He added to the message that he was very sorry for the delay, but would be there in the morning. He also mentioned that he was going to take a drive to the reservation casino and maybe flush some rats out of the sewer. He wanted Fordham to have that information, for reasons other than being polite...like in case he went missing.

Frank put the top down and made the twenty mile drive to the Indian casino. He didn't believe in valet—at least these broke days—so he self-parked and made the block walk up to the entrance.

He wasn't sure if they had metal detectors. It had been a long time since he was in a casino, or even carried a gun for that matter. He felt that if you could live long enough, bad habits like gambling, drinking and chasing women— well maybe not so much the last one—went away and you found little interest in losing money or getting drunk. It was with age that one discovered the price that was paid for such living. He thought there were very lonely people sitting on bar stools, when they could be home watching the weather channel.

Frank knew he had crossed some invisible line in life when he admitted to himself that Storm Stories was his favorite TV show. It was the same as leaving toy land. Once you found yourself there you knew you couldn't go back to your youth again. Storm Stories was a real mark in your life. Another one was finding out there wasn't a Santa, but that was much earlier. He had learned at his late age that you had to make the most of the hand you were playing. Some days you bluffed and some days you just closed your eyes and hoped God dealt you a good hand. He entered the casino with its continual sound of ding ding ding.

The rancid smell of smoke filled his nose and the slot machine noise filled his ears, all part of the never-ending, unforgettable sound of a casino. They all spoke the same language. He asked the first security guard he came to if he could be directed to the office or to a manager, whoever was in charge. The guard, through tight lips, asked why.

Frank said it was personal business and the security card said, "Who are you?"

"Frank O'Hara. I'm a PI and just wanted to give your office some information. I only need a minute or two." The guard was rather a large size member of the tribe. Size made him look formidable but Frank knew in reality he was too heavy to catch anyone on the run and certainly had not been to the pistol range with the large weapon strapped so high on his vest. Under trained and over-nourished was Frank's opinion.

The guard, after some back and forth communication on his radio, replied that no one was interested in talking to him. He was welcome to play the tables or slots and have a drink, but other than that he had no business there. Frank didn't know that a security camera during the entire transaction was watching him. Inside the main office, the on-site new manager of Kachina American Financial had been watching Frank on the security monitor. He didn't know then who Frank was or what he wanted but he did know his orders were specific: he didn't talk to anyone without Philadelphia approval.

Brad Pasqualuchi had been working with Kachina American Financial since graduating from Princeton Business School. He was told as a youngster that he was a distant relative off the famous mobster Lucky Luciano. At that time it did not mean much to him. But now, he liked that association. His grandfather and father had both been raised on the edges of organized crime though, never achieving a "made" status. As far as Brad knew, there were no murderers in his immediate family.

He was well aware that the company who hired him on his college graduation day was in the gaming business. He was also sure that the money behind Kachina American

Financial came from illegal operations when the mob was banking cash from gambling, prostitution and lastly narcotics. But he was told that the men behind it had gone legitimate. Their sons and daughters were in respectable jobs and the old days were gone. The mob as it was known had cleaned up and was actually donating money to charity.

From the Vegas days it was only a natural progression, he thought, for men with that much knowledge to get into legitimate gambling enterprises. He often told his wife that the Indians actually needed his company's help and was always taking her to a dedication ceremony when the tribe opened a new day care center or got a new fire truck. "Our contribution," he would whisper in her ear. He was far removed from Pete "The Nose" and the shadow men like Fortunato. They were four or five levels above him, or below him depending on how one looked at it.

Brad Pasqualuchi had no illusions that the organization in Philly, as he called them, could be somewhat harsh in business arrangements that didn't work out the way they wanted. Yelling often, yes, but cutting hands off, putting a hammer through a girl's head, forcing investors out, and putting a bullet in one of their brains...no that didn't happen anymore. Or so he wanted to believe. His job was to keep the gambling machines turning, the customers coming in, and make sure no one was taking what was not theirs. His title was "Advisor" to the tribal gambling operation. And although he never stepped on anyone's feet, he in reality held the control, even if the tribe didn't know it.

His call to go to Phoenix immediately, one week ago, got to him before he tucked his new child into bed. He was successfully running an Indian Casino in Colorado.

He was told to be there the week that Kachina American Financial was buying out a new casino, and that there were plans to build a new one with hotel and golf course under construction. He was to take charge of operations immediately. He set the phone down and said to Linda, his wife of four years, "You're going to like Phoenix except in the summer."

He arrived early four days later and rented a car to drive to the casino. He was shown to his office by a party who claimed to be the chief's right hand man, but hadn't seen the chief in five days and couldn't get in touch with Duncan either. Pasqualuchi soon learned they had abruptly retired and he was basically the main man. His office was off site, a block from the casino in a separate building. It was connected to all the security cameras, and had a computer setup that gave him instant reports on the hourly operations of the casinos. He had near-immediate access to payout, money taken in, and who called in sick. His business school, as well as his six years of experience in working with American Financial in the casino world, aided him in spotting an impropriety almost when it was happening. By Water and Duncan would have been gone long ago if he'd been in charge earlier.

For now, the eye in the sky watched Frank look around and walk around, then approach the cashier's cage. "Excuse me," he said, "would you kindly give this to your boss?" He handed her one of his business cards onto which he had written, "I know about the missing file that you boys aren't really allowed to have. Give me a call if you want to add to the police report." He figured this was like putting on antlers in deer season and walking through the woods, but he knew he had to get this thing moving and this note might jump start it like putting a firecracker under a kangaroo's s ass. When Brad Pasqualuchi got the card, he had his assistant call Philly to give the next boss up the information.

Frank walked back to his car. As he drove away he called Fordham again from his cell phone. "Fordham here," he answered.

"At last." Frank replied, "Why the hell haven't you called me back? I'm doing your work and not making near as much as you."

"Frank, you were my next call. I was going to ask where you were so I could send the warrant boys out to haul your ass in. So where are you, and what do you have for me?"

"Well don't be too pissed, oh and I'm just leaving the casino parking lot. But my client has an envelope with some legal papers from her friend Brenda James. I know this is a weak excuse, but she wasn't sure if it was connected to the murders. She is now, thanks to a phone call she got telling her she was going to join Brenda if she said anything about it, but we're bringing them in. And she's going to need some protection."

"Damn it, Frank, how long have you known about this?"

"Since my first meeting with her," he answered. "My excuse is the same as hers. I wasn't sure of a connection and she was frightened. But I'm telling you now, we've got a lot for you...get ready for the grand jury...and you are going to fill your jails with lots of supposedly nice people."

Fordham was obviously still pissed, which Frank understood. He continued, "It's not like I wasn't trying to call you...check your cell phone. I think it is all connected to the Indian gambling casino and I'm going out in left field with this, but I will bet the mob has something to do with it."

Fordham's reply was quick. "Shit Frank, there hasn't been any mob in Arizona unless they came to sun themselves at the Biltmore."

"Well I'm going to give you all of it, can you meet me in the morning? Your office at nine? I just dropped a bomb at the casino, to help you my good friend. If my hunch is right there are going to be some rats coming out of their holes, and you can thank me for flushing the toilet for you. I'll have the girl and envelope at nine AM tomorrow in your office."

Detective John was quick replying. "You and your client give me a statement, and then we'll talk about your toilets. And let's make that eight at my office."

"You're on. I'll be glad to get rid of it, and I told you I would give you all I got. One thing, I want my client protected. I can't give her up until I'm sure she is safe."

"Shit Frank, I can't go that far. She'll be safe, I assure you...but getting an order for police protection will have to wait until I hear what she has to say and what she delivers. She's a material witness to this thing now. My office here at the station eight AM, no exceptions. I have enough to haul both your butts in, so we play by all the rules from here on out. I'm going to have someone from the prosecutor's office in on this."

Frank was angry now. "John you know in all our years I have never screwed with you and I'm not going to now. Trust me on this I'll get her to you. Be a little less of an asshole cop and more understanding on this. She's flying in from out of town for the sole purpose of seeing you. You have my word, and that's always been good. She needs some protection. Oh and this will make you happy...you've got a crooked cop in this."

"Give me his name."

"Tomorrow at eight."

Fordham paused before responding; he had never been called an "asshole cop" by Frank. "If I don't have her in front of me at eight tomorrow morning, I'm hauling you in for some kind of charge. You know they got a smoking ban in jail so you can just look at those Cuban cigars I bring you when I visit, and they don't have Starbucks or Danish in the morning. And I want what you have on any cop that's dirty."

"See you tomorrow, and John, if it's not too much to ask, could you bring me Starbucks and a Danish to the meeting?" Frank couldn't let him get by with that last statement.

"Bullshit, Frank, I'll see your ass then; not a click later." Fordham hung up. He was not happy with Frank.

CHAPTER 25

Dominic's Lie

Brenda waited for Dominic to bring the file back. He assured her when he dropped her off the morning before that he would get everything he needed copied and she could take it back immediately. So far she had not heard a word from him...it was now almost 8 hours.

She was feeling more uncomfortable with what she had done. She also was beginning to feel dirty and used. She wondered what power she had given Dominic to get her to do this. She kept trying to justify it by telling herself that it was just a bunch of legal words anyone could look up. But she knew she had violated a strong legal code. Confidentiality, it went from the attorney all the way down to the doorman.

There was a reason Dominic hadn't shown up at Brenda's home yet. He soon knew the files after just a few minutes of reading were dynamite and worth major blackmail money, let alone what he could ask Pete "The Nose" for. This was big time, worth a hell of a lot more than a "favor" and five hundred bucks.

After looking at the documents, Dominic knew he would eventually need more than one copy. He first made two sets of copies and then would give the originals to Brenda to put back.

He hadn't figured how he was going to handle Brenda. First, he had to make sure she kept her mouth shut. Let the law firm think they were lost, or at the worst taken by someone else. Hoping she wouldn't lose her job was about the best feeling he held for her now. He knew their relationship would end. He had no idea how violently. But this would open doors for him. He knew the documents would be eventually be delivered to Pete, but he also felt he might get a little use out of them before delivery was made.

When he finally showed up at Brenda's apartment five hours later and gave her the originals for her to return Monday morning, he told her he had not been totally honest with her on why he needed the documents and had to copy them. In that time he had developed a con story he hoped Brenda would buy. It seemed that his grandfather was being blackmailed and had his life threatened and the only thing that could save him was for his attorney to see the copies. That was going to take just a bit longer but she had no worry as it would never come out. If by the very remote chance it did, no one would know that she had anything to do with it."

Before Brenda could say anything more than "No... no," Dominic grabbed and pulled her close. She fought to pull away.

"I'll take care of everything and I'm very sorry it turned out this way."

She continued pushing him away. "What have you done to me? Why?"

He kept assuring her not to worry. "It'll be okay." He got back into his vehicle and started backing out. All the time he kept saying, as Brenda stood sobbing, "Trust me on this. It's going to be okay. Besides, no one knows it was you. Come on settle down."

Her voice was loud through her sobs as he was pulling away. "Dominic, you lied to me! You can't do this to me!"

"I've got to go," he yelled back.

Brenda continued to cry as he was leaving. "How could I have been so dumb? What have I done? You used me and I cared so much for you. Please, please give me the copies you made!"

Dominic stopped the car. "I won't let anything happen to you. My grandfather is a powerful man in Philadelphia. He knows important people. Those documents will save his life. He knows the FBI and people in politics. It was a good thing you did and we will both be rewarded. I can't tell you any more, as I don't want your life to be in danger. I am protecting you as well as me but I will explain everything to you when I can, and you will see that you have saved lives. That's all I can say right now. You don't know how grateful my family will be...we are very lucky to have you. "'

"Take the originals and hide them. In fact, give them to a trusted friend. We'll need the originals, but you can put this copy back in Lewis's file as soon as you can; he'll never know the difference. I had a friend make this copy, he's a pro."

"Why do I need to give them to someone else?"

He answered firmly. "Just covering all my bases. Lewis, if he sees what you put back, won't be able to tell the difference. And if he does find them missing for some unforeseeable reason, he may think they were stolen. If the police come with a warrant, you don't want this on you. It's important Brenda. Don't mess with me on this, just do it. Don't hang on to these. There might be some bad people who could get very angry if they find them with you. We will get them back in a day or two. Then, hell, you can switch them again if you want." He had never spoken so harshly to her. It was like he was dealing with one of his lowlife cronies.

Brenda sat down, crying and bewildered and scared. She got up and ran to the street but he was gone. She hoped everything he said was true, but she had been lied to and the trust needed in any relationship was gone. She continued thinking, I don't want him to be in danger. This was so unexpected. I did what he asked because I loved him. That was the first time she had used those words. Please hurry, Dominic, she thought. Hurry!

"What have you done? What have you done to me? Why should I be worried about the police? This is not what you said...you lied to me!"

"Listen Brenda, and don't ask me anymore. My grandfather has some rough people who don't like him, and one of them would not like him to have him seen these, and they know you are with me. Some bad people may come looking for these copies and the originals. Don't ask me now, but someone big knew you worked for Lewis. They are not stupid. Just get these out of your house for a day, and you'll be okay. The last people you want asking you about these is the police. Take them to that friend of yours, but don't...and I repeat, don't...tell her anything but to keep her mouth shut. One of us will get them back. You told me you trusted her." Dominic could not make himself believe that if they ever guessed Brenda had them they would ever hurt her. And she couldn't give them what she didn't have. He thought it pretty remote anyone would come looking. But he knew the organization could be that interested.

She knew from this conversation that she had crossed a line in the relationship. She knew that not wanting to lose Dominic had compromised a value system that had been in place since childhood. For the first time in her life she didn't like who she was. Dominic got in his car when the conversation was over, and drove quickly away. She was glad to have the original, and had no intention of putting the copy back that Dominic had given her. She also knew she no longer wanted Dominic. He left her telling her she could be in danger, which he had put her in. That was not an act of love.

CHAPTER 26

The Margarita Frank

Frank put a yellow sticky note on his dashboard reminding him of the meeting with Fordham at eight tomorrow, as if such a reminder was necessary. He decided to stop by and get a margarita on the way home. Hell, he thought, maybe two or three. He thought about what in the hell tomorrow would bring into his life after he met with Fordham. Nothing good was his mental answer. He ordered his usual from the bartender who knew him by name and said, "Cigar?"

Frank replied, "Yeah, give me one of the cheaper ones."

The margarita arrived with the cigar. Frank was the only one at the bar. Such times gave him moments of refection. The kind of all of us have, such as: Who we are? Where are we going? And who gives a shit?

Lately he had been fighting with his spiritual life. Or maybe it was the spiritual life he didn't have. Frank remembered his school days and reading about St. Augustine and his battles of faith. Frank had no illusions about his road to sainthood. He just wanted someone who really knew, somewhere somehow, to occasionally let him know everything was okay and to keep trying. He tried to find it in church and daily prayer.

Frank had for some time struggled with his chosen faith, but it was all he knew, the one thing he had trouble with was the idea which permeates the Christian religion and that was the constant reminder that God so loved the world, that he gave his only begotten son. Then that gift led to the horrible and miserable crucifixion death given to Jesus Christ, as told by the Gospels. Frank thought that was a bizarre symbol of love from God, who he was taught could do most anything he wanted. Frank would have said to God (if given the opportunity back then), "Hey, how about giving everyone a cold beer and bag of peanuts or give the kids some ponies, or something like that, a big picnic for the world, you don't have to have your son beaten up like that to show you love us, the picnic will do fine." His Irish mother had taught him, when he stubbed his toe or caught his finger in the door, "to offer it up for God." He never questioned why God would like suffering until he got older, when he decided once while sitting on a bar stool that he would much prefer to offer God a cold sip of a well-made margarita or good drag from an expensive cigar, or share the pleasure he got from seeing a great butt on a waitress who walked away from his table, instead of the painful times he hit his finger with a hammer. But now he reluctantly accepted the way he now found it. Hell, he thought, he was too old to change religions and he had read a prayer by an old monk he knew named Thomas Merton, which basically said he wasn't sure if he was pleasing God or not, but that God had to be happy with the simple idea that he was trying to. For now, that seemed good enough for Frank.

Frank was raised a Catholic, as the majority of the American-Irish gene pool was. In his younger years he had always been comfortable with the relationship it gave and he had known no other. It had been a slow spin down in his spiritual life. He had claimed as a child to have had experienced the touch of God in his life. But in his adult life, the only development of a God-like sphere had become negative. His prayers went unanswered and to his thinking that meant that maybe there was no God, or if there was God didn't have much love or time for him. But Frank never gave up. He still prayed, but no longer for his own wants. Now he prayed for others, and mainly his two kids, as he needed not only God's, but also their forgiveness.

He now felt often empty and alone, and at times had a feeling of being lost during his recent life. That was expected, he thought, as he took a sip from the third margarita and the last drag of the cigar. Frank found himself thinking more about his ex-wife and his new client. In fact, he found they both shared many of the same qualities. Both were unselfish, delicate, and very easy to be with. Both seemed willing to put up with his unorthodox ways and coffee spills. Maybe he had expected too much from his marriage; maybe he should have tried harder. Frank felt like he didn't know himself anymore. For him that was the worst of it. He was only good at being a PI and the part of that he was good at was a dying breed and didn't hold much of a future. "Damn it," he washed down his thoughts and then had an idea. "Hell, I can always play the blues in some run down piano bar and end up with a woman who smokes too much. Give me another one buddy."

CHAPTER 27

What Happened to Fordham

Frank's head was pounding from the night before as the ringing of the phone startled him. "Hello?"

"Frank, I'm flying into Phoenix on Southwest and will be there at 7:00 PM. It was the first flight I could get. You will meet me, right?" He could tell she needed reassurance.

The taste of last night's cigar smoke and tequila swirled in his mouth. "Hang on, I got to get up to think." He walked to the kitchen with the phone and pulled two Alka-Seltzer tablets from the junk drawer. As the water buzzed he said, "Okay, I'll be there."

"I would feel safer just being with you and having you bring me up to date and I need to get some things from my apartment. The landlord said he had the door repaired and they picked up what they could. When is this going to end? I hope your police friend will take it all away." There was no reply.

"Frank, are you there? Frank?"

Frank answered after swallowing the glass in four gulps, with white foam left from the seltzer notched in each corner of his mouth. "Yeah, I'll get you. You know our meeting is eight tomorrow morning. That was the best I could do. No more time changes. We both will be there or we both will be in jail having stale bologna sandwich for lunch.

That is the best I could do and my friend Fordham was not happy I changed times on him again. Where are you going to stay? You definitely shouldn't use your name in a hotel."

"I was wondering if you could put me up for just a night or two. I am not any trouble, and would keep out of your hair. I just don't want to be alone and there is no one else I trust. I realize your police friend will help. But I still am scared, you understand? I know you do. My plane arrives at terminal three. Can we meet at the luggage counter?"

"I'll be there. I don't have much of a place but I never say no to someone who needs a place to lay their head. I'll put some sheets on the guest bed and some towels out. You can have the front bathroom. We see Fordham at eight AM He wanted it to be sooner but I talked him into tomorrow morning on the fact that you were not flying in until late."

"Thank you Frank, it will give us some time to talk. I'm so thankful for all you are doing. I'll see there."

"Okay." Frank hung up the phone. His head was pounding. He coughed, left over from the cigars he didn't enjoy the previous evening. He mentally promised that he would never smoke another cigar again. He made that promise once a week.

Frank looked around his home. His ex-wife had taken most of the furniture. What he'd had was replaced with garage sale bargains he had picked in the last year. He always had a thing for American Indians in his younger life and took the opportunity to decorate his walls with his version of Indian art and artifacts, as he called it. He knew most women would never permit a decorating scheme around the tomahawk (made in China), the fake Navajo rug, a bow and arrow set that he got in a gas station tourist stop on the way to Tucson for $49.00, or his most prized possession, the authentic Indian feather head dress displayed over the TV.

CHAPTER 28

Kim Returns

"Let me get that." He took the luggage from Kim's hand.

"I'm so glad you could come," she replied.

They walked out to the curb where Frank had left the BMW. He had tipped the security guard $10 for letting him park it curbside while he went inside, and had kept his promise to be out in less than ten minutes. The security guard had told him, "Tip or no tip, you go past ten and it's towed."

As he put her flight bag in the trunk, he said, "I don't have much of a place, and not much in the refrigerator. If you'd like, we can pick up some Chinese." Not letting her answer one way or the other he continued, "Let me bring you up to date. I have met with Mr. Lewis and I have fed some of the info to my friend in homicide. I still haven't figured out all the angles on this yet, but to-date, three people have been murdered and I have a gut instinct they are all connected to the Indian gaming money and connections for gambling in Cuba...whatever direction that part is going. Lewis claims to not know what the hell is going on himself; just that he is missing a file with original documents, and because of the secrecy of their deal there were no copies made by him. Even the disks and hard drive have been destroyed. He sure as hell doesn't want anyone looking at the file. We are meeting with Fordham in the morning. I bought you some time. Not much, so let's hope Lewis can shed some more light on all this. He has my card and number and I think since we met he is putting this together. He now knows Kim was killed because of it, though he doesn't know why. If he doesn't call me before meeting with Fordham, I'm sure Fordham will be calling him."

Kim interjected. "Do you think someone is still after me?"

"I'm not sure. My guess is that whoever the hell it is has a pretty good intelligence network and they knew you were Kim's friend so got your number from somewhere, or she had told Dominic. Who the hell knows at this point... but they might figure you have what they are looking for. Just speculation, but you could still be a target if not the bullseye. Since leaving my card at the casino I've joined the enemies list. I think once we meet Fordham he can give you some direction. I had Norma at my office make copies of the file. Once we give him the original, we'll keep a backup. Why? I don't really know. Just following my hunch that you may need one. For now, let's both let go of this worry, until tomorrow at least. I had a friend of mine who is a wizard at getting information through Internet records get on this. Mike Ferdinand, what more he'll find I don't know. But be comfortable in the fact that he has found something. Enough for now, we'll talk later."

As they drove from the airport he turned to small talk hoping to put her at ease. "I'm going to get us some Chinese at one of my favorite places. You like Chinese?"

"Yes, but I don't know how much I'm in the mood to eat."

"Well I don't like eating alone and I often have to, so just move your part around your plate a bit and fool me." He pulled into the restaurant, coming out with two sacks after a few minutes, then headed for his place. He was still making small talk.

"One time I was working in Vienna, Austria, and got tired of eating heavy food and was walking down the street and saw a Chinese restaurant and went in and ordered sweet and sour chicken. It was exactly like sweet and sour chicken you would get here in Phoenix. So from then on, whenever I travel, I always find a Chinese restaurant. It's the same all over the world." They pulled into his drive. It was a modest home with a manicured lawn thanks to Paul the yard man, who came and did what Frank should be doing every other Friday. It cost Frank $50 a month but he liked his yard looking nice, and Paul didn't know that Frank would have paid up to $75 to get it done.

He followed her through his front door, and then into the living room. "It's not much and I usually don't have guests. I tried to pick things up a bit, and I set some towels out in the spare bathroom." She said, "Frank this is lovely. Oh, I love your Indian decorations!"

Franks eyebrows went up, "Are you serious?"

"About what?"

"About the Indian decorations."

"Yes, it is very eclectic. I especially think the bow and arrow just sets it off the room. She walked over and looked above the TV. "Where did you get the Indian thing with all the feathers?"

"Are you serious?" Frank asked again, part of him thinking she was making fun of him or being overly polite.

"No I do like it. It's not what I would put up, but it just fits you...and this house. Of course, you living alone should have it the way you like it."

Ah, the truth, Frank thought, but he let it go. "How about a drink? Ice tea, soda? I'll even make some coffee." He got two matching plates from the cabinet and a spoon to dish out the Chinese food.

"Just some water with ice would be fine," she said. She took a seat in his red leather chair. She let her hair down from the ponytail and pulled it to the sides. Frank looking at her again thought how very nice looking and attractive she was, in addition to the intelligence he had observed in her. And the sexual part of him that still sprung to the front of his mind thought that she had a very nice posterior. His mentality didn't like the list to be in that order. Unfortunately, and somewhat sadly, that is the way most men start their list...it goes from hair down to eyes, then the figure, followed by legs and arms and then back up to the mind. It wasn't Frank's fault, or men's fault in general; it was the way nature made the male of the species. There was so much truth in the old adage about a man's brain being hidden and too often controlled by the crotch of their pants, thanks to genetics.

They ate with chopsticks, making small talk about where they grew up, their parents and childhood stories, and before long personal likes and dislikes as well as past relationships. They had been conversing for almost two hours, which was unusual for Frank. He found himself saying things he would never have told another human. And it was made more unusual by the fact he didn't really know the girl he was talking to, yet he felt there was part of him that had known her a long time. Conversation was easy and he was doing a very good job of keeping her mind away from her current troubles.

Frank had told Kim some of his teenage date stories and she laughed, maybe even harder than Fordham did when he made Frank tell them. After an hour of sitting across from each other she began to feel herself falling into a comfort zone. She hadn't had that feeling for some time, and this was more odd because of the fact that she was sitting in a man's home she had only met few days ago, under less desirable circumstances than one might find on Match.com.

She had removed her shoes, and with his silent nod of approval put her feet on the coffee table. Her thoughts drifted in their conversation to a quiet admission that she liked this man eating Chinese in front of her in his testosterone-laced Indian room. She, at this precise moment, knew she was vaguely attracted to him. Both purposely avoided discussing the file and the problem at hand. She felt there was much more to this man fumbling with his chopsticks; there was clearly a sense of her being protected and feeling a warmth for him that was suddenly unavoidably noticeable.

"Frank, you dropped some food on your shirt." He immediately looked down and saw the red-sauced piece of chicken and rice and wiped it with his paper napkin.

"Never did learn how to use these damn chop sticks. Hell, they invented dynamite and put up that huge wall... you'd think they could have come up with a fork somewhere along the way."

Frank took a sip of his drink. His eyes could not help darting down the crossed legs of his house guest. In a brief instant her eyes caught his gaze and she shifted in her seat and pulled on her skirt to make sure the view was covered. John noticed that and was immediately embarrassed but just gave the nervous cough that men do in such awkward situations and said. "How was your sister?"

Kim was lost in the thought that his home was almost exactly how one would decorate a Hollywood set of a single middle-aged man who had the slightest touch of a woman's flair, but failed miserably in using it. The curtains were outdated, the house dusty, and though the room was "picked up," it still lacked all the touches of comfort or warmness that a woman would bring it. In some ways, she found herself making mental notes of what this place needed. She broke the silence and asked if he'd had any "flings with a woman since his divorce?"

The question caught him off guard and seemed out of place. He remembered the first and last romance, if it could be labeled such, that he'd had since the divorce and the woman who led him to it. It still puzzled him; he had not yet mastered the task of figuring women out. He seemed to have a habit of saying the wrong thing, but not meaning anything about it, and having it blow up in his face.

The last memory of a date with a woman he thought he could really like, or hope to date (if it could even fit in that category) was telling her during dinner how much he liked her and missed her. Her eye began to twitch and she said, "Stop it, stop it, stop telling me that! You're making my eye twitch!" Sure enough he looked in her face and she was holding her hand to her left eye. It looked like...yes it was twitching. It was not an easy thing for Frank to digest when he was hoping to warm her heart for him. It wasn't a pleasant memory, but certainly an odd—and in some ways funny—memory.

There was a pause after Kim stopped laughing, then she looked at Frank and took the opportunity to ask him a question she had once read on an online dating service that she thought of trying and then backed out. "Frank, tell me, just for fun. If you were going to a deserted island and could only take ten pieces of music and a CD player, what ten would you take?"

He looked quizzically at her and thought, what the hell kind of question is that? "Hell, I don't know. It is important to you?"

"I'm just curious. Can you tell me? Come on try."

"Well let me think about it...for sure I would want some Sinatra. If just one by him, it would be 'The Way You Look Tonight.' Definitely Manfred Mann and 'Blinded by the Light.' Some of the best electric guitar solos in the world. Uh...'Shout,' by the Isley Brothers. Can't keep your foot still to that. Ben E. King singing 'Stand by Me,' a classic...some jazz piano by Oscar Peterson. The soundtrack to Phantom of the Opera. Gladys Knight, can't think of the name of it, but it has the line 'Superstar but he didn't get far.' Love that one. How many is that?"

He continued without waiting for an answer. "Without a doubt, an Eva Cassidy CD; the 'Live at Blues Alley' one.

Barbara Streisand singing 'When you walk through a Storm' always gives me chills. Elton John singing 'Butterflies are free.' Something by Dave Mathews...and uh...lost count. How many is that?"

"You've been so fast I lost count, but keep going," Kim replied.

"Okay, let's see. Stevie Wonder and the gang singing 'That's what friends are for.' Then the rescue boat comes, right?"

She laughed, "You are very diverse...'Blinded by the Light'? That's a little out of your age...or maybe not?"

"You ever heard the electric guitar solo on that? Oh and I would have to have someone, anyone singing 'Over the rainbow' when I get depressed on those dark island days waiting for the boat to come. Let's see, some Gershwin, at least one Elvis tune. Uh, you want me to keep going?"

She gave him a soft laugh for his answer. "Who is Eva Cassidy?"

"You'll have to buy one of her CD's...that's the best answer I can give to explain her." He continued smiling back. He found himself enjoying this game.

"Now if you were with me, I might add some more romantic ballads, hoping they might do me some good when I bring you a coconut shell." He smiled to let her know that he was teasing, but a lie detector test would show that maybe he wasn't.

"Who knows?" she said. "One could get desperate on a desert island." She was still smiling warmly. She liked his company, even though he was a little odd and unkempt. But still, there was something about Frank O'Hara. She held her thought.

"I've had a long day, and dinner with you was very nice, but I think I should say good night. I am so appreciative of all you have done. I feel safe with you, and I'm glad I called you. Your ex-wife was right; she must miss you. It will be so nice for me to get this chapter in my life finished. I want to look my best when we meet your detective friend in the morning." She got up and walked over and gave him a quick kiss on the cheek, "Thank you again." She then went to the guest bedroom, smiling back at Frank as she softly closed the door.

CHAPTER 29

Dominic No Longer Shakes Hands

Dominic had left Brenda and made a quick decision as he noticed he was driving by the cemetery to visit his mother's grave; he usually stopped once or twice a year. The cemetery only allowed plastic flowers. There was cement urn on the top of the marker where plastic flowers could be placed. Dominic, walked up and said the one prayer his mother had taught him as a little boy: God is good, God is great," and then adding the prayer of the moment said out loud, "Be good to my momma." Dominic looked around to make sure no one was watching, and then with subtlety that came from years of practice doing such things, took the plastic flowers that were in the urn next to his mother's grave and placed them in her urn before walking away. He made a mental note that he needed to stop by and do that more often as he said, "See you later, Momma."

There was a lot on his mind. The information that Brenda had given him fell into that wonderful world of opportunity. Dominic, more than all other personality traits, was an opportunist, especially when it came to making easy money, big easy money. He usually didn't think of consequences. Hurting those around him was not part of his thinking. Obtaining easy money superseded all such factors.

He cared for Brenda. He had no trouble accepting that. Hell, he thought she's a fine-looking woman. But even she would leave him if he didn't have money, he reasoned. That was his guiding light, and he was sure that she would understand and believe that he was doing it for both of them. She'll come around, he thought, they always do. He had little doubt she would eventually leave anyway and when she did, he'd still have to have money to keep going, reasoned Dominic. Brenda would understand. She was smart enough to get another job.

He had, with all his mental ability, bent the truth as far as he could, but he assured Brenda all was well. He did not feel the need to mention to her that the documents he had her steal (though he preferred the words "made available to him") and which he now had copies of were very valuable, not only to the Philly Mob, but now to Dominic.

Dominic knew that the boys in Philly were not the only organized crime family involved or wanting to be involved in Indian gambling casinos, and more importantly, an open door to a casino in Cuba. He made the decision that couldn't be undone: to make contact with Louie Marenelli, the head of the New Orleans Crime family, and let them know that he had information which could open the doors to the casino business in the southwest and Cuba via documents that could be used in bribery. The big problem for him, of which he had no illusion, was that the organization in

Philly, whose request he had more than completed, would not be happy.

Dominic knew he would need protection. He would ask—no make that DEMAND—that he be taken into their business and organization in New Orleans with full protection. All the operating crime families understood business, so this kind of information would offer not only big money but for him protection...he was sure of it.

In his twisted value system, he believed he had found the magic solution to the "big time." He carried in his satchel information on the reopening of Cuba casinos, a regime that likely would turn its head to the street drugs. He thought he was deserving of being in charge of that operation, and would ask for it. His mind was spinning at the thought.

He believed he was bringing Christmas early, and a chance to bring this deal was much better than running drugs and moving stolen cars to Mexico. It was worth much more than Pete "The Nose" and his small time payment of five hundred and a vacation, "if she wants to take you." In fact, he thought, it was outright insulting. He made some calls around Phoenix to some people he knew would have the information he was seeking, and finally found someone who could set up a meeting. Even if it was brief, it gave him a chance to push his agenda along with the information he now controlled.

The boss in New Orleans would be happy to see the stolen file he was carrying on the plane to his meeting. Dominic's only thought was, how much is this going to get me? He was going through figures on his airplane drink napkin....a million...no less than a half-million. He never once wrote down, "My two hands." I'm finally going into an organization, he thought. Running into that broad (he no longer used her name) was the best damn lucky thing I ever stumbled on.

The boys in Philly didn't like such renegade moves. You lost your hands and your life for dipping into the cookie jar that was reserved for someone else.

CHAPTER 30

The End of Fordham

Frank's eyes followed Kim into the guest room till she closed the door. She was actually going to stay at his house, and had just been sitting across from him. Frank had his first full-fledged feeling of being overwhelmed by all of this. He had totally lost the ability to communicate, at least with a beautiful woman. He was out of his element and, he realized at that moment, felt powerless. He said as he heard her close the bedroom door, "I'm turning in too. I'll have coffee made in the morning."

At 7:00 AM Frank was finishing his cup of coffee and fighting off the urge to light the first cigar of the day. Until recently, he had only been lighting them at the end of the workday, but lately had found the time frame moving up. Now he had the urge, and he hadn't even had breakfast yet. Damn stress, he thought to himself.

His cell phone rang. He knew the number was a police extension, so there was no need to go Spanish. "Frank here." It was Sgt. Brosky.

"Frank you sitting down? I have bad news."

"What?" Frank asked.

"Fordham is in the hospital, barely alive on a breathing machine. It looks like he tried to commit suicide early this morning, before work."

"Oh shit," Frank said. It was the only thing that came out. "Oh shit," again. "Ah shit," a third time. "John wasn't suicidal. That's bullshit...pure bullshit." Brosky told him what hospital Fordham was in. Frank said "I'm going to head over there."

Brosky then added, "Frank you know he had a tough time with sex crimes...and how he was always keeping and reading those suicide notes he kept in his desk. This didn't surprise a lot of us here. Lt. Barnes ran the investigation. Fordham used his service revolver to his temple. I can't believe he's still alive. I don't think he ever got over the divorce."

"I was supposed to meet him at eight. There's something wrong with this."

"Yeah we know, John told Lt. Barnes yesterday at the end of the shift that you were bringing some witness to the Brenda James...and Dominic whatever the heck his last name was...murder investigation. Barnes still wants to meet with you at nine. He's listened to all the voice mails you left."

"Wow, this sucks. Anyone call John's ex and kids yet?"

"Yeah, Chaplain was there. He may still be."

"Well Sergeant, I ain't buying a piece of it. That's not something John would do. I was as close to him as anyone, and he never once even hinted...something is wrong here... it stinks so loud. I've spoken to him three or four times in the past couple of days and he was his old self. No way in hell did he shoot himself. No way." He hung up without saying another word.

He walked into the guest bedroom. She had just finished her shower and was wrapped only in a bath towel. "Sorry I guess I didn't knock, but my mind is gone right now. I have to leave for the hospital, Fordham is there. It's an emergency. I'll call you but I have to leave now. Our meeting is on hold for now...you stay here, don't open the door for anyone. I'll be back soon."

With that he turned, picked the car key off the counter and was out the door. He didn't hear Kim say, "Call me...I'm sorry."

Frank walked into the hospital and was directed to the intensive care unit on the second floor. He first saw Fordham's brother, Paul, who was a cop in another town close to Phoenix. "They found him sitting in his car in his driveway this morning. Neighbor called it in. Shit, if he does survive he may never be right. The docs say the brain injury is real bad. I ain't buying the suicide story."

"Neither am I." Frank added, "Someone did this, but why? Can I see him? You know we were close." As if he needed an excuse.

John's brother knew that. "He was always talking about you and your damn funny stories."

John's brother knew from conversations with his brother that Frank and John both felt comfortable and safe in their conversations with each other. Not just about the work they did, but women, religion, social injustice. Above all they laughed a lot.

Fordham called O'Hara "goofy." Frank could get Fordham laughing very easily during these social outings.

Frank was thinking about those times as Paul took him back through the hospital hallway to the intensive care room. They had Fordham hooked up to the typical tubes down his throat and needles in his arms and legs. His head was bandaged and his face swollen. John lay unmoving and silent among the humming and beeping sounds of the life-sustaining machines they usually have running in intensive care rooms.

"I was just with him for dinner and Irish whiskey a few weeks ago. He was laughing and excited about taking his son to the Grand Canyon next weekend. We were supposed to meet at his office this morning."

Paul spoke to the closed eyes and drawn face of John Fordham. "Frank's here to see you. Frank O'Hara," as if the last name was necessary.

Unmistakably Fordham barely opened his right hand, intentional or not...who would know? Frank placed his hand inside it and Fordham closed his fist around Frank's hand and Frank felt him so slightly squeeze.

Frank squeezed back. Frank knew by some miracle that John knew he was there. "Hang in there," Frank said. "Hang in there."

Frank turned and walked out of the room. His eyes were noticeably misty.

He turned back to Paul and said. "Keep me posted. I'll be back later today. You know, we had a meeting. It can't wait; I need to see someone John trusted at the department. Check on that for me, and let me know as soon as you can. I know it's a shitty time to ask for such a request but I need to know soon. John was all I had. John was not suicidal, I'm sure of it."

Paul answered, "I'll let you know this morning. Let's hope in a week or so John can talk to you." Paul's hopes were still running high. "Lt. Barnes said John's service revolver was on the car seat next to him, with one shot missing. Naturally John's prints were on the pistol. There were no witnesses. He tells a story that John's divorce was the start of it, and that John had been seeing a shrink. For now the department is listing it as an attempted suicide."

Frank spoke to John, "I'll be back buddy." He walked out of the room again, with tears in his eyes.

Hell of a time for someone to put a bullet in your head, he said to himself. I've talked to him twice in the last two days, and I know he was fine. He was his old self, even giving me hell and a favor at the same time. He was highly interested in meeting with me this morning; I would have known if he was that down. Somebody shot him with his own gun. I'd bet my life on it...and may have already. He paused, while working through things in his mind. In the past two weeks four people have been killed. Didn't know any of the others, but I'm sure they're all connected. This last one was a very good friend of mine, and that fact is not going to be forgotten.

Frank got on the elevator and headed for the parking lot. Within fifteen minutes John's brother called Frank on his cell phone. "He's gone." Frank pulled over to the side of the freeway. He could not stop the heavy breathing that started with the end of that statement. "I'll find the asshole who did this John, I promise you," he said, barely audible.

Frank was closer to John then most of John's police friends knew. They seemed to have a connection that maybe they didn't even understand, a zone in their relationship that most men don't find with other men in this too-often rough and tough world. In their own way they battled the heartaches that one experiences in life, but their friendship was open and honest and they could tell each other about the hurts and the pain that came with life. It helped. Sometimes nothing was even said, but there would be a phone call and it would be one or the other just saying, "You doing okay?"

John loved to hear Frank's dating stories, and would usually talk Frank into telling them again on his second drink. John would mention to anyone sitting close at the bar, "You gotta hear this," while literally dragging them over to Frank's seat. He broke up laughing every time, as if he had never heard them before. As Frank thought of those times, he actually smiled. It was the best way to remember John. He thought of those stories on his slow drive home.

Frank had gotten a monkey when he was about twelve years old. He actually ordered it out one of those men's magazines from the early 50's, where the back pages offered "fireworks, boomerangs, throwing knives," and occasionally a cinnamon ring-tailed organ-grinder monkey. Frank, without his parents knowing, had saved his grass-cutting money and mailed a money order for fifty dollars to the address on the monkey advertisement, then waited anxiously for his monkey to arrive.

He had recently arrived at that age where you discover girls and don't completely understand why. But there was no mistake...you are attracted to them. You also learn at the same time you are competing with other boys for their attention, and Frank thought a monkey could make a decidedly big difference. He had a mental vision of himself walking up to a girl with the monkey on this shoulder, and thought it would be big advantage in starting a conversation with the blonde pony tailed girl, whose brand-new breasts barely showed through her pink sweater set that matched her pleated Catholic school skirt.

When Frank finally got a call and went to the train station to pick his monkey up, he had a local vet meet him there to examine the monkey and sign a paper stating that this new unusual pet did not have any jungle disease. Indiana had fairly lax animal laws at that time. The vet examined and signed, and Frank took the wooden box with the brown eyes and sharp fingernails sticking out between the wooden slats home. To say that monkey was pissed off would be a major understatement.

He called his best friend at the time (whose name had now slipped his mind), and the two of them opened the box up with screwdrivers and hammers, and discovered the wildest animal they had ever encountered. It has been said that a 25-pound monkey is no match for a six-foot, 200-pound man. The man loses every time.

The fact that a monkey uses all four of its extremities, as well as its mouth and tail to grab and hold on while it sinks its teeth into the finger that is reaching out to it with a soft banana, is a very painful introduction. Frank had told John that he had no doubt the monkey was living in the jungle in a tree just days before he took it out of the box, and was mad as hell about it so was not easily going to sit on Frank's shoulder as Frank tried to impress the ladies of his age—unless the ladies worked with animals in a circus. In fact, Frank could only handle the monkey (who he affectionately named "Gigi") with extra thick oven mitts. And even then he had to keep the monkey turned away from his body and beware of its tail as it squirmed and fought to turn and bite him anywhere it could. He tried and tried to become best friends with that monkey, but it was a relationship that was going take lots of time. In fact, the truth of it was that there wasn't enough time.

Sometimes Gigi would get loose from her cage in the basement of Frank's home where Frank secretly hid it from his parents. Frank would get three of his friends to come to the house and with a blanket they would corner the monkey, then throw the blanket over her. It was always one hell of a battle to get that monkey back in her cage. There weren't always enough oven mitts for everyone, and usually someone had a bloody finger or at least scratches to the face.

Frank told John that the monkey would not always need to be cornered to attack. It was not uncommon for her to pounce if you were walking too close to wherever she had decided to sit, and you had better have those oven mitts on so you could fight her off.

Once when Frank was watching "I love Lucy," his dad decided to get something from the basement during a commercial. This was a highly unusual event, as his dad never went down to the basement. Frank knew the monkey was out of her cage and lurking somewhere in the basement's false ceiling. His dad opened the door, turned on the light and proceeded to go down the stairs. At twelve years of age Frank had faced some strong character tests, but this was the biggest so far. What should he do? He decided for sure he wasn't going to yell, "Dad, watch out for the monkey!" He kept quiet, hoping that Gigi would stay hidden.

His father proceeded down into the basement and Frank sat on the edge of the chair, waiting for the scream as Gigi pounced on his Dad. His Dad had not the slightest inclination that a monkey might attack him at any minute, in what he perceived to be the safety of his own home, and he certainly didn't have any oven mitts with him.

But the silence continued. There was no scream. His father returned and sat back down in his in front of the TV. Seconds, maybe even a minute went by, until his father looked over at Frank and said calmly, "Either the monkey goes or I go."

Frank demurely replied, "I'll get it out by tomorrow."

Fortunately, he was able to get the one and only pet store in town to take the monkey. The owner soon found that it was a good draw, and the monkey lived a long and happy life. And Frank was able to buy his mom some new oven mitts the next Christmas.

The first question he was going to ask his Dad when he got the opportunity to see him again in the afterlife was, "What in the hell did you think when you saw that monkey in the basement?" His dad had never mentioned it again while alive.

John loved that story, but it was a toss-up between the monkey and the time Frank had one of his first dates when he actually got to borrow the parents' car and take a girl to the movie. Frank, at the age of sixteen, was in puppy love with the young girl. He wanted to impress her, and saddle shoes were the current rage—white with the brown swatch of leather under the white shoe laces. Of course they needed to be worn with white athletic socks, self-draped Levis, and a short-sleeved shirt with the collar turned up. This was just before James Dean appeared with the white t-shirt and red windbreaker.

Frank didn't have a pair of saddle shoes but ah, his dad did. The only thing different (besides being three sizes too big) was that his dad's had cleats on the bottom, specifically designed to grip the ground when he started his back swing on the golf course. Frank did not think anyone would notice the clicking sound as he walked on cement, or the indenting into the carpet of the movie theater. He thought he was looking good and that is what was important at the time.

It was a date that had lots of detraction, which started when the movie theater manager asked him not to wear those shoes on their carpet, causing Frank to have to watch the movie with the saddle shoes on top of his lap with the popcorn. After walking out holding the shoes at the end of the movie, he put them back on for the drive home. Parking his father's car against the slightly downhill curb, he walked his date up three flights of stairs, shook her hand and said, "good night." After thanking her for a lovely time, he returned quickly to the car.

His date had not known that Frank had to take the biggest piss, as for the sake of good manners he had refrained from telling her on the drive home, during which the messages sent to his brain from his bladder and kidneys were growing more persistent with each mile. After leaving his date at her door he returned to his parked vehicle. He could hold it no longer. He perceived the street to be dark, with no one around and no one watching, so he opened the car door. Standing in the guarded space created by the open door and the car, he took what might have been the longest leak of his life.

He finished, zipped up and got into the car and turned the key, but there was no sound. Nothing. Then he saw that the car was stuck in neutral, and it would only start if it was in park. The gear shift wouldn't move. He got out and walked back up the three flights of stairs and his young date answered the door with a surprised smile. "My car won't start," Frank said. "Can I use your phone to call my dad?"

Frank had not seen his young date's older brother sitting in the living room but hearing the conversation he jumped up and said. "Let me take a look first." Frank was secretly thrilled, although the brother did ask what the clicking noise was as he followed, and looked down at Frank's shoes. He must have mentally thought, this poor kid has huge feet for his age. The brother got a screwdriver and flashlight, and Frank and his date walked down the stairs with him and out to Frank's dad car. He shined the light around, walked to the front of the car, and had Frank pull the hood lever. Frank remembered him saying something like "the over and under admixture attenuator may be stuck," and if they pushed the car and got the wheels to turn, it might unlock and Frank could get the gear in park and start the car.

Frank, the date, and the brother proceeded to push the car just far enough that when the brother walked back around the car with flashlight shining, he said, "Whoa!" He had noticed a stream of liquid flowing from where the car had been down to the curb, and forming a pool which had slowly become a tiny stream gently flowing against and down the curb.

Before Frank could say a thing—even if he would have said a thing—the brother bent down to the pool, stuck his finger in it, and took it up to his nose. He gave it a good smell, not once, but twice, before looking at Frank and pronouncing in the mechanic's voice he hoped to be someday, "You got big trouble, you've lost all your transmission fluid."

Of course there is no way Frank could say, at least in front of his date, "Ah, no I think that's my piss."

Frank never told the girl or the brother the truth of that fluid, but it was a memory of his young life that would never leave him. He went home laughing to himself and placed his dad's "saddle" golf shoes back in the closet, vowing not to wear them again until either they fit or he had a golf club in his hand. When Frank got older he would think about that event and had decided he didn't know one woman who would ever stick her hand in something from underneath their car if they didn't know what it was, hold it to their nose, and smell it. On the other hand, he thought, there wasn't one man he knew who wouldn't. And that statement alone explained more than any relationship book ever could on the marked difference between the sexes.

But the story that John loved the most was the time Frank was in college and took a date to a Christmas formal dance, after attending a wedding in the afternoon. It was a rushed shotgun wedding at which the refreshments consisted of a cheap keg of beer, salami, and baked beans. By the time Frank picked up his date, he was having what technically is flatulent gas. Anyone who has ever had flatulent problems caused by beer, baked beans, and spicy salami knows that they are silent but deadly, with the absolute worst odor known to man.

Frank believed that if your eyes were real good, you could, on occasion actually see what is known among men as a beer fart. Frank said to John, "It had to be a green color but translucent." A beer fart was not something for which you just said, "excuse me," while on a date with a girl in a formal dress, and then politely rolled the window down and tried not to notice as she gagged and her corsage withered. A fart on that date night definitely would be known as a show stopper. But here Frank was, driving down the road in winter, and he felt one coming. There is a remarkable burning sensation, which seems to be right on the anus and is the only warning you get.

Frank knew it was bad from earlier experience so with what he perceived as taking quick action, he stopped the car on the road and jumped out of the car. However, in his haste he forgot to put the car in park, so much to the surprise of his date (Frank too, for that matter) the car continued moving forward down the freeway at between five and ten miles an hour with no one behind the steering wheel.

The young girl, in her Christmas formal, began screaming. Frank, who by this time had passed the beer fart into the cold country air, was running in his tux as fast as he could to catch up to the car. The date was still screaming and trying to get control of the steering wheel, with no appreciation at that moment of what Frank had done for her.

Frank finally caught up with the car and was able to climb back in behind the wheel. He looked at his date and said, "Sorry, I thought I felt something bumping...maybe a bad tire." He slowed the car to a stop and got out saying, "I'd better check it again." In an effort to continue to sell this story, he kicked the tire on the rear driver's side twice before announcing, "We're okay."

The girl never went out with him again.

CHAPTER 31

Seven Days Earlier

Dominic returned from New Orleans the following day, after what he thought was a good trip. He had been given a two thousand dollar payment toward the delivery of the file copy, and was assured that it was a confidential transaction. Both parties seemed to be elated with such fortune falling their way. The New Orleans organization said they would meet his demands, and if Cuba came to be, "Yes, he could be in charge of the narcotics sales," and no problem with protection. They would call Philly and tell them "hands off" today.

Dominic planned to deliver the copies to the boys in Philly. He told the people he met in New Orleans that he would, after they strongly suggested he do so. After all, it had been their request, so it was the honorable thing to do. They would appreciate his fulfilling his assignment. He was told Philly would have let New Orleans in on it anyway, so he had no worries. Plus, he was under their protection.

Dominic, after hearing all of this, had a sense of safety, plus he was the only one who knew where the original file with all its secret potential was located. He hadn't even gotten to the part about blackmail, but knew those rich boys would pay nicely to keep their names out of the papers. My next move, he thought, will be to contact a few of them. His big payday was growing faster than Apple stock, or so he believed. He just had to figure a way to get the original file back from Brenda.

It didn't take long for the New Orleans people to contact the Philly Godfather. It had not always been that way; Dominic was considered "lower than whale shit" by both the crime families. In these times you didn't want, couldn't have, and tried to completely avoid, family wars. Those truly were a thing of the past. There were no crime family Mafia wars in these times. Oh yes, an occasional hit, but complete family wars didn't exist anymore. These days they all cooperated, and in essence helped each other. Each had its own interests in local unions and liquor control, and times had gotten so bad they'd had to get out of numbers since the state started running their own numbers racket in the form of the lottery. It had become a tough business. Loan sharking was still good, drugs and prostitution were always good, but the well was running dry in their old endeavors. Most Godfathers always spoke with each other and they were more business cronies then enemies. Dominic was on the plane thanking his good luck when the New Orleans people called the Philly people to meet and see how we divide this up." The elimination of Dominic was the last item mentioned before both parties ended the business conversation.

Dominic's Phoenix killers were called that afternoon. Not just to end his and his girlfriend's lives with a strong message, but to locate the original stolen file. Dominic received word the following day that two unknown men were in the Chock and Hen asking for him or Brenda, which was his first tip things might not be going so well. He called who he thought were his new friends in New Orleans, but they wouldn't take his calls, let alone return one of his several messages. He knew this was bad. He called Brenda and told her to get that file out of her house. No questions, just do it. He was under the erroneous assumption that as long as he was the only one who knew where the original was, he held a very important bargaining chip that gave him added protection.

They were waiting outside of Dominic's high rent apartment in North Scottsdale when he pulled up and hit the lever to his garage door. He noticed the car pulling in behind him with its lights out, and he reached under the seat of his car for his gun. As he was pulling it out, a huge hand grabbed his wrist and said, "Hey, we're friends," as the other hand went around his throat. Dominic struggled for a second, but the other man had already pushed himself into the passenger side and took the gun from his hand.

"Hey, why the hell'd you do that?" There was no doubt Dominic was no longer in control as the gun hit the floor. "What do you want, what do you want?"

"Nothing much...Philly sent us. They heard you were doing a little business with some papers they wanted. They thought you were their friend...thought you would give them back to us. Help us straighten this out; where is the legal file you had your girlfriend steal for you? They told us not to leave here without them. You know how they can be when they don't get their way."

Dominic was no fool, he knew bad shit when it comes and this was bad shit. "I got protection from New Orleans. I'm under them now. You got no authority in this."

"They told us they pulled that, and you are open meat on the market. Now do we do this the hard way or you going to give us the file?"

"Hold on, I got them, let me get out of the car. Come on up with me." Dominic was stalling, looking for a chance to break away. The guy next to him released his grip on his neck but Dominic could see the barrel of a gun pointed to his head. He kept talking.

"I wasn't doing nothin', really. I wouldn't mess with Pete. I was going to give him all the shit I got today. He would know that." He knew he didn't have the papers. He had left all the copies he had in New Orleans, and had given Brenda the originals back with a copy to put back into Lewis' file. "Come on relax. I can get them for you. Give me some time. You come back in an hour. I don't have them here. I'll give them to you with some cappuccino."

It was not a good answer, the man in the driver's seat reached over and with the knife in his hand sliced Dominic across the face, deep into his cheek. Dominic groaned as he felt the blood run down his face and onto his nice crisp white shirt. "Hey," he said, "come on, I can get them."

"Who has them, shit face? Give me a name or I'm going to match this cut on the other cheek."

Dominic did not want to give them Brenda's name. He was stuttering and fast-talking as they pulled him from the car. His right hand was covering the deep slice to his cheek.

"I got protection, call New Orleans and check. I'll give you the number...you both are getting your ass in trouble."

The bigger of the two took Dominic to the front of his car and pushed him face down over the hood. "Listen, you piece of shit, you got shit protection, and we're not going back to Philly without them papers. We ain't waiting till tomorrow, so you'd better make them show up now."

Dominic was trying to protect Brenda's, as well as his own, ass. He kept thinking, I need time, but he knew he was short of that. He could not think. "I can get them, but you need to understand it will take some time. I'm also going to call New Orleans and get someone you can talk to who will tell you I'm now with them. Give me a little time. This will all work out." He was pleading at this point, rather than asking.

With that the man with the knife grabbed Dominic's hand. His other Philly friend was leaning on Dominic and pinning him to the car as the first began to slice off Dominic's left hand at the wrist. Dominic tried to scream but a rag had been pushed into his mouth almost to the back of his throat. With the first push of the knife, Dominic felt the nerves in his wrist shooting pain into his arm, then into his shoulder, and then into his brain. He kept trying to scream. His hand, the fingers still twitching, hit the cement floor of the garage. Dominic not only heard the sound as it hit, but could see it from the corner of his eyes.

"We don't want anything from you but the file, or address of where those papers are, and if you don't give me a quick answer you're going to be signing your Christmas cards this year with a pencil in your mouth." They grasped Dominic's other hand and took the rag from his mouth;

Dominic was in shock and pain and did not reason past that point. He knew the only way he was going to save his life was by giving them Brenda. "She doesn't know anything, don't hurt her."

"Hey," the one holding the knife said, "you think we hurt women?"

"Her name is Brenda. She lives at 6634 East Mesa Drive, but she has no interest in this at all, she doesn't know anything about this, don't hurt her. Don't hurt her. As he was talking he didn't realize he was pissing on himself. With that answer, the knife went through the second wrist. It was very sharp, serrated, hunting-style knife; the kind you normally would use to gut a deer. When the slicing to the bone was complete, the blade was flipped and the pressure against the wrist bones with the serrated edge completed the job. Dominic watched as his other hand hit the floor. "That's just to make sure you're telling us the truth."

He was moaning too loud for the Philly boys, so they shoved the rag back into this mouth and carried him to the trunk of their car. Dominic saw the trunk door come down. He was thinking of his momma when a short time later they pulled him out and laid him on the ground. The bigger one sat on his chest, looking into his eyes, and the other one tied chains around his legs and arms and padlocked them shut. Then they rolled Dominic over and said, "Pete wanted you to know just how unhappy he was with you, so he wanted us to take you swimming with no hands and some chains around you. Oh and just in case you got some seal in you, he asked us to do this." With that the silenced gun went off. After the 22 entered the back of

Dominic's head, they both kicked him three or four times until he rolled over into the Central Arizona Project Canal. It was shortly after nine PM Their next stop was to find out what they could about Brenda, but in reality they didn't feel optimistic about her future.

CHAPTER 32

Two Weeks Later

When Frank returned from the hospital, Kim was dressed and sitting at his kitchen table. She could see that he was immensely bothered. "How is he?"

"He's dead. They say it was a suicide but he was murdered."

"How horrible!" She put an arm around John. "Why would they lie?"

"I don't know, but they are. Someone didn't want us meeting him this morning, or giving him the file, or maybe even something to do with you. He told someone we were meeting, and a quick stop was put to it. You and I are in a big bag of shit to put it mildly. We've got no one on our side, and it seems a lot of enemies on the other side. We can't really trust anyone at the police department, because there's at least one crooked cop there. I made a big mistake leaving my card at the casino. Lewis is worthless. I need some time to think...and my mind won't stop spinning with John being gone. I'm not sure I can even go to his funeral. There's no question my name and your name are at the top of someone's 'get rid of' list. You don't have any rich relatives that own an island in the South Pacific do you?" he asked sarcastically. "I'm too long in this business. Most of my FBI friends are dead or retired. John was my last real contact. I can't think of his last name but John mentioned a good friend of his he must have trusted. He talked about him in good terms more than once. They had some big homicide cases together. I don't know if I can trust him or not; with John it was in the bank. I don't know yet, I will feel it out and see where we go. We might just turn the whole fucking thing over to the Attorney General and leave town for a month or so." He smiled and said, "You like Tahiti?"

She stared back and started to answer, but he interrupted. "Hey I'm not serious about Tahiti...that's just the wishful part of my brain speaking. Let's make a follow-up with Lewis; that stuffed shirt might have some information by now. At least it's worth another try. We got an hour or two before we need to disappear."

CHAPTER 33

How It Works

Dominic was not aware that whoever sent him swimming with no hands already had Brenda's address. Their intelligence network was in good working order. It had to be known that she took the documents from the law office, and the common thought was that Dominic got what he needed and had given them back to her for a speedy return trip to the file. Their information was correct, and it made no difference that Dominic, in the last minutes of his life and in extreme pain and shock as he was losing his hands, gave them Brenda's name and address. He was going to be a dead man no matter what. The instructions were to kill Dominic in a manner that would send a message that you don't mess with whoever is ordering this. Dominic was a dead man, just hours before Brenda. Frank told Kim he was not sure who they were leaving messages for, but it may not be that hard to figure out. To kill a cop is a big deal, but Frank didn't really think the mob was responsible for John. "They don't operate that way, it brings too much heat. They're much more into killing their own and bribing anyone on the outside." Frank went into detail explaining mafia dealings to Kim.

In addition to killing Dominic, the instructions were to locate those files. There was a very nice deal going down, sweet in many ways...you run a casino, you could clean up drug money that came from Columbia. Vegas had been cleaned up when the big corporations got involved. The Teamsters had their pension fund guarded by legitimate people, and organized crime had tired of fighting the Jamaicans, the Latinos, and the black brotherhood who had all found the profit in narcotics. They fought mainly between each other, with the old time grandfathers shrugging their shoulders and deciding to be distributors to these young punks who wanted to shoot each other. There was way too much heat in the narcotic world, so organized crime decided to take a back seat. If those punks with all their gang tattoos and gang-related scarves on their heads wanted to kill each other, it made no difference. The next day there would be a new punk who would buy their product and sell it on the street. The Godfathers were far removed from the transaction; it went from Columbia to a district manager, to a zone manager, to a city, hell to the border towns of Mexico. Then to some local manager and then to a street party who finally found it in the back of his trunk, neatly bundled up. No one knew the others' names, and everyone knew it was better to go to prison for 25 years then to give up the connection above you who was the only one you ever knew. It wasn't always death, but whatever the punishment was, there was no question that prison was far better and at least held some hope for keeping your mouth shut.

There were street stories of a man's whole family being burned alive at home when fire broke out and all the doors had been nailed shut along with the windows. And of seeing a man, who used to have bundles in his trunk, now in a wheelchair, unable to move anything below his mid-back where a knife had entered and purposefully severed his spinal cord. Once making 500 grand a year, tax free, he now had a bag on one side for his piss and a bag on the other side for his shit, wearing those half gloves on each hand as he rolled his chair around. The worst of it sometimes was that the former friends of the man in the wheel chair wouldn't even talk to him as he rolled himself around his neighborhood. He was a snitch, so he got just what he deserved.

No, the boys in the high end had insulated themselves well. Soon news of Dominic's death and lack of hands would hit the street, and a whole new shock wave would roll around, with the message that you don't mess with the hand that feeds you. Frank said, "That message is now for us too."

Kim sat stunned at Frank's words. "My God, then who had John killed?"

Frank looked her in the eye and said, "Someone from our good old police department, or someone on Lewis's payroll, or both."

CHAPTER 34

Give the File to Kim

Brenda hadn't heard from Dominic since he left her house; he hadn't returned her calls. She wasn't sure where he lived, but she went to the Italian restaurant he had taken her to on their last date, where he knew the waiter and the bartender by name, and who gave him the usual first class service. She entered alone and waited at the stand until the maître d' approached her. "Can I help you?"

She replied, "I am a friend of Dominic Serrano, and I was wondering if anyone had seen him lately? He usually calls me a lot, sometimes three or four times a day. But I haven't heard from him, and it's not like him to not call. I was just worried."

"I'm sorry," he answered, "but we haven't seen Dominic for a few days. If you want to give me your name and number, I will give it to him next time he comes in."

She took a pad and pen he gave her and put down her name and phone, then thanked him and left. When she got into her car she had an uneasy feeling that someone was watching her. She sensed, as women often do, that eyes were following her as she walked. She looked around, and made sure the car was locked and the windows up as she pulled away. Looking in her rear view mirror, she saw a car that might be following her out of the lot. She kept glancing into the mirror, finally running an almost-red light. The car behind her stopped and she pulled away.

When she walked from the covered parking spot in the rear of her apartment to her door, she found the whole experience of Dominic's sudden drop out of sight, and the sense of being watched, making her very uneasy. Her danger sense only went higher when she thought of Dominic saying something about being blackmailed. But she had no comprehension of the depth of the danger she had brought into her life. She went into her bedroom and pulled opened the second drawer of what used to be her mother's dresser. The file with the original documents was still there. She picked the phone to call the police, but then stopped. Dominic will call me soon, I'll wait. Then she thought of Kim. Just in case, I'm going to run these over to her. What if someone gets them and I can't put them back into the file, she thought, I could lose my job. She dialed up Kim, and as soon as Kim answered she said, "Not a lot of time to explain but I am going to run some papers over to you. I just want you to keep them for a day. I can't tell you now, but I just need to trust someone for a day. Dominic had me do something I am not proud of and now wish I wouldn't have done, but if you can just hold on to these, I'll pick them up from you by tomorrow. Please don't say no."

Kim could sense fear in her friend's voice. "Sure," she said, "I'm just about to jump into bed, how long will you be?"

"I'm leaving right now."

Kim knew that Brenda was less than a mile away, so she turned on her porch light and waited. In a matter of minutes Brenda pulled up, left the car running in the driveway, and ran up to Kim's door.

Kim immediately opened the door and Brenda handed her the sealed package. "Here, I don't know what this is all about, but I think Dominic might be in some kind of trouble. He needed these to stop a blackmail and I helped him get them, but I don't want them in my house. The police may search my house, that's what he said. I can't get in touch with him. I will get them in the morning. It's imperative that no one find them in my house. Don't tell anyone, especially not the police, please." She sounded and acted desperate. "I'll get them in the morning. Thank you so much, you are a true good friend."

"Sure, sure," Kim answered. "That's what friends are for, like the song, right?" She was trying to lend lightness to the strange situation with her statement, but Brenda didn't even seem to hear her, as she was back in her car and out the driveway. She yelled back to Kim, "I'll call tomorrow!" and left. Kim shut the door, wondering what the envelope contained. She took the envelope, opened the closet door, and threw the package on the top next to the seldom-used umbrellas, then went to bed. The reality of what she had agreed to do hadn't registered with her yet.

Brenda returned home, relieved to have the legal papers out of her house. She just felt better when she couldn't see the documents and, better yet, didn't have them in her immediate possession. She had no concept that Sal and the boys in Philly not only didn't like the idea of Dominic trying to cash in with his stupid scheme, but they wanted no one else to have seen them, read them or even know about them, in any form. It was one thing to have joined forces with the New Orleans crime family. But it had to stop there. When Dominic gave them back to Brenda, he might have well as put a knife in her heart. It was a fatal decision.

Dominic's crooked friend, Dizzy, didn't last long in the back room of the garage in south Phoenix. He was switching VIN numbers on a stolen truck when some local hired hoods of the organization found him. They let him know that Dominic was dead, and how he had died. Dizzy defended himself as best as his intelligence would permit. "Hey, I only helped him collect on some debts...nothing big." They told Dizzy he was going to die. They wanted to know all he could tell them about Dominic's girlfriend and anyone else Dominic had been dealing with or talking to in the last few days. They told Dizzy that if he was honest, he would die an honest death, He could say prayers and there would be no pain. If not he was going to suffer, and in the middle of that suffering he would wish he had taken the first deal offered. Dizzy knew they weren't lying. "I don't know much, really. Her name was Brenda James and she works at some law firm downtown. He met her at some bar. That's about it. He never really introduced me to her, and I only saw them together a couple of times. She was real good looking."

They wanted any information he could tell them about a legal file or Dominic going to New Orleans. "I don't know nothin' about what was in it, just some file he got. He was going to blackmail someone with it, he said. He flew to New Orleans and was just gone overnight."

"Do you know anything about his girlfriend taking any documents from her law firm for him?"

"Yeah, he mentioned it to me, but I don't know what they were or nothing about them. He never told me. Just that he was coming into some big money."

"Did you know why he was going to New Orleans?"

"Yeah, I gave him a ride to the airport. Said he had a big time meeting with...he called them the 'big boys'... said he was going to show them some papers. Said we would be moving there and then Cuba, if it all worked out. He mumbled something about he might be meeting with Castro's brother. I didn't know what he was talking about, just thought it was his usual drug deal. You know he was a big talker. I never believed half of what he said. He didn't have a lot of friends, but did have lots of women."

"Dizzy you've been honest with us. You deserve a good death." The tallest of the three thugs pulled a 22 from his belt.

"For what? I didn't do nothing...come on," he pleaded. "I didn't do shit with him."

"Get on your knees and start praying." Dizzy was still pleading; between sobs he started "Our Father...who...come on, I ain't done nothing...art in Heaven," he continued. The sound of the bullet was still bouncing off the inside of the garage wall when Dizzy's head hit the floor. Mercy had been granted. The three men walked out, with one more connection to Dominic and the file gone.

The boss in Philly hung up the phone after giving instructions for a hit on Dominic's girlfriend. They would take no chances on what she knew. "Pete wants no one to have any doubt about this. He said not to even ask the bitch for the documents. They got a copy from New Orleans. He figures she stored the originals somewhere. The accountants told him that even if it comes out, Kachina American Indian Financial is in the clear. He hates to lose the income, but we're isolated. They want zero chance that anyone goes public. He wants us to hit her in the head with a hammer, get any phone directory we can find, and get out fast. This could be messy, I've never been told to use a hammer; what the hell is that about? Let's go get this over with, shit, I'm getting out of this business, shit," he said again as they drove down the street and parked the car a block from Brenda's townhouse. Brenda did not know that a GPS tracking device had been magnetically attached under her car's frame, when she briefly stopped to ask about Dominic. The boys from Philly had located her home and actually had already had a duplicate key made from the one Dominic had given them in his pain. They were not in the least concerned about where to locate her without Dominic's help. The order to hit her in the head with a hammer was unusual, but like the good soldiers they were, they didn't question it. They didn't like it, but orders were orders. "Damn," Vince kept saying, "Pete really wants us to send a message on this one."

Brenda took a shower when she returned from Kim's and put on a terrycloth bathrobe her niece had given her. It was her favorite for that reason alone. She turned on the CD player, and Rachmaninoff started playing. She went over to her red lounge couch and turned on the table lamp. She set her Ann Lamont spiritual book in her lap and brushed her still-damp hair back with both hands. She was exhausted. Her thoughts were running between worrying about

Dominic and being angry at him for taking advantage of her. She knew she had to be up early Monday and get those papers back into Lewis' office. Why hasn't Dominic called me? She was tired and upset; the day's events had taken a toll. Spiritual books always made her feel better. She took the book from her lap and began reading.

Rachmaninoff by the Boston Symphony, with Van Cliburn at the piano, swelled over her like the sound of ocean waves. She turned the page. Then something made her turn her head.

CHAPTER 35

Frank is In Too Deep

Frank realized he was much closer to Fordham than even he had realized. It would take a long time for his loss to heal...if he ever did. The other problem with Fordham dead was a more practical one. With Fordham gone, he now had no one he could trust in the police department about the events in which he had now found himself involved. Even worse, he could now land (and rightfully so) in jail, charged with obstructing justice, concealing evidence and whatever else someone at the department might throw his way when it came out that he had been holding an envelope with legal documents that were—there was no doubt about this—crucial to murder investigations.

He had told Fordham by phone in one of their last conversations about the documents. Fordham had not yet seen them. Someone, somehow, knew he had talked to Fordham and John was killed for that information; of that Frank was sure. Frank knew by instinct there were no saved messages on John's phone.

Frank needed to tell Kim that they had to get clean on this, and right now, but who to tell and what to give them was an issue. He did know he wasn't taking Kim or himself into the police department. The situation was now that Frank was very much in trouble, and would lose his license and be arrested. Add that to the fact that his client was running, scared for her life. At least four people were dead, all connected by this case. How the hell he got into this for a lousy $1,500, was looking like a big mistake. The flip side was that his client was smart, stacked, good-looking, and staying at his house. Having that unprofessional thought at a time like this just pissed him off.

She was dressed in tan shorts and a red t-shirt, when he walked in his house. He sat down, looked up, and said, "We're not going to any meeting." Kim was surprised.

"The lid is off. Fordham would have had to put this info at the top of the pile. Everyone connected to the fine Mr. Lewis would be in line for a homicide investigation interviews. Now we are at ground zero. I doubt if Fordham told anyone everything, but he had to mention it to someone. I'm not good at lying to the police so unless you got a hell of good reason not too, I need to turn these over now to someone...the FBI, Attorney General, hell maybe the IRS will cut a deal for you and me. They are the most ruthless people I know. It's a foolish hope that whoever we go to won't ask how long I've had them, but that is like Dorothy wishing she was back in Kansas before the good witch showed up. It ain't gonna happen."

Kim was no longer silent. "Frank, my name and address will be out, plus how I got the file from Brenda. I'll never be safe."

"Well the good news is that when this comes out, whoever reads the paper is going to know you gave them to me and I gave them to the police and you don't have them anymore. So they will stop looking for you. Let's look for some luck on this...we need it."

"I hope it is just that easy." Kim replied. "But I'm worried about when and how this will end?"

Frank stood up and took her hand. "Soon, soon," he assured her. "Your friend got you into this. You got me into this. We are both going to get out of it. I'm not going to let anything happen to you."

She needed to hear that and pulled herself close to Frank, putting her arms around him. "I don't know what I would do without you." Her actions seemed out of place but genuine.

Even under these circumstances Frank hadn't felt a woman in his arms in more than two years. He could feel her hair against his cheek, and the fresh smell of her perfume. He hugged back. Then they both looked at each other and he kissed her. It was much more of a kiss then Dominic's first kiss from Brenda. It was a kiss that seemed overdue. He finally pulled back and felt embarrassed, as if he had crossed some imaginary boundary, or been caught doing something wrong. Instead she said, "I needed that. In case you haven't noticed, I like you, a lot."

Frank felt the rush one gets from that kind of information, which didn't happen often enough. He smiled back and said, "It's my turn to thank you. You have certainly brightened up my life." He paused and added, "To say the least." And with that a smile crossed his face.

Kim smiled back. With her arms still around his neck, she gave him another quick kiss on the lips and said, "I think you are going to be my hero, or knight in shining armor, which do you prefer?"

Frank answered, "Whichever one gets the most loving." She liked his answer and replied, "We will have to wait and see for that. Your job right now is—and I don't mean this lightly—to keep me alive so you can collect the reward."

"I will, don't you even get other thoughts about that. Get your purse. Let's go down to my office and see what Ferdinand left me. Then we'll call some governmental agency and get my ass in trouble."

They drove to Frank's office, and right under the coffee machine mat was the indexed file Ferdinand had left for him. There was a note on top: "Good luck, and don't call me for any bond money." It was a job well done, with highlights and yellow sticky notes. All was indexed in front, telling where and how each name was connected, the money involved, taxes avoided, and the unsavory information Lewis had kept on each investor. Frank was smiling when he showed it to Kim. "Only Ferdinand could do this. An 8th grader could follow this. First we find Lewis, and then we find someone to leave this with." Frank picked up the file and said, "Let's go."

An unpleasant surprise waited for them upon their arrival at Lewis' law firm. Frank and Kim learned from the receptionist that Sid Lewis, the senior head and one of the founding members of the firm, had turned in his notice and said he was resigning immediately for personal and family reasons which included his health. He was gone fifteen minutes after dropping off the resignation letter. He didn't even bother to clean out his office. The member attorneys, associates, and secretaries were "shocked."

He evidently wanted the community to know about it as well, as he had his firm give a press release to the local television stations and newspaper. It was hardly first page news, but he wanted to make sure it was somewhere in print and on the airwaves. Sometimes on slow news days, when space-filling material was needed, a retirement release of a local prominent person could get on the first page of the second local section. "Sometimes" was the key word. Lewis was lucky; it was a slow news day.

The law firm members joked that something must have happened over the weekend, because the last time most saw Mr. Lewis he was joking with the cute secretaries like he always did on Friday afternoon. He was trying to get one of them to go out with him for a drink and appeared to be perfectly healthy on Friday. He sometimes came across as the "dirty old man" of the organization, but was a failure at that as he was out of touch with the younger crowd, and his tired jokes and come on manner had been history long after Woodstock.

What the law firm members and the Arizona public didn't know was that Mr. Lewis had no choice but to retire. He had, that weekend, put his house up for sale, and planned to get out of town as quick as possible.

By the time the junior members of his old firm were contemplating the why's of his sudden departure, his home had a For Sale in front and his wife was on the phone unhappily arranging for a moving van with a storage center. Lewis had only told his wife that she had to completely trust him on this unexpected turn of events, that their lives were in danger, and there was no choice in the matter. And most important of all, she could only say, "It was an emergency," to her friends, neighbors, and whoever the hell else wanted to know, with no further information.

He didn't tell her that the last words from the Philly organization were that they expected to read about it in the paper and they would have a Realtor contact him about his house. Most importantly, their message contained a reference to a Biblical story: "Once you leave, don't look back or you might end up like a statue of salt," was said as the smaller of the two men had put his cigarette out on Lewis' oak desk. Lewis had already told them who he had discussed the file with and that included a local private investigator named Frank O'Hara who was working for a friend of the murdered paralegal from Lewis' firm. Mr. O'Hara, he said, "seemed to have more information then he revealed."

Mr. Lewis' secretary was told her job was over when Lewis called her Monday morning. He told her the file wasn't actually missing, and in fact the whole file was now a closed issue. She could get a $5,000 check for her loyal years of service, and a nice letter of recommendation at the front desk. The file was gone (stolen, according to Lewis) and he had no idea where the documents were. But the PI O'Hara had said he had a copy or even the original of it.

It was lucky for him that the organization from Philly believed, him, because he was close to having one of his hands jumping around in the parking garage next to his car. Or worse yet, listening to his wife's scream as the dynamite was lit under the rear side of her dress. Mrs. Lewis didn't know that her prominent attorney husband—a founder of one of the most prestigious law firms in Phoenix—had been visited by the same spokesman for Kachina and Indian American Financial, and was made to understand in very simple plain language and action that it would be better for his current business situation if he were to leave town as soon as possible after he transferred all of his interest to them.

As he was being told this in the sanctuary of his office late Friday afternoon, one of the well-dressed gentleman had picked up the picture of Lewis and his family taken during an Aspen skiing vacation ten years earlier, ripped it out of the frame, and began tearing it up and letting the pieces fall on his large oak desk.

They further told him that as far as he was concerned there were no missing papers from any file. In fact, from this minute forward there was no involvement of his firm in any casino deal. He had no idea what anyone who thought differently was talking about, and he should make sure he conveys that to anyone who asks. Just say he did some minor legal work, and didn't even write it down.

As they were leaving, the one who ripped up his ski picture turned to let him know that he must be a cheap ass hole, as his personal donation to Brenda's memorial account was very skimpy, and if he'd had any idea how much she liked working there, how she had to give up reading her last book just for the sake of his firm, he would have given more. Also, if they ever heard mention of the missing file from his mouth, the casino, or their visit, he should especially kiss his wife goodbye, then bend over and kiss his ass right after that. They left certain that Lewis understood and would comply with their request Lewis immediately started cleaning out his drawers.

When Frank had tried to see Lewis at the law firm that Monday morning and was told that Lewis no longer worked there, he was stunned. He pulled up what he could through motor vehicle registration and driver license records and called Norma to check assessor records, thus obtaining Lewis' home address. When he and Kim drove up to the house, they saw the for sale sign. Lewis' car was in the driveway. Frank rang the doorbell.

Sid Lewis was like the proverbial cat in a room of rocking chairs. He peeked out between the closed blinds in the living room and saw the red BMW parked behind his car. He went to the door and asked who it was. Frank answered, "Frank O'Hara. I need to talk to you."

"Get out of here," Lewis said, "I can't talk to you. Please go."

"Come on, open the door, what the hell is going on? I'm going to the police, open up. I need to ask you something first. It could be some help for you."

Slowly the door opened and Lewis said through the crack in the door, "You don't understand, just go. I don't know anything. I am not talking about anything. My wife and I are leaving tomorrow morning. I want nothing more to do with any of this or you. If I were you I'd shred the file you stole from my office and leave town immediately."

"Mr. Lewis, I only need to know who would have been interested in those files other than the investors. Anyone in the casino side, or the tribe? I've been there, left my card... not one person has called me back. Give me the name of someone you talked to, that's all."

The answer back unnerved Frank. "There was no file, nothing, no connection to anyone, I have no idea what you are talking about. Nothing, you understand. I am done talking to you." The door started to close, and as it did, he suggested that Frank should take "whatever you have and burn it; take a vacation, forget the police, forget everything...let it go." With that, the door slammed shut. The next sound was the dead bolt closing from inside.

Frank beat on the door but it was no use, Lewis had closed up shop.

Frank returned to his car, talking to himself. What the hell is this about? No file, what the hell? Kim was sitting in the front seat listening to him mutter. He finally composed himself and told her about his conversation with Lewis, finishing with, "Someone or something has scared the crap out of him and his memory. He now says there isn't any file and he's leaving town. What the hell is up?"

Frank rubbed his brow, "Let's go to my office and think this through. Damn, Fordham, you picked a hell of time to leave your old buddy."

CHAPTER 36

Things are Getting Out of Hand

The Godfather in Philadelphia liked the initial reports he got from Phoenix that Dominic was gone; it left a big lesson to others. His girlfriend, who unfortunately had gotten her nose in this, was also gone. It was messy, but quick, and she shouldn't have felt a thing. He was comfortable with that; didn't like the idea of her suffering. Like swatting a fly on the kitchen counter. He figured, with his smattering of religious background, that she must be up with God in heaven. Hell, if anything she should thank him someday. He made a mental note to make a donation to her fund, of course through someone else. Things were getting under control. He wasn't even that upset about having to cut his friends from New Orleans in on the Cuba deal. He figured he would need the help if it panned out anyway. He longed for the old days when you drove a truck in from Canada with some whiskey and sold it by the case for big cash profit. Now it was casinos, heroin, Mexican cartels, and street gangs. Damn, he longed for the old days. But, he thought, one thing hasn't changed...you don't get whacked unless you got it coming. Or, in the case of that young girl, walked into a place you were not wanted or welcome and there was no way out. They could never have her tell anyone about a file that they did not want public. Poor broad, she was dead the day Dominic asked her to have the first drink.

Lewis was gone, had left town. And all the investors had graciously renounced their investment, happy to get a little of their money back. Unfortunately one of them had a bit of a struggle with it and had to be dealt with; but all in all, he thought, it's turning out nicely. The casino deal is rolling along nicely. There will be no outside interference anymore, no partners who don't act grateful. It was turning out well, except for one small part. Who in the hell is this private investigator and his dumb broad client? He needed to find that out and deal with him. He knew they had the original file.

And don't forget that whoever got to that cop has to have a permanent memory loss. It would not be good to ever have that attached to any of this business. His intuition told him it had to be someone on Lewis' side. That suicide story had better hold up. Frank did not recognize yet that the Barnes listed as one of the payees in the file was the Lt. Barnes, Fordham's boss.

Pete "The Nose" took the call, and told Sam Benito not to worry, he was already on it and would "talk to the PI in a very nice way." He hung up the phone, laughing. They had already located the name and last address of Frank O'Hara. He was basically known as a guy who, lately, was down and out. Now he mostly chased ambulances and did some not-too-heavy insurance defense work, but at one time had a substantial practice. Not much else was known about him, and at best it was sketchy, but from the looks on paper he should not be a problem; maybe just needs to be roughed up. A bullet through the knee, or something like that. An out-and-out hit might not be necessary, and the organization in Philly and now New Orleans wanted no more heat after all the recent murders. They wanted things to slow down.

In addition, there were also those local crooked casino contacts. By Water and Duncan needed to know not to be talking, and may need to be reminded of why they don't do such things, but first things first. Find the PI and his client and get their mouths closed and memory dimmed. Give them a chance; if they don't take it, they vanish. With Cuba on the horizon they wanted no one around who could screw that up.

Their intelligence also learned from reading the file that there was a crooked cop named Lt. Barnes working for Lewis and they knew he was aware of the PI coming in to the station to see someone and turning over the file to the police, which was reason enough to have this cop Fordham whacked. They guessed (correctly) that Lt. Barnes had something to do with the cop's suicide. They wanted nothing to do with a cop killing. Talk about lighting a fire.

Frank and Kim walked into Frank's office, and he motioned for her to take a chair. He sat in the chair behind his desk, picked up the phone, and called Paul, John's brother. "Hey Paul, Frank here, got a name of someone for me?"

"Frank, no one I would trust and bad news for you. Lt. Barnes, John's boss, has a warrant issued for you that says you have concealed evidence and a witness in a triple murder investigation, and you are to be considered...get this wording...'armed and highly dangerous.' They're out looking for you, and don't put your hand in your pocket or they will be shooting to kill."

"Are you trying to tell me I might be the most popular kid on the block?"

"Something like that. And add your client. They have a name, Kim Dawson."

Frank's red flags went up." How did they get her name? I never even told that to John."

Paul answered, "I don't know, but Lt. Barnes wrote both warrants and hand carried them to the judge for immediate release. Best part...he has her listed along with you as armed and dangerous and 'will resist arrest.' Sounds to me like they don't want to bring either of you back alive. I'm sure he went through John's notes and voice mails."

"Well," Frank replied, "let's get him off our friends list. Now I know who the son of a bitch was who set John up for a suicide, and probably even ran the forensics people on it. How nice. He's going to fart real loud if he doesn't shit his pants first, once I find the right people to get this info to. Nice morning so far. Got the cops after me, and pretty sure the mob would like to find me. I have to think about all this, but first need to get out of my office. Fast."

While he was saying that he could see from his second story window a SWAT team exiting a van in the front of his office. He had a feeling they weren't here just to arrest him; he was sure there was a body bag in their van somewhere. "Got to go, call you later," he said, and hung the phone up before he got the last word out. The SWAT team was about to enter the building and up to his office. They obviously saw his red BMW in the parking lot.

He grabbed Kim's hand and pulled her out his office door and across the hall to Norma's office. He opened the window, and putting his hand gently over her mouth so she would get the message to stay silent, led her out the window to a six-inch ledge. They started moving slowly down the ledge to the office next door. Kim was petrified and pulling so hard on Frank's arm that she damn near sent them both over.

"What are you doing?" Kim whispered, petrified. Frank pulled her arm off his shoulder and placed his hand into hers. "Steady," he said, as they inched along. "Don't look down, there's a SWAT team on our ass." Frank said. They finally got to the window of the next office. Frank kicked the window in and, reaching up his hand to the lock, pushed it to the side and pulled the broken window up.

Frank's office neighbor was an insurance agent who was not so inclined to be Frank's friend, as his memory burned harshly with some big payouts in years past to attorneys who employed Frank's services. "Hey what the hell are you doing?" he yelled.

Frank went through the window bringing Kim right behind. He had the original copy of Lewis' file indexed in his tight clinched fist.

"Uh, locked myself in. Or is it out? Hell, I can't remember." He walked over and, knowing he would regret it, crossed the insurance agent's chin with a hard right fist that knocked him out of his chair and onto the floor. "Excuse us, but we're in a rather big hurry. I'll explain someday."

Frank led Kim down the back stairs and out a fire door that entered the alley. They ran toward the street to the rear of Frank's office building. Frank could hear the fire alarm screaming from the alarm tripped on the fire door. The SWAT team had not reached this exit yet. "The hell with the BMW," Frank said. "See that bus coming; run for it. Jump on it now. Frank was waving his hands so the bus driver wouldn't miss them. The bus pulled over and Frank handed the driver five dollars. "Keep the change. And if you don't mind, please floor it. We're about to miss a plane."

Frank's office door was kicked in and the SWAT team, with guns loaded and drawn, rushed in. They checked each room. "Clear," they shouted. "He's gone!"

CHAPTER 37

Frank and Kim Make Their Break

After switching buses and hailing a taxi, Frank and Kim arrived at the airport. He went straight to the rental car agency and said to Kim." I hate to do this to you but do you have a good credit card?"

"Sure," Kim said, and handed her visa over. Frank rented a sedan, had Kim sign her name, and they were out the door.

"Where are we going?" she asked.

"Not sure," Frank answered, "but we've got to find someone we trust. What we have is better than all the rest—the truth, my dear. And that has got to get us out of the gun sights of those who don't want us to have it. Or use it." He paused, then said, "We are short on time, as they will soon be checking credit card charges. We must get this original file turned over to some official agency. My best bet is the IRS. Nobody corrupts those guys and they so enjoy going after someone's ass. They will love to read it. We can deliver it; we'll wait for dark and slide it in there. Then head for the hills 'til the shit hits the fan...and hit it, it will. God how I miss Detective John," Frank said softly as he and Kim left the National car rental lot.

Lt. Barnes was not happy with his SWAT team. "What the hell do you mean, you missed him? I had his office staked out and we saw him go in. How the hell did he get by you? Issue a full pick-up on site and if he makes one move, shoot his ass."

The officers under Barnes were surprised by his order. "It's like he wants this PI shot and killed." "No, he's just warning us...he wants no chances taken."

Lt. Barnes' ass was in the cooker with Lewis and the rest of his crooked partners. He knew he could be connected, especially by Lewis if he broke and talked. He believed he could explain his way out of that connection, but he had no idea his name was in the missing secret file that clearly demonstrated he was in all the way, and being paid a tidy sum to help keep the casino deal and all the bribes that went with it running smoothly.

"I want him found now...and you can shoot if you have to" Barnes reiterated. He made it plain in the warrant that this PI was not only armed, but connected to the previous murders by the very fact he was hiding evidence and a witness, and failed to surrender himself, as well as the witness and evidence she had, as he had promised Detective Fordham. He also stated in the morning briefing for his officers to take no chances and to shoot if Frank's hand so much as dropped to his waist.

Before the room cleared after the morning briefing Lt. Barnes called out to patrolman Gazio. "Hey Gazio, hold on." Jack Gazio was Lt. Barnes' nephew and had had trouble getting on the force due to some juvenile crimes that appeared in his background check, which he had failed to disclose. Lt. Barnes went around and behind the system to get his nephew cleared for entrance to the academy, and ultimately a job on the force. He owed his uncle, and his uncle was calling the debt in.

"Jack, I want this guy dead." Lt. Barnes handed him a weapon. "Put this next to the PI once he's down, and don't let anyone see you. I don't care where, just clean it and get it next to him. You understand?"

"You sure?" Jack whispered.

Barnes reacted quickly, putting his face inches away from his nephew. "Damn right, I'm dead serious. My career and yours depend on it."

What he didn't tell his nephew was it was a pistol taken from Detective Fordham's house. He told forensics he would turn it in later; he just needed to run a couple of ballistics tests for use in the final investigation of the suicide. Basically no one in the department questioned him. They knew they had the gun that killed Fordham. If the lieutenant wanted to run some more tests on another gun, then so be it. If Gazio got caught, no one would believe him and Barnes would hang him out to dry. He had written in his report from Fordham's death that he had Gazio search Fordham's house, which wasn't true, but no one could deny it. He was putting a noose around Gazio's neck, in case questions came up.

This will add a new twist, Barnes thought, smiling.

CHAPTER 38

Hide Out

Frank and Kim drove to the mountains of Payson, Arizona, ninety miles northeast of Phoenix. Frank decided it would be a good place to hide and lay low until about ten PM when he planned on driving back to Phoenix to somehow get the envelope and file into the hands of someone at the IRS. He knew that wouldn't immediately end their problem. It would take time for the IRS to find the right person to start digging into the file and then pass it on for investigation for their criminal division. He planned on having his picture taken by Kim as he marked the envelope and got it into the IRS Building in Phoenix. He also was going to have a copy made at one of the local Payson grocery stores, photos taken of him mailing the envelope at the post office. He thought of an old joke; this will be much like the English Ambassador to Brazil who was cabled from his home in England that his mother-in-law had died and did he want her cremated or buried? He cabled back, "Both. Let's not take any chances."

Frank knew the police were looking for him and for sure an organized crime family. Phoenix was not a good place for him or Kim to be. "No shit," he said out loud after that thought.

Kim responded, "No shit about what?"

"You don't want to know. You just watch out for police vehicles and do not let me speed. I'll get us a room here with phony names. You got cash to pay? Remember they can trace your credit card."

She handed him a hundred dollar bill, saying, "Most men who would take me to a motel would pay for it."

"Real funny," Frank replied. "Just for that I'm getting twin beds. We need to stay here 'til after ten, and maybe a bit later, then go back to Phoenix. Even after we drop this off and mail it, it will be some time before the bad boys are picked up. Then we turn ourselves in, and we will be witnesses...and in the news. Got anyone you don't want to find you? Get Anderson Cooper's autograph for me, I've always liked his show. Oh and also Brooke Baldwin's phone number or Susanne Malveaux, either one. Don't mention my name. The IRS is always looking for me. When I die I want them to put on my tombstone, 'Don't tell the IRS he's here.'"

"Oh Frank, please be with me through all of this. Also, no chance on Ms. Baldwin's number or anyone else. She wouldn't be your type anyway. For starters, she wants someone who doesn't drip coffee on his shirt within fifteen minutes of putting it on. Or isn't worried about the IRS, and can pay for the motel room."

"Thanks, I was just starting to feel good about myself."

"Oh Frank, I'm teasing. Just have enough to buy her coffee."

"Funny," Frank answered. "For the first time in my life, I hope they do find me." He continued, "Don't you worry, I'm here with you, unless she calls. Want me or not, it's much too late to get out of this now. By the way I can always wear a dark shirt."

Kim, recognizing a jealous feeling for the first time, answered, "I would like to think it's because you now want to be with me, instead of just me being a client."

Smiling, Frank answered, "You know you had me the day I met you in the red sweater, and then telling me you liked my Indian decorations was the icing. I'm not going anywhere as long as I keep my Indian headdress and bow and arrows." He reached over and squeezed her hand. "And if I hadn't already spent it I'd give your money back." Kim squeezed back.

CHAPTER 39

Pull Off the Dogs

"Any word on that PI?" Pete "The Nose" asked.

"Nothing," his wise guy associate answered, "But we did get a reliable tip. The police have all points out for him. From what I hear, it's a shoot-first operation."

Pete responded, "Bet he's got that broad with him, and the file. We think he's going to turn it over to the police. The organization met, and it seems we're willing to let the whole thing go if we can get into the Cuba deal. We got people working on it now. Told them Lewis is out and Kachina Financial is now driving the deal. Frankly, I don't give a shit about that PI now that we got Lewis out. Call our boys off him; he can't hurt us.

One of the younger members of the crime commission said, "Hell, lets knock off Fidel ourselves and get this deal moving faster." He was quickly rebuffed by one of the older members. "We tried that with the CIA under Kennedy in the early 60's, and it didn't go well for anyone. Don't bring that up again."

Another older respected member added, "We wait, Fidel is knocking on hell's doors, won't be long now. Learning about the reopening of the Cuban casinos was the best thing to come out of all of this. We move the day after his funeral."

Frank and Kim had spent most of the time in the motel room talking. She talked about her childhood and how her brother got messed up on drugs and how her father tried all of his life to help her brother. Then they learned he had been sexually abused by a priest for more than a year around age thirteen. She told Frank how it really messed him up for most of his life and at the age of 38, still on hard core drugs, he took his own life by hanging himself in the garage at their home. Their mother found him when she hit the automatic garage door opener coming home from work. It devastated her entire family, it was especially hard on her dad who seemed to age ten years after his only son's death. She told Frank how the father didn't find he was abused until he read the suicide note his son left. The local diocese ignored it for the most part, and never once told her father they were sorry. The guilty priest had long ago died.

Frank didn't know it but his good friend Detective Fordham had kept that suicide note with the others he had collected.

The story of her brother pissed Frank off and he didn't have any trouble showing his anger. "You know the damn church has forgotten what Christ was all about. They need to make all the priests and bishops and hell, even the Pope and his cardinals, go back and read the Bible to find out what in the hell God had to say and taught about how you treat people. You leave the 99 to go after the one. You eat dinner with tax collectors and go out of your way to be nice to prostitutes." Her story reminded him of the problems he had with religion.

Kim replied that the worst part was that her dad was her brother's hero and her dad never forgave himself because he was the one who sent him to the priest in the first place.

Frank and Kim left the motel that night and started the drive back down from the mountains into Phoenix. He again told Kim to be on the lookout for any police cars, and to remind him of his speed...not too slow, and for sure not over the speed limit. Just right at 55 so they would attract no attention.

The conversation went into silence as they continued coming down the curvy road from the mountains into Phoenix.

The first stop was the IRS, where Frank hurled an envelope with the entire file in it over the chain-link fence. That was the best way he could get it to them without getting into trouble. The next stop was the downtown post office. Frank had Kim take a photo of him mailing the envelope to the FBI. He wrote the time and date on the outside so it would correspond to the photo Kim took.

Frank said, "That will have to do, now let's get the hell out of here for a few days. We need to wait for the news to get out before we come out of hiding. You like trains and oceans?"

"Yeah, but what's it going to cost me?"

"Well let me just say you need to have about a grand left on that Visa card...and that's eating cheap." Frank replied.

"You are damn lucky you met a girl who worked in bank and knew how to save money. Where are we going?" Kim asked.

"We are going to drive to LA, catch a train for Portland, Oregon and then I'm going to drive you to the Oregon coast and get you some of the finest seafood around. You ever eat Petrale sole?"

"No, tuna is as far as I've come."

"Well you are going to be thanking me after this meal I'm going to order for you, with a nice soft glass of red wine. I don't think I've ever enjoyed hiding as much from people who are trying to kill me."

"Not funny, Frank. Stay focused, and get us to the train. A sleeper car with two beds, I gather?"

"Of course, and you get the top bunk. Much more comfortable up there."

Kim was quick with her reply, "You don't snore do you?"

"Don't know for sure, it's been so long since I slept with anyone close enough to complain about it...but if I do you can kick me, okay?"

CHAPTER 40

Everyone Leaves Town

Lt. Barnes was still grumbling because they had not found Frank. He was even more upset that Lewis had not returned any of his calls. "I killed a cop for that piece of shit," speaking low to himself, "He'd better get back to me." He called the law office and was stunned to hear that Lewis had abruptly resigned. He knew some of the other players, especially By Water and Duncan. He signed out and told his assistant he had to run to the capitol.

When he got to the capitol he found Duncan's office and was told he had resigned from being the tribe lobbyist. He had left abruptly, like Lewis. He was also told that By Water was still chief, but didn't have anything to do with the casino. Some new company had taken over.

"When did all this happen?"

"Duncan said it was too much trouble, so he resigned and took his family on a long cruise somewhere. Didn't say where, just that he would be gone for a few months or more. Happened real fast," the office manager told him.

"I'll bet." Barnes knew that something had happened. He had no idea what, but it was not good.

He called back to his office and ordered the homicide sergeant under him to run Kim Dawson's credit report, get all of her banking information, and run all of her credit cards. He knew, without being told, that she and PI O'Hara were together. He also wanted the same information on Lewis. He knew Lewis was the only one who could connect him to the murder of Fordham and he was determined not to let that happen. He soon learned that they found a car rented by Kim Dawson parked in LA at the airport.

It didn't take long before he was called again on his private cell and told that Lewis had purchased gas in Flagstaff, Arizona. Barnes called his office and said he had some unexpected family problem and would be out of contact for the rest of the day. "Keep checking on Dawson and O'Hara." He took his wife's car and drove north on I-17 to Flagstaff.

Barnes knew that Lewis was keeping his location secret from everyone and was on the run. He had heard Lewis speak of having sums of money in different banks, so financially it was not going to be a problem for him to get out of the country. He pulled into Flagstaff at dusk. He knew where he believed Lewis would stay. Only the best, it was The Little America motel, which had several buildings. He drove slowly around till he found what he was pretty sure was Lewis' Lincoln Continental. The personalized plates that read, "S L ATTY," were a giveaway.

Barnes went to the office and walked up to the young girl working the front desk. He was aware that his questions as well as his face could be picked up from security mounted video cameras. For that reason he wore sunglasses as well as a baseball cap with a fake mustache and hooded sweatshirt, and purposely bent over in an attempt to confuse detection should the film they contained be examined later. "Hi, I'm supposed to leave a message for Mr. Lewis, he should be a guest here."

She was very polite," Yes sir, let me look." She took some time going through the registration book. "I'm sorry, I have no Lewis registered."

"Thank you. He might not have arrived yet. I'll check later." He was purposely vague as he knew they were likely to interview this young girl later. As he left he pulled the hood of his sweatshirt up over his head keeping his head down.

Barnes went outside as though he was leaving. By now it was dark. He pulled his car up across the lot from Lewis' Lincoln. He would wait him out. It didn't take long before Lewis, along with his wife, came out to get into their car. It was a completely dark and moonless night.

Barnes immediately approached Lewis and said, "Sid, I need a word with you. It's very important." Lewis was taken aback. Barnes was the last person he expected to see.

"What are you doing here?" His wife was sitting in the front seat of the car. He walked over to her.

"I'll just be a minute. I need to talk to this man he's an old client of mine. You wait here."

"What are you doing here?" he asked again, as he walked toward Barnes who was standing outside his open car door.

"What the hell are you up do, resigning and not letting me know? Duncan is gone, and I need to know what is coming down. I don't want my ass being pulled into something. You have got me into some deep shit. I took Fordham out for you. You're leaving my ass to take the fall?"

"No, no...it's just that some things happened. I don't know how to put it." Barnes cut him off.

"How about just saying what is going on...that's how to put it."

"The control of the tribe is under new management. It happened rather quickly. I didn't have time to call you." Lewis sounded like a man starting to plea for his life.

"By who?" Barnes asked. "Who has that kind of muscle?"

"I'm not sure, but it wasn't friendly, if that helps you to understand. It was organized crime. Your name was never mentioned."

"What about the file on all of this...and the homicide? Speaking of which, who knows about Detective Fordham?"

"No one, I promise you!"

"I'm having trouble buying that. You left without a word to me. You're not even registered here. Using a different name, house up for sale, I found out. You know I'm not going down on a murder rap for you."

"No, I would never let that out. You know I would never be a part of that."

"Like hell you wouldn't. You get a plea deal and I'm gone."

At that moment Barnes knew he had no protection. He also knew Lewis would be the only one to finger him for the murder of Detective Fordham and he had caught Lewis running away from something. He knew Lewis too well, as a man who would turn in his mother if it meant saving his own ass.

"No...never!"

It was too late and not convincing. Barnes knew he had to protect himself. It was good that Lewis had registered under a fake name.

Barnes pulled out a 22 pistol with a silencer. He aimed it quickly at Lewis head. Lewis had no time to react. Barnes pulled the trigger at the same time putting his arm around Lewis to hold him up. He opened his rear door and set Lewis onto the back seat. Lewis slumped over. The bullet had entered just above his left ear, and he was dead instantly.

Lt. Barnes exited the lot with Lewis' wife still sitting in the front seat of her car listening to the radio and waiting for her husband to return and take her out for Mexican food as he promised. She didn't notice the man her husband was talking to even leave the parking lot. Being a moonless night and her having poor eyesight helped Barnes leave unnoticed. There was no one who saw or heard the shot.

Barnes was twenty miles away before Mrs. Lewis got out to see where her husband was. It took another twenty minutes before the hotel clerk called the police to report that "a woman lost her husband. No, not dead...she says she lost him."

The police were not in a big hurry. A wife call on a missing husband was not at the top of the "needs immediate attention" list. When they finally got there and listened to her story, it sounded like he just left with this stranger she didn't know. They told her to relax and he would be back. There were no immediate alarms set off by anyone other than the worried wife.

Barnes was almost back to Phoenix at midnight when he came to the construction site he knew, with a large hole dug for an eight-acre golf course lake. He pulled off the interstate and drove on the gravel construction road as closely as he could, careful not to leave any tire tracks in the mud. He pulled Lewis from the back seat, pulled a spade from his trunk, and dug a hole approximately in the middle of the golf course lake, as wide but not as deep as a grave. He knew it would all be under water in two to three days. He carried some big rocks over and covered Lewis' body in the hole, then filled the hole in. He had emptied Lewis' pockets and taken his watch, his wallet, and the receipt from the hotel so that if he was found it would take some time to identify him. Barnes' next problem was getting rid of the car with the blood all over the back seat and floor.

CHAPTER 41

Still on the Run

Frank and Kim boarded the train in LA It would be an all day and all night ride in a small sleeping car, getting into Portland the next afternoon. They sat across from each other with the drapes pulled to give them privacy.

"Ever travel in a sleeping car before?" he asked.

"No," Kim answered, "but it sounds like you are real experienced."

"Experienced enough to grab the bottom bunk."

"At least I feel safe. How long do you think we need to be gone? Or, as you say, when is the 'shit going to hit the fan'?"

"Well the IRS will have someone looking at it hopefully within a day, and when they get ready Lewis and his friends will be hauled in. I'm sure we will see it on the news. From what I read in the file, and what Ferdinand laid out, there are some Congressmen, and a Senator or two who will be hauled in as well. I figure after it breaks we can make a call and they will be happy to see us. Give it a week. Until then, enjoy the Oregon coast, the great seafood and my amazing companionship."

"We've got a few hours on this train. Let's talk about how glad you are that I called you to help me."

"Glad may not be the best word, but I'll admit I've had some clients that didn't look anything like you. I'm not sure yet, but I think...I might miss you when this is all over."

"Really?" Kim replied with raised eyebrows.

"Hey, have I ever told you anything less than the truth? You know I've told you all about my lost loves and heartbreaks...what about you? Now there's an area of discussion that should take some time. Let me know what I should do if I want to keep you smiling."

"Frank, I must be honest. You are a little old for me. I may or may not get past that. You're making me pay for our getaway trip. I know I'm your client, so I shouldn't say too much about money to someone who is saving my life. You are, without a doubt, the strangest man I've ever snuck out of town with. And yes, I find you to be very interesting... so maybe when this is all over, and you can afford it, we could have dinner. You have to wear a dark suit and a dark shirt to hide the spots that will undoubtedly appear during dinner. But security is important to me. As for any past loves...I've had a few. Never came close to getting married, but someday hope to. I'm pretty particular. You do make me smile, and that's important to me. Let's leave it there for now, and you can escort me to the dining car. I'm famished."

"Follow me and order anything you want. I'll get the meals." He neglected to tell her when you ride in a sleeper the meals are free.

The rest of the trip was a delight to Kim. The scenery of northern California, along with Frank's stories about some of his past investigation capers, seemed to make all the turmoil of her past week slip away. She did find herself very much enjoying his companionship. Riding through California along the coast reminded Frank of a case he had worked on some years before. Frank shared that adventure with Kim, about a client who had lots of money and owned a hotel on Catalina Island, and had hired Frank to do some work on an investment that he had been sold. In a nutshell, he gave some "gentlemen" five million dollars to buy a small used ship which was supposedly going to be used to haul food and supplies, as well as other equipment, back and forth from the California coast to the oil rigs stationed far offshore out in the Pacific. He flew Frank to his hotel on Catalina where he gave Frank a box of legal documents to go through. His client had not heard from his "partners" in a week and had no idea where the ship he purchased was.

Frank spent two days going through the documents and decided the first thing to be done was go to Houston, Texas, to speak to Shell Oil who wrote the contract for the services to be provided by this five million dollar ship. Frank left the next day for Houston. It took only an hour to discover that no one at Shell Oil knew anything about this, and had never seen the contract. It was well done fraud, but it was unreal. "Slick" was Frank's word for it.

The false contract called for Frank's client to provide the necessary funding of five million for an 18.5 million dollar contract to be paid by Shell Oil for three years of performance. The contract between Frank's client and these "partners" called for a 50/50 split of the 18.5 million with the partners paying back Frank's client 75% of the ship's purchase out of their initial half of money. Frank flew back to California to inform his client of the unfortunate news. The client wanted his ship back, but first it had to be found. Frank, using all the documentation he could locate, found documents that clearly stated his client was the owner of the ship

Frank next notified the Coast Guard who, after a few days, contacted him to inform him that the ship was in Seattle where it had refueled. By this time his client had prepared legal documents to give to the Coast Guard, to give them legal authority to seize the ship.

Frank flew up to Seattle to deliver the documents to the Coast Guard authorities and left feeling comfortable that his client might not get his five million back, but at least he was going to get the ship his money had purchased. Unfortunately, that optimism was short-lived.

Frank received a follow-up call that the ship had left the Seattle port after refueling and before the Coast Guard could seize it. The ship was now in international waters and the documents to seize it were not valid unless it stopped at an American port. Frank was told the Coast Guard, as a matter of courtesy to Frank, would keep a watch out and monitor the stolen ship.

About two weeks had gone by before Frank heard anything from his contact at the Coast Guard who informed him that the stolen ship had docked in a port in Japan to refuel. He was also told that he needed to call someone in authority in Japan to assist him in this ship's recovery. Now the paperwork was beyond Frank's expertise. To get to the end of this caper Frank cut through all the details and told

Kim the end of the story was that the ship had been sold to some Japanese freight company.

Frank's client was livid upon hearing the news. 'How the hell can they buy my ship?"

"Don't know," Frank replied, "but somehow they did." Five years went by before Frank had a reason to call this former client about another case he was working, and in the course of the conversation he asked, "Whatever happened to your ship, did you get it back?"

"Not yet. I've spent more than four hundred thousand in legal fees on attorneys here and in Japan, but I'm not stopping." Frank thought, if only people did some good research before handing over a five million dollar check. There are some big scams going on out there. Some with such knowledge have said," The bigger the scam, the easier it is to pull off."

They finally arrived at the Portland train station. It reminded Kim of a scene out of an old World War II film. All it needed was some soldiers and women with white hankies drying their eyes.

They only had carry-on luggage, so they stepped down from the train, and Frank led Kim to the street and transit train, which would take them to the bus depot. He didn't let Kim know, but he had some worries. They couldn't rent a car, because her credit card could be traced, and she couldn't use it for a shuttle, for the same reason. Frank asked, "You still have some cash?"

"Not after paying for the train. I've got a twenty and some ones."

Frank went to a phone booth, and called Norma on her cell phone.

She answered immediately. "Frank where are you? The police are looking for you and a rough-looking guy who was NOT a bill collector came by the office."

"It's not important; just don't give out any information. Tell them I'm dead if you have to. Listen closely. I need you to wire me $200, by Western Union. It's for...uh, need a name...make it for Bill Norton. And tell them I'll need a certain code, as Bill Norton has no ID. So make the question be what is Bill Norton's step-father's name? The answer is Clyde. They'll do that. Now don't send it to an address, just the main Western Union in downtown Portland. Do it immediately. The cops will be on it soon enough. I'm sure they have Kim's credit card info, but by that time we will be out of here."

"Who's we? You got Kim with you? Just in case you don't know it yet, they have warrants out for both of you."

"Yeah she's with me. I dropped some documents off with the IRS, as well as mailed them to the FBI. As soon as they start making arrests I'll be back. Keep your eyes on the news. You can't call me, but I'll be okay. Get that money sent now."

Norma answered, "Do I add this to my check that you are now three weeks late in paying? Don't answer...I just will. It's on its way. Frank, please be careful. The paper this morning said that Lewis disappeared from a hotel in Flagstaff. Said he was with an unknown party. His wife was waiting in their car while he talked to the man, and he never returned. Paper says they don't know what to make of it. He was registered under a false name."

Frank took a few seconds to respond. "He's no longer with us, I'm sure. Keep your eye on that story. I'll get in touch with you in a couple of days." He hung up and waved back to Kim.

"Get your twenty out, we'll get Starbucks. Norma, my secretary, is wiring some money. We need to find a Western Union close by and then get to the coast. By the way, there's an article in the paper about Lewis disappearing into thin air in Flagstaff. Seems he left his wife and was either forced or drove off with a stranger. My instinct tells me he's on a one-way trip. All the more reason for us to lay low."

"Frank, I'm getting frightened again." She took his hand as they crossed the street and entered the Starbucks.

It took an hour but the money came, and the ruse about not having ID and the code question worked. After taking their cut, Western Union handed Frank $170, then they were back at the bus station where Frank purchased two one-way tickets to Cannon Beach. Once they got there, he had a close tie in with a hotel right on the beach, the Inn of the Four Winds. He had stayed there many times before and they would let him register under an assumed name and hold the bill for a few days. He knew he could be found, but he also knew it would be difficult and was going to take some time.

CHAPTER 42

Time for Everyone to Run

Lt. Barnes drove his wife's car to the Indian reservation on the outskirts of Scottsdale. He had purchased a five-gallon can of gas on the way back from Flagstaff. It was a moonless night. He pulled the vehicle off in a remote area and then poured gas all over the inside off the vehicle. He pulled a two-inch candle and placed it on the front seat of the car. Carefully he lit it. He had previously called his nephew Gazio who was waiting to pick him up. The fumes would soon blow the car up and then the gasoline would do the rest.

They had barely pulled away when the fumes hit the lighted candle. The car exploded in flames. Even as dark and remote as it was, Lt. Barnes knew it would be found soon. But he also knew that cars found burning on the reservation were not an unusual event. He had his wife, who knew no differently, call her car in as stolen. He told her it wasn't outside when he left. He hoped all traces of Lewis would be gone before the police and fire department from the tribe arrived. It was close to 3 AM, so the late hour would be some help.

He didn't tell Gazio there was recently a bleeding a body in the car. He did tell him if he wanted to keep his job he was to tell no one about picking him up or about the burning car. He also asked about O'Hara. "Any word on that crooked PI and his client?"

"Only that we haven't found him yet. Homicide is running everything. His car, her car, her bank accounts and credit card, and we got a warrant to tap his office and home phones. Same with hers. We're also checking cell phone records. Just got the warrants issued last night so they are ready to go."

Barnes was not happy. "What the hell took so long? You should have had those going yesterday"

"Prosecutor didn't have them ready till just before four, and then we had to get the judge to sign them."

"Well stay on top of them and let me know the first break we get."

"Will do. Say, do you know that Lewis, that attorney, was turned in by his wife as missing?"

Barnes, acting surprised, said, "No shit? He'll probably turn up."

Fazio dropped him off in front of his house. His wife had been married to him too long to ask any questions but one," Did you forget and leave the keys in my car?"

"Must have, or they hot-wired it."

The IRS was in its second day of going through the file Frank threw over the fence. It was initially hard for them to believe it wasn't some kind of a hoax. Fidel's brother meeting with a Phoenix attorney in Costa Rica. Kickbacks from phony charity organizations. The casino repaying a building loan that wasn't through a government-regulated company. Local Phoenix city council members receiving cash payments for votes on water rights. Congressmen and senators being paid to help reopen trade to Cuba for the singular purpose of Americans obtaining gambling rights to future casinos after Fidel died...a fact he was not going to be happy about. Cash sent by a Phoenix attorney representing a group of investors through the Mexican Consulate in Costa Rica to give to Fidel's brother, Raoul. These same investors neglected to list income, obtained legally or not, on their tax returns going back, in some cases, six years. The name of a Phoenix police lieutenant who had received monthly payments as a consultant to Lewis Law Firm, which was also unreported on his return.

There was too much to cover for one day. The next day there was a whole floor of the IRS going through it. Washington had been called and was sending agents out to the Phoenix office. The U.S. Marshals were placed on alert. Like Frank predicted, "the shit was about to hit the fan."

Frank woke up early, as he always did. It was another of those things that came with age.

He looked out at the beautiful ocean on the overcast day, stretching his arms over his head. He had rented a suite and Kim had taken the room to the rear. He made coffee on the machine provided with the room, and turned the TV on to CNN to see if there were any stories originating out of Phoenix. He kept it low, not wanting to wake Kim. They had arrived after sunset and she did not see the ocean. He expected her to be blown away when she walked out and got her first look. He had planned to take her for a hike later in the day, and to the stores downtown, which he figured was every woman's pleasure. He planned to buy a good book and wait outside while Kim shopped and looked at all the tourist knick-knacks and expensive art stores.

Kim came out of the back bedroom a little before ten. She had her robe provided by the hotel on and had only brushed her long dark hair. "Frank, why didn't you wake me? It's almost ten. I can't believe I slept so long." Then she looked past Frank who was sitting on the second story patio outside the room.

"Oh my God in heaven...how beautiful is that?"

Frank motioned to a chair next to him. "Here, sit down and I'll fix you a cup of coffee. Cream, right?"

"Yes. Frank, this is simply stunning...and hardly any people. I see you have the news on. Anything up yet?"

"No nothing. It will be all over the news; we won't miss it. The water is very cold, so you don't find a lot of people swimming, even in the summer. It's a great beach to walk on. As soon as you're ready, I'll show you the sights and we'll get some lunch at Duggar's. I insist that you try some Petrale sole, pan fried."

"Okay. But I also want to walk on the beach. I can see why you like this place so much."

"Well relax and enjoy it; we could be here a few days. Don't answer the phone and don't you use your cell phone. We're registered as Mr. and Mrs. Hernandez. I stay here a lot and they will cover for me. They'll also let me know if anyone is calling or looking for me. They'll deny that O'Hara is here. I don't think anyone could track us from Portland. But I have friends who know I like this place, so there is a remote chance someone might talk to one of them, and Cannon Beach could get mentioned. We can never let our guard down. But no worries today. I'm guessing in a few days the nice people at the IRS will be looking for us too, but that will be in a good way. You'll be pleased to know that they'll probably pay our tickets home."

"Well outside of getting my coffee and putting me up on a beautiful beach, that's the best news I've heard today. Answer me honestly...you'll let me know if things go bad?"

"Hey did I walk you down that ledge and kick a window in for you?"

"Yes. And knocked out your office neighbor."

"What better answer can I give you?"

Kim stood up and said. "Give me twenty minutes to shower and get dressed." She then kissed him on the cheek and walked back to her bedroom.

It took Frank less time. He had already showered. Now he shaved, and waited for Kim in his yellow sweater. She finally appeared. There was a worried and apprehensive look on her face.

"Frank, I need to tell you something that might be an issue. I wasn't thinking when I did it. I'm so sorry, but I called my sister last night to let her know where I was. I didn't think of anyone being able to check my cell phone, and still find it hard to believe they could. As soon as I hung up, I told her not to tell anyone. I only spoke to her less than a minute. I also knew I had to tell you."

Frank, obviously upset, immediately inquired. "What exactly did you tell her?"

"Just that I was okay."

"Did you tell her where you were?"

"Just safe and in Oregon...that I was with you and you were taking care of me."

"Well, I'll bet the warrant covers your cell phone calls, and now you've added your sister to the list. I feel bad saying this, but it was a stupid thing to do. Your little comfort phone call has most certainly put our lives in danger. It doesn't make me happy but I appreciate you telling me. We're going to have to assume they will either find us through phone records, or from your sister. You may not give a shit about your own life, but I still got some living to do. We can't stay here now. Get your stuff together. I'll check on a bus that can get us to Seattle, and either you throw your cell phone—turned off—into the dumpster outside or I will."

"Frank, I really am sorry. It was a stupid mistake. I didn't realize."

At the same time Frank was finishing his admonishment of Kim, Lt. Barnes was being informed that they had received a hit on Kim Dawson's cell phone. He was told they traced it to a phone tower in Cannon Beach, Oregon. It covered the whole town. They also traced the call to a phone in Denver, Colorado. It didn't take long for them to identify that the call was made from Kim to her sister Helen.

The "organization" in both New Orleans and Philadelphia also had pulled Lt. Barnes' name from Lewis' secret file. They knew Lewis had at least one crooked cop on his payroll along with the rest of his nefarious partners and bribed officials. They didn't like publicity and preferred to operate in the shadows of their endeavors. They knew that this file was in the hands of others who could bring such publicity. In a lengthy phone conversation, the two crime families made a decision to back off. They felt that having their hands in the running of the Arizona casinos was too good of a deal and they knew, like Frank, that the "shit was going to hit the fan." They didn't want their names connected to the four murders they had ordered, since there was a very good chance they all would be connected to Lewis. Time would show they were correct. They guessed correctly that the PI, Frank O'Hara, would turn the files over to some authority. Just knowing that Fidel's brother had an interest in bringing gambling back to his island was good information. They weren't sure what Fidel would do, if he didn't send his brother to a grave for dealing behind his back; they knew he or his brother wouldn't be around much longer in any event. It was agreed they would stop all activity and sit back and wait to see what dictated their next move. They knew there was no connection to them in the file. Kachina, or Indian American, was a legitimate casino operating company that paid its taxes. Lewis and his friends may well bring an examination of this company which now held total control. A call was made to Brad Pasqualuchi to clean up all records and bring in some smart accountants immediately to fix all the books. They told him Kachina and Indian American were about to be examined by the IRS. They also knew that none of the former members could do much. They were buried too deep and there was no record of them turning over their shares. They had all been making illegal and unreported taxes for too long. They decided to let the PI have his run at turning them in. Brad and his wife were told to get out of town. Brad's wife had a smile on her face as she packed and called the moving van.

They called Pete "The Nose" back to Philly. "Send word to Vinnie and Sal to lay low, maybe take a trip to Florida along with the two who took care of Dominic." It was a damn shame, they all agreed. But the smart business move right now was to get out. No heat is good heat; it was time to shut down, sit back, and wait for Fidel to have a nice funeral. Until the Lewis file they had no idea they could get back their once-flourishing casino business in Cuba. All in all, things could work out nicely for the "organization."

CHAPTER 43

It's Jail Time

Lt. Barnes, with his nephew Fazio, caught the first flight to Portland and drove the rental car to Cannon Beach. They had called before leaving Phoenix and the police chief in Cannon Beach had been notified that he had a suspected murderer, along with his female witness, in the area. He was faxed a copy of the warrant for Frank and Kim with photos from their drivers licenses, along with a detailed description of their alleged crimes. The police department in Cannon Beach only had a staff of five, and this was not something they were prepared to handle. The chief of police assigned two of his most experienced patrol officers to assist Lt. Barnes upon his arrival. They also began to check all the motels and hotel in the area.

Kim's sister was contacted by the Denver police department. She knew her sister had nothing to do with any murder and "told them she was in fear for her life." She told them a PI named Frank O'Hara was only protecting her. She also told them her sister and Mr. O'Hara were on the Oregon coast. But she did not have any more information, other than that her sister felt protected by Mr. O'Hara who had been helping. She gave them the date that Kim had flown back to Phoenix, because she knew that Mr. O'Hara had picked her sister up. The Denver police relayed all the information to the Phoenix police department.

Frank and Kim took a taxi to Seaside, Oregon, a town just 10 miles north of Cannon Beach. They got dropped off at the local shuttle terminal which would take them back to Portland where they could get a bus to Seattle. Frank knew they were on someone's radar. He checked the paper for any news about the IRS going after some Phoenix residents. There was nothing. Damn, he thought, what is taking them so long? He told Kim to stay seated while he waited outside. He could smell the cops coming. He hoped it would be the local boys in blue. He did not want Barnes involved. He knew there was a chance Barnes would not be all that interested in taking them back, except in body bags.

It was quicker than he expected when a Seaside, Oregon blue and white pulled up. He wanted no games. If they had to be arrested, then these were the right cops to surrender too. He was prepared to have them call the IRS. He doubted they would right away, but that's where he was going to start. Then he'd use his phone to call the best criminal defense attorney in Phoenix and tell him to get his butt up to Oregon immediately. He walked up to the first officer. "You are looking for me. The young lady is inside. We will not resist. But I want this to be in your arrest report, that the officer coming here from Phoenix is crooked and connected to an illegal organization in Phoenix. He would like to see both of us dead. You will note neither of us is armed. We are peacefully giving ourselves up. I also do not want to be left alone or placed in this Phoenix officer's control. I wish to immediately be allowed to call an attorney in Phoenix and ask to be taken before a local judge for arraignment immediately. Neither I nor the young lady will agree to be extradited to Arizona. I also want you to call the FBI or IRS in Phoenix and tell them you have us. Believe me they will be happy with that news."

The arresting officer had never encountered a speech like that. "Turn around and place your hands behind you. I have a warrant for your arrest."

They then entered the bus terminal and Kim, seeing Frank, stood up.

Frank said to her, "Don't say a word. I've spoken for both of us. Let them cuff you and be peaceful. It's going to be okay."

Kim did as Frank told her, but then tears started. Frank felt bad, but also resisted reminding her that this was all because of her damn phone call.

It only took minutes before Lt. Barnes was told they both had been found and were being brought to jail in Seaside. Lt. Barnes had the Cannon Beach chief drive him and Fazio there. "I need to talk to both of them, and would prefer to do it alone. Can you arrange an interview room for me? Oh, and I'll need a tape recorder. Bring in O'Hara first."

The chief answered, "I think we can arrange that, but you know it's Seaside jurisdiction."

Frank was placed in one cell and Kim was placed in another. Lt. Barnes walked in. He spoke into the Seaside officer's ear. "I need to interview him if he'll talk to me.

Can you get me alone with him in an interview room? I'll need him cuffed."

"No problem, but you'll need to leave your service revolver outside."

Barnes pulled his service revolver and handed it to the office. As he did so, he said, "I'll read him his Miranda rights. You got a recorder?"

"Yeah." He handed Barnes a recorder.

"I don't want this videotaped."

"No problem, there isn't one working in that room. Got smashed last week by some mentally disturbed person who thought we were aliens. Still waiting for the city fathers to okay a new one."

Barnes was well-muscled from his daily weight lifting. His shirt looked tight on his torso. He was 41 years of age and in top condition. Most criminals were intimidated by his size alone. He stood over six feet, four inches, and weighed a taut 260 pounds. Frank, at five feet, ten inches, and 180 pounds including his stomach paunch, was no match.

The door was opened and he walked in to find Frank handcuffed to a chair sitting behind a table. Frank was not intimidated. "I'm not talking to you, period. I want an attorney immediately."

Barnes set the recorder on the table. He purposefully showed Frank it was turned off.

"Didn't hear a word you said. I think you're an old man who has lived too long." He leaned over and put his face just inches from Frank's. "You have caused me a lot of trouble... and I am going to see that you don't cause me anymore."

Frank was still silent.

"You know, you're a has-been PI. Your little girlfriend is over in a cell by herself. I'm going to be a little harder on her, if you know what I mean. I'll enjoy being alone with her."

Frank now responded. "You piece of shit. You have no idea what Lewis wrote about you in his little secret file that the IRS now has. You are heading down. Send me a card from prison and I'll have $5 put on your books for extra smooth toilet paper."

Barnes smacked Frank in the face with his open hand. "You show respect."

Frank turned back his cheek bright red from the blow. "Turn on your recorder and let's talk."

Barnes was not fooled. "Tell you what I'm going to do. I'll take your cuffs off, and then you are going to make a break for it. And even if you don't, I'm going to throw your ass on the floor and say you attacked me, and then I'm going to put you into a police choke hold until your lungs stop sucking any air." Lt. Barnes ripped his shirt in the front and messed up his hair. He then took his badge off and took the pin from the back. Staring at Frank, he put the pin to his chin and dug it in hard enough to draw blood. He then reached down and took Frank's right hand and stuck the pin into his finger while twisting it at the same time. Frank's finger was bleeding profusely. Barnes then wiped some of Frank's blood on his shirt, then slowly took off the first of Frank's cuffs. It was the one holding both hands down.

Frank jumped up, and ducking under Barnes' swinging fist, beat on the interrogation room door. "Help!" he yelled. Barnes recovered and quickly had Frank in the choke hold.

Frank could still use his feet and kicked the door, praying they would hear it. Barnes was cutting off Frank's air. Frank kicked the door again. Still no help came. He took his free right arm and reached up trying to scratch or at least poke Barnes' eyes.

They were both spinning in the room until Barnes tripped Frank and got him on the floor. The pressure on Frank's neck increased. He could no longer breathe. With his free hand he reached for the table trying to get some type of leverage. He kicked the chair and knocked it over.

At last the door opened. The Seaside officers rushed in, not to help Frank but to grab him in an attempt to help Barnes who they evidently didn't notice had complete control.

"We got him lieutenant, you can let go." But Barnes was not about to let go, until Frank was no longer breathing.

"We got him...we got him!" the Seaside officers yelled again.

They could now tell Barnes was not letting go, and Frank was going under. The initial officer who arrested Frank remembered what Frank had said. He grabbed his revolver and slammed it against Barnes head. "Let him go now!" He then swung again.

This time the blow was hard enough to make Barnes release his grip. As he did so he said, "Son of a bitch was making a break for it. Said the cuffs were too tight, and I was trying to be a good guy and loosen them, then he attacks me."

The Seaside officers lifted Frank up. "Get him some water. You okay?" they asked Frank.

Frank, not able to talk yet, nodded his head yes. He was gasping for air.

The Seaside officers pulled Barnes from the room. The one that hit Barnes with his service revolver said, "Looked to me like you were trying to kill him."

Barnes appeared indignant. "Bullshit, it was the other way around. I'm just glad you guys got in when you did. I was afraid to let go of him, especially with you guys having your weapons. Look what he did to my shirt." As he was talking he wiped the blood from his chin. "He could have killed me."

The Cannon Beach police who had arrived just moments prior said to Barnes, "You need to fill out a report on this."

"No problem," Barnes replied.

The Seaside officers both agreed that they needed to take control. "Listen, we've called our chief, and we are going to ask you to go. Your officer too," pointing at Fazio. "This fellow told us when we arrested him that he wanted to call his attorney, so we are going to grant him that. I'll read his Miranda rights." They took the unused recorder from the floor where it fallen when Frank kicked the table over.

Barnes and Fazio left with the Cannon Beach Chief of police. Barnes knew he had missed his chance. He was also pondering the comment about his name being in the file Lewis kept. He knew Frank had given it to some authority. The bad news continued. Barnes got a call on his cell riding back with the Chief. "Barnes here."

"They found your wife's car, burned out on the reservation. They also think they found blood in the back seat. Plates were gone, but we were able to get the VIN number. Homicide is on it. We've had the car, or what is left of it, pulled in. Forensics is going through it. They already stated that an accelerant was used. You might want to call your insurance company. It's no longer listed as a missing stolen vehicle. I'll keep you posted. Good news they got that PI. Nice job, Lieutenant."

Barnes was guessing, rightly so, that Lewis never had his DNA pulled. If they did manage to find anything in the burned out car to run DNA on, it would not help them. He knew he had covered his ass on this one. He also felt comfortable with the Fordham murder. There were plenty of witnesses who would say John was depressed. His fetish for keeping suicide notes was standard gossip around the station. Adding in the facts that his own service revolver was used and no other prints were found would make it difficult to send his death in any other direction then self inflicted.

He blindly thought, so what if my name is in the Lewis file? I was a consultant. They can't prove otherwise. It will be uncomfortable at best, he hoped.

CHAPTER 44

Lunch in Jail

Frank made his call to an attorney he had worked for in Phoenix. He explained his current situation, leaving out as much detail as possible. He said there was a lot more he could tell him, but for now he and his client were being held on "obstruction of justice, concealing evidence in a murder investigation, and as possible murder suspects." He also told his attorney friend that soon some news was sure to break which would be very beneficial for both his client and himself. Meanwhile they were both going to fight extradition back to Arizona. Frank told the attorney that the Seaside jail was a safe place for both of them. He just wished he could get them to bring him some Petrale sole for lunch. His attorney was going to call the Seaside court and see when the arraignment was scheduled. He told Frank he and his client should just plead not guilty to all charges, and tell the judge they refuse extradition. Also, not to worry about bail, as neither Frank nor the girl had that kind of money. The attorney would get back to him.

Frank was in agreement with all of the advice. He asked the attorney to call the court and arrange to talk to Kim and let her know what was going on. He knew she had to be worried out of her mind. The police had confiscated their luggage which had the Lewis file underneath Frank's boxer shorts packed loosely at the bottom. He didn't mind the Seaside police having control of it. He asked to talk to the officer who saved his life.

Within fifteen minutes, Officer Cunningham entered the small cell block and stood outside the bars, keeping Frank locked up in his five by ten feet cell. Frank started by thanking him and telling him that, whether he wanted to believe it or not, Lt. Barnes was trying to kill him. "I trust you. Right now you are all I have. I need you to get my luggage and pull out a legal file and hold it as evidence. Under no circumstances should you let Lt. Barnes see it, read it or have it. It's crucial evidence in a matter that is soon to put him in jail and blow the top off Arizona politics. That girl you have locked up is my client and I am a licensed PI. I've been one for many years, probably before you were born. We did not kill anyone. Soon the file you will be holding will be requested by the IRS or FBI. It is the original of a file sent to them. Please don't question me on this. That's all I can tell you. You will soon know the truth of it all."

Officer Cunningham was young, as Frank perceived. Also, he was as honest as Frank thought. A cop the people needed who had wanted to be a police officer since grade school. "Okay I'll do that. And no one else besides our prosecutor will see it. If he says it is evidence, then it's locked up and will not be given to another jurisdiction unless they go through the courts, which I can't stop. But until then, you have some time."

"Thank you," Frank said.

Officer Cunningham turned to leave. He stopped and said, "You doing okay in here? Anything you need or I can get you?"

Frank smiled and said, "You've got all my money, but I assure you I'll pay you back. Any chance you can go to Duggar's and get me and my client a Petrale sole lunch?"

Cunningham smiled. "I'll see what I can do." He turned and left the area.

He returned in two hours and delivered Frank and Kim the requested lunch, with a note attached to Frank's: "This is on me."

CHAPTER 45

The Shit Hits the Fan

Federal marshals showed up at Lewis' law office early the next morning. They had warrants issued by the federal court for all documents and financial transactions with the local tribe. Also, taken into custody in Washington DC, was Arizona Senator William Castillo and Arizona Congressman Gerald Doran, with warrants were also served on their offices for all financial documents...warrants so broad that their attorneys were quickly filing motions to stop what they termed was a "fishing expedition" in the production of documents requested.

In Phoenix, with the exception of Lewis (who couldn't be located), each and every one of the parties named in the file were picked up from their homes and offices, as well as two from the seventh hole on the golf course of the Tomahawk Country Club.

As Frank predicted, CNN and some other networks picked up the story, and before the day was out it had been leaked that these people had plans to build a casino in Cuba and had actually met with Fidel's brother. Fidel was very unhappy, and of course his brother denied everything and referred to the story as Capitalist lies. He said he met Lewis in Costa Rica to talk about getting the ban lifted on exports. He said Fidel was very sick at that time and he had simply forgotten to tell him. After all, it was Fidel who put him in charge. For now Fidel believed his brother, simply because it was easier.

It was a field day for news outlets as more and more documents were released, and soon arose the murder of Brenda James who was believed by all who searched through the file to be an innocent victim of these parties. There was no mention of the Mafia as of yet, but the warrants for Kachina and American Indian Financial were not going to be issued until the following day. Lewis had done a very good job of keeping his personal hidden file. It literally was on its way to taking down many in high Phoenix society. Several wives were as unhappy as Fidel when they learned their husbands had mistresses and "favorite hookers" they visited frequently.

The IRS was preparing audits for more than 35 of Lewis' cohorts. Duncan and Chief By Water also had warrants out for their arrest. The feds were writing subpoenas faster than they had since the Bernie Madoff case. When the Department of Interior contacted Kachina and Indian American Financial for a request to see their operating agreements and union contracts, they also advised them that they were very interested in how they obtained controlling interest just three weeks earlier without evidence of paying anyone for it.

And Frank was sitting in the Seaside jail eating Petrale sole and enjoying the knowledge that back in Phoenix the shit was hitting more than just one fan.

Officer Cunningham came up to Frank's cell pushing a portable TV. "Hey Frank, thought you'd be interested in the news." Bingo, there it was. Arizona and national corruption at all levels of state and federal government. This was big news, and it had gone national. There was even a story about how the police and federal marshals were trying to find Lewis. By this time, the local story was all over the news saying that Lewis had set up his own disappearance to avoid prosecution.

Frank knew it was just a matter of hours until the IRS or FBI came to get him and Kim. Phoenix police still had some homicides to deal with; that of Brenda James, Lewis' former partner who was killed at the golf course, and of course Dominic Serrano. They had no leads on any of them. Frank knew they never would, as those were professional hits. He would tell that to the FBI but even he could not explain any connection other than Lewis and his file, which contained no underworld connection or reason for why they would want to kill for it. Frank reasoned correctly that their only interest would be in running the casino, and getting into Cuba's door before Lewis and his friends. He knew they had taken out Dominic and Brenda James, but he couldn't prove any of it. As for Lewis' partner...hell, Lewis could have ordered that just like he had probably ordered the hit on John Fordham. Lewis had wanted no one to see that file, but his ass had been in the cooker much earlier than he knew. And Frank doubted he was alive now to care. Frank thought through the past couple of weeks' events as he sat in his cell.

Frank knew Barnes had been there, or at least knew who had shot Fordham. Brenda was killed simply for meeting the wrong guy at happy hour and working for a crooked lawyer. Frank knew she had stolen the file. It was wrong, he thought, but hell he had done much worse. She just wasn't smart enough or wise enough to see through the punk Serrano Lewis's friend was a greedy businessman, that's why he died.

Frank knew he had to find John's killer. Not just find him, but get him convicted.

Officer Cunningham walked in and unlocked John's cell. "Frank O'Hara, there's someone here to see you."

Frank followed him out to the small foyer of the Seaside police department. Kim was standing there with two men dressed like they worked for IBM.

"Oh Frank" she ran and through her arms around him and kissed him on the lips. Frank was a bit taken aback, and couldn't resist his first words: "You must have really liked the Petrale sole."

"Frank, I'm so glad to see you. I heard you got roughed up by that Phoenix policeman."

"That's an understatement. Let's leave it with I'm glad to be here to get that kiss."

The taller of the two gentlemen standing behind Kim spoke first. "Mr. O'Hara, I'm Agent John Robertson with the FBI." He reached to shake Frank's hand. "And this is Richard Ballinger with Internal Revenue."

The second shorter man reached his hand out. "It is a pleasure to meet you Mr. O'Hara."

Frank responded, "I haven't heard that in quite some time."

Ballinger continued. "We, as I'm sure you know, received the documents you dropped off. We also have now in our possession the original Lewis file. We have quashed all warrants for you and Ms. Dawson. We have detained Lt. Barnes, who is under arrest and being sent back to Phoenix where he will be booked. To-date we have made 22 arrests, thanks to your diligence in getting a copy of the file to us. We would both like to debrief you and Ms Dawson. We have questions regarding your roles in obtaining the file. Who you spoke to about it and who else, if you know, may have copies of it or seen copies of it. Do either of you have any objection to that?"

Frank had not forgotten how to negotiate. He hadn't shaved in two days and he knew his body aroma was not as nice as he liked. He didn't believe that even the Polo aftershave he usually sprayed on each morning would be much help. "Do you mind if we both get a shower, a change of clothes, and maybe a couple of hours to enjoy freedom first? And do you mind doing this after we get a meal of Dungeness crab? You know this area is famous for it. We will be much more cooperative and happier to work with you." The agents looked at each other. Both nodded in agreement. "Where are you staying? We will be glad to give you a ride back. Then say, pick you in three hours to interview you at the Cannon Beach Police Department?"

"Sounds perfect," Frank answered. "How about you Kim, sound okay?"

"The shower part sounds the best."

Frank continued, "You've got a deal gentleman. There is one small issue, which I'm sure the United States

Government could take care of. We did not pay for our room yet, and I've maxed out this poor girl's credit cards. Can you handle that for us?"

"Ballinger, you have a problem with that?" the FBI agent asked.

"Not as long as I get a receipt." The IRS always wanted receipts.

"Okay, Mr. O'Hara, let's get both of you checked out of here and back to your hotel."

Frank and Kim signed for their confiscated luggage and money. Then Frank asked to see the Seaside Chief of Police, whose office was a short distance down the small building hallway.

The Chief came up. "Mr. O'Hara, you wanted to see me?"

"Yes, I just wanted to tell you that Officer Cunningham saved my life, and that he should be promoted as soon as possible. I'll be very disappointed if I learn he isn't. As you can see, I have some real important friends." He pointed, as he spoke, to both the FBI and IRS agents in their meticulous suits, shined shoes, spotless white shirts, and ties.

"Mr. O'Hara, I'll make sure your recommendation gets noted."

With that, Frank, Kim and the two agents headed out, and Frank and Kim were soon back at their Cannon Beach Motel. Three hours and fifteen minutes later, Frank and Kim were giving statements to the IRS and FBI agents in separate and small interview rooms at the Cannon Beach police department.

Frank told how he had initially been hired by Kim. He started with their first meeting at Denny's and took the agents detail by detail up to the time of their arrival at the Oregon jail. He showed them the photograph of him mailing the file to the FBI as well as the photo of him throwing the envelope over the fence at the Phoenix IRS building. He told them of his strong belief that Fordham had been murdered, and told them why he thought that. He told of his meeting with Lewis and told them why he thought Dominic and Brenda James had been murdered by professionals. He believed that Brenda James had given the file to Kim on instructions from Dominic, who must have known someone from a crime family organization was trying to locate it. He told them he was certain Dominic was going to sell it to some crime organizations and had evidently reneged on the deal as Fordham had told him they found the body with its hands cut off.

Kim's story was much the same. She told how Brenda had called her frantically wanting to leave something at her house. How she said she would get it the following morning but had never came. She told about not wanting to tell the police about it and then deciding she should, and at that point hired Frank to assist her. She told how her apartment had been ransacked. How she flew to Denver to see her sister. How she flew back to meet Frank and was going in to see Detective Fordham the next morning and give the file to him. She told of taking the train from LA. to Portland and making the mistake of calling her sister in Denver. But she knew her sister was worried, and felt a short call to tell her she was okay would be okay.

The interviews lasted four hours and Frank and Kim left nothing out. One question Kim couldn't answer was the last one when the FBI agent wanted to know if she and

Frank were anything more than a working relationship. She paused and said, "Sometimes I think so, but I really don't know. He has protected me and taken care of me, and I have grown close to him. But in all honesty, I can't say one way or the other. Have you asked him?"

"Yes. His answer sounds just like yours. Except he wasn't sure if he named the right ten songs...does that makes any sense to you?"

CHAPTER 46

The Net Is Closing

The wheels of justice were on a fast track. Kachina Freedom and Indian American Financial were soon suspended from the Arizona Corporation Commission and the Internal Revenue Service had confiscated all financial records of both corporations. Lt. Barnes was out on bail the following day. He was ordered by the court to not leave the city, call in twice a day, and not carry any firearms. His future looked bleak, as he was placed on leave from the police department pending the outcome of the investigations. It was highly doubtful he would ever have a badge again. He was, according to how much was learned and proved from the Lewis file, looking at some serious prison time. He was listed as a consultant by Lewis in the file, but so were all the congressmen and senators. They all received payments that were not listed on their tax returns, payments in cash that were listed by Lewis as too large to ignore. One doesn't just receive $75K in payments in one year and forget to note such funds on one's tax return. Unfortunately for them, Lewis had them sign receipts for each payment. It was part of the covering his own ass process that Lewis rigidly maintained.

Barnes was the only one who knew that Mr. Lewis would not be talking to anyone. He had a few knots in his stomach when the department decided to reopen Fordham's death. This was after they had read Frank's interview and his insistence that Fordham was going to meet him the morning he was found dead in the driveway of his condo garage; that Frank had been having daily conversations about the Brenda James murder with Fordham and was bringing Kim and the file in to give to Fordham that morning.

It was well documented after Fordham was found dead and thought to be a suicide that Lt. Barnes had had a conversation with Fordham the night before and that Fordham had told Barnes, as his superior, that O'Hara was bringing in some girl who was his client and some documents she had that were relevant to the Brenda James and Dominic Serrano murders. Barnes had told Fordham he wanted in on the meeting. Several others in the office had heard him make that request. The FBI agent, after interviewing Officer Cunningham concerning the fight in the cell he had broken up by hitting Lt. Barnes, and reading the report Barnes had been required to fill out, was highly suspicious of Lt. Barnes. This was even before they had the complete breakdown on Barnes and his involvement with Lewis.

There was still an all-points bulletin out for the arrest of Lewis. His wife insisted he had made no mention of meeting anyone. She also said that they were in a hurry to leave, but she didn't know why and was as shocked as everyone else at his resignation and decision to leave town. Her last statement was that no, she hadn't heard a word from him.

The police were pulling all of Lewis' banking and telephone records. They were also interviewing all of his employees at the law firm. They were going through the tribe's file and comparing all transactions to the original secret file Lewis had maintained. The police now agreed with O'Hara that the file was taken by Brenda at Serrano's request. She obviously thought she would return it before it was noticed missing. But for who Serrano was getting it was still unknown. All agreed it was a blackmailer's dream.

Kim and Frank were given airline tickets on Southwest back to Phoenix. Norma picked them up and gave Kim a ride to her place. "You'll be okay now, but call me at any hour if you need to."

Kim gave Frank a hug and looked at Norma. "Is he always this much fun to run around with? No, you don't have to answer. Frank I'll be fine, and I'll give you a call in the morning. It's all over the local and national news about the file, and me not having it. That makes me feel a lot better."

Frank exited the car with her and walked her up to her door, making sure she got in. He walked in first to check all the rooms out. "Okay, talk to you tomorrow." Then to Norma on the ride home, Frank looked over and said, "No remarks about her...nothing, okay? It was strictly business."

"Right, Frank, why would I think any differently?" Norma replied with raised eyebrows of disbelief.

CHAPTER 47

The End of Vinnie

It's not very common for a lifelong wise guy who becomes a made member of a crime family to find in his later years that he indeed has a conscience. But it became clear to Vinnie that he was troubled by the thought of his last assignment. Hitting that young girl in the head with a hammer had never left his mind. He would wake up in the middle of the night thinking about it, and sleep would be gone until the following night, when the process was likely to repeat itself. He also was rediscovering the thought of a power in the universe greater than the Godfather.

He was drinking more than he ever had and was avoiding all of his usual hangouts. His small circle of friends had noticed the changes in him. His hands were shaking, he was seldom seen smiling, and more than not, he stayed home becoming a wine drinking recluse. At one point in the middle of one of his lonely and sleepless nights, he got on his knees and asked whoever was listening to forgive him for taking that young girl's life. He had read the papers and knew finally the reason she was killed. No one had stolen from the organization. He didn't feel bad about others he had eliminated. They were in the business and understood the rules. But this young girl, he thought, she just happened to do a poorly-planned favor for a man she thought she loved. He knew and felt he was being watched. So far other than the corporations being shut down and removed from the administration of the tribe there was no connection to the crime family. Someone growing weak like Vinnie could change that.

He was sitting home one night looking at maps of the Florida panhandle, searching for a place to go after he turned in his notice and told the Philly Godfather he was done. He heard the doorbell ring. He got up and looked out the window next to the locked door. It was Sal smiling at him and saying, "Just dropped by to see if you were okay. Boys say you don't come around much anymore."

"Just a second," Vinnie said. He walked back to his room and picked up his 32 caliber pistol,

He made the sign of the cross and said softly, "Lord this one is for you." He had no illusions as to why Sal was at his front door, as he hid the pistol behind his back and opened the door. Sal took two steps inside the door and Vinnie pulled up the 32. Before Sal even saw the gun, the bang of the pistol sent a slug straight into his forehead. Sal was dead before his head bounced once from the impact into the floor.

Vinnie got down on his knees looked up and mouthed, "Sorry about that young girl and the hammer." He wasn't sure, but he hoped someone was listening. He the put the pistol inside his mouth and pulled the trigger again. The top and back of his skull were blown out and, like the spots from the hitting hammer, had splattered his blood on the wall and floor behind and above him. He fell over face first. The police would find both bodies less than three feet apart. Maybe if Vinnie's mom had known his last thoughts, she would have been proud after all.

Frank had faith that God has His own way of working out the little paths in life which, at the time, we know nothing about.

CHAPTER 48

The End and the Beginning

The FBI was hot on the investigation of Lt. Barnes. They were going through the debris of his wife's burned out car, and had pulled some floorboard underneath the back seat carpet. It was sent to the FBI lab and sure enough they were able to pull some DNA from it, but there was no match in the database. They knew, though, that Barnes was crooked and had been so for some time and they had little doubt— but also little proof—that he was trying to kill Frank up in the Oregon jail. They also now believed that Fordham was no suicide, and believed Barnes had some part in Fordham's death.

Lewis was still missing, but the FBI located his son, a street alcoholic who was still fighting sobriety and gambling, living in a shelter. They asked for and obtained a sample of his DNA and within a week had confirmed that it matched the DNA found in Barnes wife's car. There were only three possible conclusions: One, that Lewis was randomly bleeding in the back seat of Barnes wife's car; two, that he somehow stole the car and was killed in it and someone took his body out; or three, that he got into this car at the Flagstaff hotel and was murdered, with his body was transported in the back seat.

The FBI were locked onto to number three, as the car belonged to Barnes wife. When Barnes was told they had identified the blood as belonging to Lewis, he was stunned to learn Lewis even had a son. Lewis was not the type to speak about a son who had, in his eyes, been a weak failure living on the streets. Barnes knew they were slowly building a case against him, but at least they didn't have a body. Two agents were on their way to Flagstaff to interview the desk clerks and pull any video they could locate that might show Barnes was at the hotel the night Lewis disappeared.

Barnes could feel the heat, and went to the bank and pulled all the money out. His bail was set at $250,000 and his wife had put up their own home and her parents' home to cover the bail bonding company request. Barnes had little thought of their loss as he drove from the bank to a small airport in Mesa, Arizona. He got on a budget airline plane nonstop to Des Moines, Iowa, using a fake ID that he'd had since he worked undercover ten years earlier. He had kept the dates current. It wouldn't be until the following day that they would find him missing. The first call the bail bond company made was to Frank O'Hara, as a PI they had used many time in the past years to help them locate someone who had skipped bail. They rarely sent anyone else.

"Frank, Rudy here from Garcia Bail. Got a jumper who I think you know. Lt. Barnes from the Phoenix PD. I know you can find anyone. You still in business?"

"Rudy, this one's for free. Fax me everything you've got on him. I assume you notified the police and FBI as well.

They will not be happy about this guy ducking out. We can use all the help available."

"I called them to report it after he failed to call in this morning. We sent someone over to his house and his wife says they hadn't seen him since yesterday around noon. The FBI are checking the airlines, buses and all the usual. I told them I was also calling you."

Frank hung up and dialed Kim. "Good morning, I hope." She answered knowing it was Frank from the caller ID.

"Not to worry you, but I wanted to let you know Barnes has jumped bail. He shouldn't be bothering you. But just in case anyone has an idea we don't know about, keep your door locked and don't answer your phone if you don't know who it is."

"Oh no," she answered, "will they find him?"

"If they don't, I will. I know he is not going to be looking for a home here."

"Frank you've done enough. Stay out of it, please. Let the police take it from here."

"This son of a bitch killed Fordham. I'm not going to let him miss out on finding justice and cleaning up the shit he left. If I play it right the police will take care of it for me."

"I can see there is no talking you out of it. Just be careful and please keep in touch. I'll be very worried if you don't call."

"Promise. I may be gone for a bit. I don't know where yet, but I will call you."

He hung up and then began reading the information faxed over by the bail company. Frank was going to contact Barnes' nephew to see what he knew, but he got bad news. Officer Gazio, the nephew, had resigned from the department the day after Barnes was arrested, and there was no lead on where he went or where he was going. Gazio took his wife and son and left town, knowing with Barnes gone he would be fired anyway. Gazio also knew he could never have killed O'Hara. He was glad his uncle was gone, and he planned to lay low as long as he could. He abandoned his house and literally left everything, even money in his bank accounts, with no mail forwarding. He and his family were heading to California, with no city in mind.

Frank knew that Barnes would have used fake identification. He also knew it was common for officers who ever worked undercover to have a set that was foolproof. He contacted the agents from the FBI and IRS who had come to Oregon to get him and Kim out of jail. They were aware that Barnes had skipped bail.

Frank asked them both to use their connections to find out what undercover IDs Barnes had been issued in the past, and then run those ID's on all auto rentals, airlines and bus services leaving Phoenix. He told them they would have been used yesterday. The FBI had already learned he withdrew all the money from his savings and checking account. It was a tidy sum built up from the years of working for Lewis and not paying taxes on that money. He left town with a little over $97,000.

It didn't take long for the FBI to share their information. He had undercover ID that had been in storage since his third year on the force, currently under the name of Cedric Revis. It had been used to purchase a one-way ticket on a regional carrier that left the Mesa airport at 1:20 PM. yesterday. The plane flew straight through to Des Moines, Iowa, and landed at 4:00 PM their time. He was next picked up renting a car from Nationwide. He'd said he was in town for a funeral and would be returning the car within a week, and used a fake credit card in his undercover name to rent the vehicle. The Des Moines police department was alerted, as was the state police. Unless Barnes moved fast, they would have him soon. Frank wanted to be the one who nabbed his ass.

Frank caught the same airline and was in Des Moines the next day. He had a copy of an arrest warrant and bail bond papers, and was able to get the young girl at the Nationwide rental counter to give him a copy of the rental agreement with the make and license plate of the rented vehicle. He got some maps to see where in the hell he would go if he were Barnes. Then it hit him...straight north to Canada. There are areas above him in Montana and Minnesota where you can simply drive across the border with no check points. It was his best shot at getting out of the country. He would be able to steal or obtain Canadian ID illegally. Then, who knows, eventually Europe, Frank thought. The guy who assassinated Martin Luther King got out of here and all the way to England, and Barnes was a hell of a lot more sophisticated then that guy.

He would switch plates on the car, and travel only at night, which meant he would be at a motel within 150 miles north. A motel with parking in the rear. There was no sense checking the roads in daylight. Frank didn't bother calling the local police or his new friends at the IRS or FBI. He wanted to take Fordham's killer dead or alive by himself. Frank had to remind himself that he didn't carry a gun.

He started driving north, taking back roads and staying off freeways. Every time he came upon a small town, he would search out motels with parking spaces in the rear and go inside showing his warrant and information from the bail bond company. The desk clerks were cooperative, and would go through the registration for the past 24 hours checking the name and type of vehicle Barnes had rented. To most it would seem like searching for a needle in a haystack. For Frank it was simply following tracks in the snow. He knew how Barnes would think and act. It was those 30 years of experience and that second level of thought in operation. Frank's brain was playing boogie woogie.

He continued driving north on back roads and continually stopping and checking motels. When he stopped for the 16th time in the 7th city he got the prize he was looking for. "Yes," said the clerk looking at the driver's license photo and the arrest warrant. "A man fitting that description checked in here early this morning. Said he was driving at night as he could make better time. He only wanted the room till nine tonight, and paid in cash." He showed Frank the registration and gave him the room number. As Frank thought, it was his alias. The clerk was getting ready to dial the local police when Frank stopped him.

"Let's make sure first. I don't want to bother the poor guy if he's not the one. I'll walk back and check it out...give me five minutes." Frank walked slowly back to the rear of the motel. He checked the cars parked in the spaces in the rear, and found it three spaces down from the rented room. The drapes to the room were slightly open, so one could see out without anyone seeing in. The lights were out.

Frank, keeping out of sight as best he could, went to the rear of the vehicle. He unscrewed the tire cap on the right rear tire. Slowly and methodically, using his car's key, he depressed the stem and slowly started letting the air out of the tire. When he felt it was low enough to hinder driving he crawled to the left rear tire and did the same. This vehicle was not going far or fast with two very low back tires.

He went back to the office and told the clerk to contact the local police but to let him speak to them first. He then used his cell phone to call his new friend at the FBI who had taken his interview. Finally he called the bail bondsman. He let them both know he had found Barnes.

The local police finally showed. No sirens or lights as Frank had advised. He showed them all the paperwork he carried on Barnes jumping bail and being sought by the FBI as well and they have been be notified. He told them Barnes was a former police lieutenant who was certainly armed and would not go down easily. They should expect a gun fight. He let them know he had disabled his vehicle. He also told them he had an idea how they might get him out of the room. He said, "This guy hates my guts and would love to take me down. I'll call him. Convince him I'm alone. And see if he will agree to come outside to meet me."

The police turned him down. "Too dangerous, if what you are telling us is true. Let's wait him out. He's got to eventually make a move. Or try and get him to surrender."

"Okay," Frank replied. "But if I tell him that he can turn himself over to me you'll get him outside quicker." By this time the FBI had called and said they were sending agents by helicopter from Des Moines.

Frank wanted Barnes now. He asked the clerk to ring his room before the local police could stop him. The phone in Barnes' room was not answered immediately. Barnes could see when it was from the front desk. Finally he heard, "Yeah what do you want?"

"You," Frank said. "I'm here for the bail company and I'm all alone. I knew that's the way you would like it. Just you, me, and the memory of John Fordham."

"You know where I am, come get me." Barnes replied with a menacing tone.

"Doesn't work like that. You can look out your window and you will see me waiting. I'm unarmed. I'll need to cuff you and then let's go back peacefully. If you don't want to do it that way then I call the locals."

Barnes said sarcastically, "Frank O'Hara, the has-been PI, trying to make a name for himself again. Stand outside my door so I can see if you really are alone."

"I'll be next to your car. Again, I'm unarmed. I didn't think a cop would want to risk a murder conviction."

Barnes hung up. Frank looked at the local PD and said. "He'll come out, and he'll try to shoot me. So I'm relying on your pistol range scores. When his gun comes up you shoot. He doesn't need a second chance."

"You don't think we should we should give him a chance to surrender?" the youngest of the local small town police asked.

Frank was firm. "I'm certain this guy killed a cop working under him in cold blood, and he tried to make it look like a suicide. He's running from a warrant. He's also been crooked since he took his oath. Save us all the trouble. If he raises his gun you shoot his ass. He won't be taken alive. No one is going to complain, trust me." Frank, with the two locals, walked back to the rear where he took a position behind Barnes' vehicle. The two cops with weapons out were crouched down behind him.

"Hey Barnes, I'm right here," Frank yelled. The drapes to the room parted slightly for just a second. Next the door opened and Barnes stepped out in boxer shorts and a blue t-shirt.

"You actually think I'd let your sorry has-been ass take me in?" With that, he raised his 38 service pistol and fired at Frank. The bullet hit the top of the door Frank was standing behind, barely missing him.

Frank ducked down behind the car as the two officers jumped up still thinking there was an easier softer way. One yelled to Barnes, "Drop it!" The other one took Frank at his word and aimed his Glock service revolver. Barnes got another shot off and barely missed the officer who had yelled. The other officer kneeling behind Frank fired twice, and he was right on the mark. Two bullets hit Barnes, one in mid chest and one in the shoulder. Barnes fell back and then to the ground. He moaned just once and then fell limp. He was dead. Frank walked up the stairs, bent over the dead body, and said softly, "That's for you, John." The local police called for an ambulance and called in the shooting. It was a search that ended as Frank hoped it would. His ears were still ringing from the gun fired just above his head. The young officer behind him asked if he was okay. Frank smiled and answered, "Couldn't be better." He called the bail bond company, and homicide at the police department. He agreed to come in for a debriefing in the morning.

Frank called Kim from the Iowa airport and asked her to pick him up when he got back into town. He told her briefly what had happened and about Barnes death. She told him how worried she was, and that she would be there. His flight was smooth and on time. He walked outside and Kim was standing by her car in front of the terminal. She ran to him and threw her arms around him. He held her tight and said, "Well, it's over for both of us. You are safe now."

"I'm just so glad you're back…do you think I can stay over at your place?"

"Sure, you know where the bathroom and towels are."

"What are your plans now?" she asked.

Frank smiled and answered, "You and I are coming into a little money. I have been told the IRS has a reward for us for alerting them to tax cheats. I gather it's about 75 grand each. I think that you were my last case. I was thinking on the plane on the way back that I'm going to take my share, go back to the Oregon coast, and write a book about my life as a PI. Hopefully someone will find it interesting. I don't think I can ever do this work again. That was my last case. I don't know whether to be happy or sad. But I've often been told that I have a book in me somewhere. What about you?"

"Frank, I'm going to miss you. You have done so much for me. I am so lucky and fortunate to have had you in my life. It is very difficult for me. You know you're a bit old for me, and yet I'm still attracted to you. However, I don't think in the long run we could work as a couple, so for now I need some time to find out where I go next. I think I'm going to take some time off and go see my sister. Maybe move to Denver and find a job. I just need some time alone. By the way CNN is going to interview me. I haven't forgotten your request. Can we stay in touch?"

There was a silent pause, then Frank spoke. "Sure, you have my number. I think after what you just said, it might be best for you to go home. You are safe now. Why don't you just drop me off at my house? I would find it hard to not get up in the middle of the night and sleepwalk into the guest bedroom. You understand?"

"Yes, I do. I might have the same problem with the master bedroom."

They both smiled, and soon she was in Frank's driveway.

"Will you let me know when your book's completed? I'd love to read it."

He stretched across the seat and kissed her gently on her lips. As he pulled away his eyes said much more than the kiss had. "Now there's a memory that's got to last me for a long time," she said. There was a long silence between them as if neither wanted to leave. Frank finally reached and opened the car door.

"You'll get the first copy." Frank said as he closed her car door and walked without looking back into his house.

The following month, some divers were searching the golf course lake north of Phoenix looking for golf balls to sell when they stumbled upon the remains of a human body held down with large rocks under water. The police and county morgue were soon there pulling out the remains.

The body of Sid Lewis was so badly decomposed that identification took almost three weeks. Cause of death was a gunshot to the front of the skull. It was listed as a homicide. It would forever remain a cold case murder that went unsolved.

Two weeks later Frank received his check from the IRS. He immediately purchased a cashier's check for ten grand

and mailed it without a return address, to the mother of three children whose husband was killed by an errant nurse at a Phoenix Hospital Emergency room, keeping a promise he had made to himself years earlier. It failed to purchase back the thoughts he carried concerning his character. But he knew, for him, it was still the right thing to do.

Frank left Phoenix for Portland on the first flight out the next day, rented a car, and drove over Highway 26 to Cannon Beach. It had been two months since he last saw Kim. She was still on his mind. He requested and rented the same room they had shared. It was a nice reminder.

It was early in the morning. He had picked up a Starbucks drink at Safeway and was walking on the beach through the morning mist, sipping his coffee and in his own way praying and thanking God for such a peaceful place. He had made a promise to himself to again turn to prayer. He knew it was an important part of his past life that he had ignored in the past years. He also knew he had many things in life to be thankful for...starting with just being alive.

It was overcast, as usual, with a slight misty rain hitting his face. He was passing Haystack Rock when his cell phone rang. He fumbled trying to get it out of the frayed, hooded, Notre Dame sweatshirt an old girlfriend had given him for Christmas years before. He finally pulled his cell phone out and immediately recognized the number. He smiled and then answered, "What took you so long?"

Kim said, "You want some company? Figured by now you needed someone to pay for a meal, so I thought I'd get the next flight out."

Frank was grinning with his reply. "You know when you get here I want you to name ten songs you'd take with you to a desert island. By the way I've added another one to my list. 'Ev'ry Time We Say Goodbye,' by Carly Simon." Frank could hear Kim smile. He couldn't ignore the warmth of her memory. "Dinner depends on your answer."

"I hardly think that's fair as I'll have to pick up the tab."

"You won't believe this but I still have reward money," Frank replied. "I'll see you at the Portland airport."

He hung up with a smile on his face, and walked back through the sand to his beach hotel and up to his second floor room, kicking the wet sand from his shoes before entering. He sat at the desk. The sound of the waves crashing on the beach could be heard through the open deck door. He could look out through gray mist and see the large waves breaking on the shore. It was a soothing gift as he thought back on his life and his PI career. He had been told by many friends that he should write a book about his life as a private investigator. He opened his laptop, not quite sure where to start.

Then he realized there was only one place to start, and that was at the beginning. He wrote the title, chapter one, then his first two sentences:

The Beginning and the End

The sound of the hammer hitting the side of her head was not nearly as loud as he thought it would be. More like a muffled thump.

THE END